Telling the Dark

Telling the Dark

Henry Mitchell

Bridge House

British Library Cataloguing in Publication Data
A Record of this Publication is available from the British
Library

ISBN 978-1-917854-06-1

This edition published 2025 by Bridge House Publishing
Manchester, England

Cover photograph © Henry Mitchell

To Charlie,
who knows the Way

Contents

FOREWORD

By Stephen Drew

From the earliest time I became aware of Henry Mitchell's work, I just knew he'd make a fine walking mate. Now and again he'd write of a ramble, and it always felt like an invitation. I could easily imagine us together on some fine granite slab next to a fast-running river deep in a wood. He'd be standing there with a mischievous twinkle in his eye, leaning on a slightly crooked walking stick that seemed to be an extension of him as he scanned the river, not missing a single blessed thing. Together we'd listen to the rushing water tell us an ancient story from the place where stories begin. We both know a wise river when we hear one.

Alas, there's just enough earthly distance between him and me to confine us to the written word alone. Fortunately, it is here where entire worlds are made evident, and in this realm, Henry is masterful.

The stories held within *Telling the Dark* presume a fundamental principle the author clearly holds dear. There is much more to this world of ours than appearances suggest. I would dare say there is a Celtic sensibility to this belief running about between the lines, where mystical experience rises out of the most quotidian beginnings; portals to the unseen open out of the thinnest of places. Although there may be some harshness, dystopia, and even a bit of terror sprinkled throughout these expeditions into the liminal darkness, there is kindness and compassion to be had as an odd, yet gentle, band of wayfarers is often on hand to usher the unsuspecting through.

But beyond the sheer fun of reading this entertaining collection, I would offer that one could come away from this traveler's tales with a lingering reminder to look between

9

and beyond the sensate experience of our world to find what is real, to hear the language of the elements as they speak their truth, and to be quiet of thought enough to notice it all.

I commend you to join in the fantasy of Henry's stories, his lilting Appalachian voice, and his gentle, loving language as he shares with us what he's gleaned from the wise river.

Stephen Drew is the author of *Into the Thin: A Pilgrimage Walk Across Northern Spain* and *Around the Forever Bend, Remembrances of Wondering What Lies Beyond Death*. Drew is a contributor to *In Search of Simple*, an essay collection.

AN UNACCUSTOMED MUSIC

Jonathan closed his eyes and listened to the water. Whenever he crossed Dark Fork on the big chestnut log his grandfather had felled over the stream, Jonathan stood halfway across in his self-imposed darkness until he imagined he was falling into the roiling creek below and the water spoke to him. He would be on the brink of understanding the liquid language at the point he was sure he was toppling into the flood, then he opened his eyes to find himself still quite upright above it, and the water just noise again with sunlight flashing from its surface and glimmering among the rounded stones in its depths.

Dark Fork was named not for the shadows that cloaked it except at the height of a summer day, but for Jonathan's great-grandfather, Edwin Dark, who first claimed the steep and stony land along its upper reaches where the creek roared and tumbled and plunged down a narrow, bouldered gorge, so sequestered from the sun by the high shoulders of mountains on either side, that most who knew of the place called it simply, The Dismal. The original human inhabitants of the area believed the Dismal was a way into the underworld, a place inhabited by ghosts and demons. Most would not even drink the water from the stream that flowed out of it, so they suffered Edwin Dark, pale and solitary, an outcast even among his own kind, to occupy his chosen acreage undisturbed. When he seemed to thrive in a place where there was scarcely enough sun and soil to grow a scraggle of corn, they decided that Edwin must be himself a devil.

It was a mystery, even to his own descendants, how he ever persuaded the woman named Dream Eater to share his exile, or why her people would have allowed their improbable union. Each Dark generation made up their own stories about Grandmother Dream Eater, but the stories were more

11

revealing of the imaginations of a clan of inveterate storytellers than of any verifiable history. Edwin's children had children before the Darks knew by name the nearest neighbors of Edwin's own race and saw little of them but chimney smoke on a winter morning when the trees were bare and one could see for miles down their cove. The Darks preferred their own company above all others, and unless they were in search of necessities like tools or wives, the Dark men tended to avoid places where humans gathered in numbers. They were honest, hard-working, not mean nor cruel nor greedy, but by no definition sociable. They were, to a soul, passionately contrary to anything ordinary. Their forbidding, inhospitable slice of the earth seemed to suit their perverse natures, and for generations the broader world left them to it.

Jonathan Dark, his elders decided, would be the first of his clan since Edwin to stay long and far from the forbidding country of their hearts. He had a scholarship to the state university in Asheton, two ridges away across the mountains south and east. Jonathan thus became the first among his kinsmen to be burdened with great expectations beyond discovering and becoming fully himself. He did not protest, but he did not wear his load easily. He suspected he might be about to participate in a life where he was passably good at all manner of things he'd just as soon not be doing.

Jonathan never anticipated the complications Starblossom Dorn would bring to his young life. She came to their homestead with her father who was inspecting a small tract of timber he considered buying from the Darks. Jonathan, as boys will do, made fun of her name. She told him her mother had named her after the weed that grew around their steps the morning she was born.

"What about you, then?" she said.

Jonathan puffed himself like a lovesick toad.

"I was named after the son of a king."

"You're too scrawny to carry around such a heavy name," she said, all solemn and serious. "I bet I can beat you to that tree yonder." She pointed toward an old pine across the yard and Jonathan took off for it. Despite his head start, the girl touched the scaly trunk first. Star laughed, and Jonathan stalked off into the woods, breaking any branch within reach he thought he could damage. He never looked back. He was afraid she would see his defeat glistening on his cheek.

Jonathan didn't see Starblossom Dorn after that until he rode the bus down to the county high school at Drovers Gap and glanced covertly at the dark-haired girl assigned the seat next to him. By then she had blossomed into a ripening young woman. The sight of her slender neck curving up between her collar and her hair rendered him as breathless as their childish race.

Starblossom caused Jonathan to be suspended from school in his junior year, though she didn't know it at the time. He watched her from afar, never daring to speak to her, or of her, to anyone. She for her part, appeared to him oblivious to males. Her only observed conversations were with friends of like gender. Jonathan knew that boys were watching her. It rankled him that some would speak of her as if she were a young ewe or heifer awaiting inspection at a stock auction.

When Jason Embers nodded toward Starblossom in the lunch line one day and snickered, "My boys, would I like to poke around in that now," without a thought Jonathan hit him square in the face. Jason was by good measure the heavier. He would have doubtless wiped the floor with a Dark mop but his tray flew at the blow. Jason slipped in the wet of his spilled milk and went down, cracking his head on the corner of a bench and rendering himself unconscious. Fortunately, no

13

lasting damage was done. Jason spent a few days at home recuperating from a mild concussion, and both combatants were suspended from classes for a week. When they were allowed back, after stern warning and threat of permanent expulsion in the event of recurrent hostilities, neither ever mentioned the incident again, and their friends feared to bring up the subject in their presence. The altercation only ensured that Starblossom remained studiously incognizant of both participants. When Wallace Keller, son of Drovers Gap's only practicing attorney, took a polite fancy to her, she encouraged his attention, and Jonathan gave up whatever hopes he might have nurtured to ever find her favor.

No real road led to Dark Fork from anywhere. A rough track barely fit for a tractor provided their tenuous connection with the larger world. The school bus stopped where this trail met the county road two miles down the mountain, and Jonathan and Starblossom walked home from there. Every day, she would charge ahead, daring the boy to keep her company, and Jonathan would hang back, content to catch a glimpse of his heart's desire at every bend. After a mile, he passed her house, and his long legs made better time the rest of the way. One rainy September afternoon, Starblossom slipped getting off the bus and fell sprawling in the mud, ruining the new dress her mother had made for her, and sending her books and papers flying across the puddles. The driver, a scrawny old bootlegger named Silas Sykes, looked out the door. "Youns all right there?"

Starblossom limped to her feet, wiped futilely at her muddied dress, and with tears tracing down her face, answered in a voice trembling with more rage than hurt, "Don't you mind, Sykes, I'm fine."

Jonathan stepped down behind her. Silas closed the door, and the younger children pointed and laughed as the bus pulled away. Without a word, Jonathan gathered up the scattered books, put them back into her bag. When he saw she was in pain, he shouldered the bag himself and held out his hand.

"Don't you touch me, Jonathan Dark," she spat at him, angry for no reason except he had been witness to the spectacle she had become.

"Touch me, then. You're hurt," he answered. Starblossom put her hand on his shoulder, and they hobbled away up the path until Jonathan saw a sapling small enough for him to cut with his pocketknife, but stout enough to keep his companion upright.

"Wait," he whispered. When he handed her the walking stick, carefully cut and trimmed, they went on. Starblossom didn't protest when he put out a hand to steady her on a rough patch, or when, once they reached her house, he carried her books to the porch.

"If you'll wait up on me Monday," he said, "I'll tote your bag for you to the bus, only if your foot ain't better, understand." Starblossom offered no word at all but met his gaze and nodded. Jonathan went on his way back to the Fork, sensing that something had changed between them, without any vague notion of exactly how or what. The two days between Friday and Monday stretched longer than long. He thought Starblossom, muddy and lame and angry at life, more beautiful than ever he'd seen her.

Jonathan Dark never meant to hurt anyone. Even after it was over, he could not have said who took advantage of whom. When Starblossom invited him on a picnic, an afternoon in her company was all that was in his mind. They spread their food on a flat boulder beside the little waterfall above the crossing log over Dark Fork, just beyond sight of the path. The first kiss was Starblossom's idea. The second was

Jonathan's. Their swim in the pool at the foot of the fall was a conspiracy. Afterward, they lay in the sun drying on the warm rock. Starblossom's taut breasts and flat belly drew Jonathan's gaze until he could see nothing else.

He reached over and lay his hand in the hollow just beneath her ribs and felt her life under his palm, throbbing and surging like the stream beside them. When she took his hand in hers and pushed his fingers down to the moist nest between her thighs, they turned to one another and lost themselves in mutual exploration and ecstatic discovery.

Jonathan Dark was walking Starblossom Dorn home one last time, although this trip, there were no books to carry. "What have I done wrong, Star?"

"It's Starblossom. You know that. My name is Starblossom."

Jonathan, frustrated almost to tears, willed his voice steady as he answered, "but you were my Star, and I was your Jonny until graduation. Then all summer you treat me like a stranger. What did I do?

Starblossom's face flushed. "You're going off to college. I'm staying here. Everything will change now."

"But I'm coming back. We talked about that. We've given ourselves. I'll always come back to you."

Starblossom shook her head, looked away, wiped her face with the back of her hand. "Go and forget about me. I would only hold you back." Jonathan would have said more, but Starblossom ran on ahead. "Go. Leave me to myself!" she shouted at him without looking back lest he see her terror streaming down her face.

Jonathan threw up his hands like a plea for heaven's intervention, but he did not run to catch the fleeing Star. *It wasn't anything you did, my dear foolish boy*, Starblossom screamed inside herself as she ran. *It was what we did that day. It was our only day. I wish now there had been others, that I could carry more sweet memories to my end.*

When she reached her house, Starblossom kept running. Nobody was out to see her pass and call her back. She ran until her chest ached and her stomach hurt. She pressed against it with her hand. Her stomach always hurt of late. She kept it bound tightly so the life growing inside her wouldn't be public. She walked on until she came to the log across Dark Fork, and once across, she left the path and made her way up to the little waterfall that had witnessed her undoing. She was still sitting there, adding her own dark tears to the flow of the Fork, when Jonathan crossed the creek later. She heard him stop and call her name. She didn't answer, though she half-wished she had after she heard him walk on up the path toward his own Darks.

Starblossom was not ignorant of her own body. When the moon had turned twice without drawing her blood, she confided her fears to her friend Martha. Martha whispered the name of Lizzie Charon. The old herb woman lived up on a high bald accessed by no road at all, just a single trace for two-legged or four-legged beings afoot. Starblossom knocked on the door and waited. While she summoned nerve to knock again, it opened, and a wizened face appeared out of the shadows beyond. Starblossom would have turned and fled away home, but two eyes bright and sharp as a hawk's nailed her fast where she stood. Lizzie's thin mouth shaped something resembling a smile, radiating unfathomable calm while she held out her hand. When Starblossom took it, Lizzie led the girl into her dark little house and sat her by the fire, then sat herself before her guest, their knees nearly touching.

Against the silence, the flickering fire sizzled and cracked and sighed like a flock of starlings taking flight. Other eyes

17

than Lizzie's were watching her from the shadows in a corner, throwing back at her the hot glow from the hearth. A large hulking bird, an owl perhaps. She couldn't tell. Her heart raced and her breath shallowed on the verge of panic, then slowly she began to settle into Lizzie's peace. She stilled and waited, patient beyond expectation. After a minute or an hour, the Herb Woman spoke, "Was it love or lust? Did he force himself?"

For no reason she could think, Starblossom wasn't surprised that Lizzie seemed to know without asking why she had come. She felt that she was seen through and through by this old crone, that there was no way now to be but honest. "I invited him in. Had he not been so willing, I might have begged him for it."

"And has young Dark refused his child?" Starblossom had left all her secrets at the door.

"He doesn't know, and I can't tell him. He would come to hate the burden of us."

When Lizzie reached out and touched her knee, a warm current welled through Starblossom, resolving in tears. Lizzie leaning close enough that Starblossom could feel her breath, whispered, "And will he love you longer if you pluck from life the fruit of all his longing for you?" Starblossom stared at the old woman. Lizzie drew back and shook her head. "That is what you want from me, isn't it? I can't give you what you've come for. You took to yourself a right-hearted young man. He wants no more than to be true to you. Deny him that, whatever you think it might cost him, and there will be no end in this life to his hurt or yours."

"But you don't understand," hissed Starblossom. "He's leaving Dark Fork."

"Then you best go with him if he does. Go or stay wherever, you will be together."

Starblossom stretched out her hands, knelt like a supplicant at a chancel rail. "Please help me. Please?"

Lizzie took the young hands in her old ones and stood, her own eyes glistening with tears when she said, "I've given you what I have. Let your Jonny give you what is your right and his."

"I can't. I can't. I will not hold him back from his life." Choking on her sobs, Starblossom ran out the door. As she fled across the yard toward the concealing trees, she heard Lizzie's door slam behind her. Whether it was the old woman, or the wind that closed it, Starblossom didn't know or care.

Lost in the song of the little waterfall, Starblossom played her visit to Lizzie over in her mind. The old woman had helped others, why not her? She knew Lizzie was right. If she told Jonathan about their child, he would abandon his dreams and stay to care for them both. But his family would judge she had ruined his life. The Darks kept long score. At every given opportunity, they would remind Jonathan of all he had sacrificed for love and pity's sake, until at last he would come to agree with them that Starblossom, or any woman, was unworthy of such cost.

"No. I can't," she whispered to the gathering dusk. She took off her dress and folded it neatly on the rock beside her. Her sister had envied her for it and could have it now. Then Starblossom slipped into the pool, and when she had accustomed to the chill, lay back into the dark water.

When he felt his vertigo build to certainty, Jonathan Dark opened his eyes. As he expected, he was still upright on the chestnut log. Below him, flashing amid sunstruck waves and ripples, the bright stones of the creek bed, and among them, brilliant under the morning, an object he recognized even before he fetched a branch from beside the stream and snared it to his hand. He held it a moment, dangling from its broken chain, the locket he had given Starblossom for her birthday, back in the spring. "So, she thought no more of me than that," he said aloud to the day, and threw the trinket as far down the creek as he could.

This seemed to be Jonathan's day for rejection. He had planned to tell Star today what he told his family the night before, that he had never wanted to go to university, and wouldn't. After a long silence, his father said, "You're old enough to be your own man. But you'll have to do it someplace else."

Jonathan had anticipated this turn. Jason Embers was working on a carpentry crew in Poplar Spring, building summer houses for rich people, and said there was a job there for Jonathan if he wanted it. Jonathan broke into a loping run. He didn't want to miss the bus to Poplar Spring.

Drowning turned out to be not so easy as Star imagined from the picture of Hamlet's Ophelia in her literature textbook. She heard thunder from a storm somewhere beyond the ridge as she settled into the cold creek. While she contemplated her final act, the water was rising. Somewhere up the mountain the deluge had already commenced.

As soon as the cold became tolerable, Star held her breath, closed her eyes and slipped beneath the surface. She thought it would be quiet underwater, but she could hear the rush and tumble of the stream loud in her ears. She opened her eyes, let out her breath, watched the last of her life bubble past her face and sail away on the current. Her world reduced to a green murmur. A vacant peace blossomed in her mind. She was ready now.

But the first flood of water through her head and throat propelled her sputtering and gasping toward the light. If she wanted to die, some soul within her pined to live. Star scrambled and grasped, fell and floundered, barking hands and feet, elbows and knees. She fixed her eyes on the blue dress by the shore and plunged toward it, but the quickening stream swept her feet out from under her and hauled her downstream. Something snagged her birthday necklace, and by the time she reached for it the chain had parted, and it was gone. The footlog across the fork passed over her like the shadow of a huge bird, wings spread wider than her vision.

She might have drowned as she had plotted had not a mossy boulder midstream stopped her short, stealing her breath as it impacted her back. Star flailed blindly. Her hand caught a limb of a fallen maple tumbled crown-first into the water. She held on, found a purchase among the tangle for her feet, and as soon as she could see again, made her way branch to limb, until she gained the trunk. She lay with her face resting against the rough bark while the rain washed all her sins away. When the rising water touched her dangling palm, she inched along the nearly horizontal trunk until she reached the bank.

Shivering, gasping from the cold, all but naked to the elements, Star was nevertheless alive and glad of it. When she reached home, she climbed into the barn-loft and hid in the hay until she saw her father leave. Then she came down and limped toward the house to face her mother's wrath and beg her mercy, having already abandoned all hope of forgiveness and restoration.

Showers slathered the windows off and on while the bus swung and strained between close hills along a road hugging a silty river, still high and boisterous from last night's storms. By the time the dozen or so passengers were jostled to stillness in front of the courthouse in Poplar

21

Spring, the clouds had broken and run away down a sky blue as a robin's egg.

Jonathan filed off the bus with three other strangers to stand like mourners at a burial, waiting for the driver to retrieve their luggage from underneath the coach. A young woman with a little boy and a solitary old man received their belongings and walked away. The driver secured the luggage hatch, climbed back behind the steering wheel, and when he was satisfied the town was not going to grant him any paying passengers, closed the door and carried away the souls remaining in his custody who had better places to go.

Jonathan stood with his rucksack watching the bus swerve off through the town toward more mountains beyond. Then he turned and stared at this place where he could claim no belonging. He had no idea what he was supposed to do next, or why he had talked himself into coming here in the first place. He pulled from his pocket the wrinkled envelope bearing the scribbled address of Jason Embers. Clueless as to where to find his purported friend, Jonathan hoped it wasn't too far to walk. He didn't have much money, certainly not enough to waste on a cab.

He was still pondering where to start asking directions when the blast of a car horn provoked a momentary mingling of panic and annoyance. Behind him, a muddy Ford sat muttering in place next to the sidewalk. Through the cracked windshield, Jason's sunburned face leered at him, the mouth bowed in a satisfied grin. Not for the first time, Jonathan suppressed an unreasoned urge to push that smile as far down Jason's throat as his arm could reach.

"No, Ma, you don't understand. I invited this. Jonny only did what I wanted of him. If he knew, he would throw his life away for me. I couldn't bear that."

Irene Dorn shook her head. "It wouldn't be throwing his life away to take his responsibility for you. You have a life, too, one more than your own. You didn't get into this fix without his help."

"I can't tell him, Ma. Not now. He's just left for college."

Irene held Star's face between her palms, gazed intently into her daughter's eyes. "You know what your father will do when he finds out."

Star wondered now if her drowning would have caused less suffering than her life. "He would kill Jonny, Ma. Oh, what am I going to do?"

"For now, you're not going to do anything. I'm going to write to your Aunt Margaret in Asheton. She will write back and tell me she is not well and needs someone to stay and help her cope for a while. I'll show the letter to your father, and he'll likely suggest that we send you to Asheton to watch after my sister. If he doesn't, I will. My sister has experience of the world. You will be useful to her while you are there, and she will assist you through your present difficulties. But, Star…"

"Yes, Ma?"

"Sooner than later, you are going to tell Jonathan Dark what he has done for you and give him a chance to be a proper man. Do you understand me, girl?"

"I understand, but Ma…"

"No buts and maybe's left to you, daughter. You've played away your choices. All you've left is necessity. Now go clean yourself up and get on some proper clothes before your father gets back here and sees you so ungathered. While you tend to your state, I'll make you some soup. You're shivering, pale as a bone. It wouldn't do to have pneumonia achieve what the creek didn't."

Starblossom Dorn pulled the old quilt tighter around her shoulders and stared at the fire. She was emptied now of all

23

will and questions and hope. "Yes, Ma," was all she had left to say.

Jonathan Dark opened his eyes and stared at the rose vines twining up the wallpaper for a full five seconds before Jason Embers' snoring from the bed across the room confirmed his situation.

Charlene Edgerton, their landlady, seemed skeptical at first, when her sometimes boisterous and perpetually late-paying boarder introduced his friend from over the mountain. Jonathan's shy charm eventually wore down her caution. Jason had a spare bed in his room. For an extra twenty dollars a month, they could share the room.

"Remember," the old woman said, struggling to look sterner than she was accustomed to presenting herself. "No liquor, no girls, no loud music. I keep a quiet and restful house for hard-working decent people who need their night's sleep. Breakfast is at seven. If you're late, I can't promise more than a cold biscuit."

Jonathan looked at the big clock ticking on the dresser. He had fifteen minutes to prevent a cold biscuit. When he turned the faucet in the bathroom, air in the pipes set a grand thumping in the walls, immediately answered by a shoe or a fist pounding against the other side. When his face was clean, Jonathan stared through his headache at his reflection in the mirror. He'd have to shave after breakfast. Clothed and on his way to sustenance, he passed Jason, still sitting groggily in his bed.

"Save me some," he said as Jonathan closed the door behind him.

Last night, Jason had been intent on showing him the town, even though Jonathan was more eager to get acquainted with his bed, and Jason had insisted on buying Jonathan a few drinks at the bar down the street. Jonathan wasn't a drinker. Two drinks had been enough to make him wish he'd kept his throat dry. Jonathan's headache now was his sole souvenir of the evening's festivities. He couldn't remember what sort of concoction he'd imbibed but made a mental note to avoid it in the future.

Whatever it was, Jason had consumed in greater quantity, and it had put him in a hilarious mood, although he turned suddenly sullen when Jonathan tried to shush him coming into the house so they wouldn't disturb Mrs. Edgerton. By the time Jonathan found the key in Jason's pocket and unlocked the door to their room, Jason was leaning against the wall, snoring softly to himself. Jonathan guided him to his bed, and Jason collapsed face down to lie like a dead dog until morning.

Starblossom Dorn waited by the road nearly an hour before the bus rounded the curve, and when she raised her hand, slowed and sighed to a stop. She picked up her suitcase, heavier than when she left home that morning, and climbed aboard, grateful her father had not been there to see her leaving. He would have been full of admonition and questions, would never have spoken the blessing Star wanted to hear, the blessing he would have bestowed freely had she been his son. It was easier to be gone without goodbye.

"Where you to, Missey?" said the driver, speaking as if she were a child rather than with child. For now, her secret was still hers to keep.

"Asheton," she said, handing over a wrinkled ten-dollar bill from her mother's cornmeal jar.

"You'll have to switch buses in town, but you won't need to wait long. Everybody's on time today," the driver said, handing Star her change. "I ought to stow that bag, but it ain't far now, just keep it by your seat."

Star folded her money in her purse, scanned the eight other passengers, nobody she knew. She took the nearest seat, had it to herself, and pulled her suitcase in beside her as she sat by the window. Before she had time to think on her transgressions or contemplate her future, the bus was jolting through the town, past the school where she would never set foot again, past the Methodist church and Owens Hardware and Sundries. For an instant, she thought she saw Jonathan Dark going into the store as the bus swept by, but she knew it couldn't have been him. He'd be away at State College by now. A part of her life that she'd best pretend to herself she'd forgotten, although she knew she never could. The memory was growing inside her now day by day, becoming her future.

After the bus deposited her in Drover's Gap, Star sat on the bench in front of the post office, courting the scant shade of an ailing maple, waiting for another bus to Asheton, and praying nobody she knew would see her sitting there. The driver said her wait would be about thirty minutes, and after twenty, Martha Thompson, her sister from another mother, the only living soul on earth who knew all Star's secrets, waved from across the street, calling Star's name loud enough for the whole town to hear.

"Blossom. Blossom, honey, how youns been, girl?" Star was glad there would be nobody in Asheton prone to call her Blossom.

At the first break in traffic, Martha darted across to Star's bench, hugged her so tight Star wondered if she could feel the roundness below her ribs. "Where you off to? Martha blurted, without waiting for an answer. "You still sweet on that Jonny Dark?"

"I ain't seen Jonny in a while, Martha. He's off at State now, I reckon. Probably forgot all about this little mountain child already."

26

Martha's face clouded with puzzlement for an instant, then brightened. "I can't say what he's forgot, but he didn't go to college. Jason Embers told me Jonny might be working with him building houses for Cliffbilt yonder to Poplar Spring. You really haven't seen him in a while, have you?" Martha eyed the suitcase, leaned close and lowered her voice, even though nobody else shared the bus stop, "You ain't still in trouble, are you, Blossom?"

A bus turned the corner and started up the street toward them. The sign above the windshield said, *Asheton.* "I have to catch my bus now, Martha," Star said. holding her suitcase with both hands in front of her, like a shield.

"Hey, Jonnyboy, You ready to go yet?" Jason Embers hollered even in the quiet. Jonathan thought his roommate might burst if he ever had to whisper.

"I'm going to stay in tonight, Jason. I have a letter to write."

Jason hooted, slapped Jonathan hard between his shoulders. "I bet you're writing to that Blossom Dorn, begging her to take you back."

"I told you, there's nothing now between Star and me. I'm writing to my ma. There's no phones up on the Fork."

Jason snickered. "You're always writing to your ma. Why don't you write to your dad sometimes?"

"He wouldn't be interested."

"Come on," Jason said, "we haven't done anything lately worth writing home about. I'll buy the beer, unless you think you're too good to drink with me."

Jonathan sighed, finally looked up from the book he was holding. "I'm not the least bit good. I'm just tired. We go out every night and drink and talk to girls I don't want to know, and I go to work next morning hung-over. That's no way to live."

Jason's laugh sounded like rocks falling into a wheelbarrow. "You get to know them better, you wouldn't have to talk so much. You ought to have been a preacher, Jon. You think it's a sin to have a good time."

"There's lots of ways to have a good time, Jason."

Jason put a hand on each shoulder, put his face close and stared hard into Jonathan's eyes. "You know what, Mister Dark, sir, I think you just don't want to be seen in my company."

Jonathan pushed the hands away. Jason's breath smelled like he already had a head start on the evening. Jonathan reached up, patted Jason on the cheek, a gesture calculated to irritate. "Let's go, then," he said.

The bus crossed the mountain only thirty crooked miles to Asheton, but to Starblossom Dorn, it looked and sounded and smelled like another world. She had been here twice before on school field trips, once to an exhibit at the art museum, and once to tour a stately castle proclaimed to be the largest private residence ever built in America. It was a grand and glorious ostentation, but Star's reaction had been that it must be lonely to live in such a big house.

Aunt Margaret was waiting at the bus station. Star had been a child the last time she saw her aunt. She'd thought Margaret Boone the most beautiful and exotic human she'd ever encountered. Margaret still looked beautiful, but to Star, she also looked old. One Day, Star thought to herself, *You'll look just like that*. The thought didn't frighten Star at all. Old or not, Aunt Margaret looked like a woman who owned her life, and if family gossip was to be believed, she did.

Margaret took hold of her, hugged Star mightily, squeezing the breath out of her, then stepped back, beaming as if they were on their way to a party. "Look at you now. What a grand young woman you've become. You must be starving." With that, Margaret took possession of Star's suitcase and strode away, beckoning the younger woman to follow. "Let's not stand in the hot sun all day, we've places to do and things to go."

Margaret stopped behind a tan Plymouth, lifted the trunk and tossed in Star's suitcase, then unlocked the passenger door and held it while she ushered Star inside, as if she were a chauffeur. "Watch your toes and fingers," she lilted, and slammed the door hard enough to rock the car. Star sat bemused and unspeaking while her aunt went around and slid in behind the wheel.

"You have a car?" queried Star, finding her voice at last.

"No dear," said Aunt Margaret, turning the key in the ignition. "But it's too far to walk and this one looked nice. I thought we'd just borrow it for a while." She glanced at Star, who clutched her seat and stared straight ahead as if she expected to be ejected from the vehicle. "Of course I have a car, dear. One has to get around, don't you know. Everyone has a car."

"We don't have a car," said Star, almost in a whisper.

"How quaint," Margaret said. "Why not?"

"I don't know. I guess there's just no place to go. Pa has an old truck, but it doesn't run half the time. If we need to go to Drovers Gap, we just take the bus."

Margaret kept her eyes on her road, reached across, patted Star's hand and chatted on brightly, "Well, Darling, in Asheton there's more places to go than any sane mind would ever wish to. You'll be wanting to learn to drive. I'll get Robert to teach you."

"Robert?"

"Robert is… well, Robert is a business associate and my closest friend. You'll be seeing a lot of him. He'll like you and you'll like Robert. Yes, I think Robert would be an excellent driving instructor for you."

"Why can't you teach me, Aunt Margaret?

Margaret hit the brakes suddenly, stopping a foot short of the van halted just ahead. Star got her hands in front of her just in time to prevent her chest colliding with the dash.

"Because, dear one," Margaret continued as if nothing had happened, "I'd very much like us to still be friends after you've learned to drive."

"Don't you want to talk to me?" the dark-haired young woman said, a declaration more than a question.

Jonathan looked up from his warm glass, still half full of beer. "Sorry," he murmured, as much to himself as to the woman, "I don't have a lot to say."

She sighed, patted him on the arm, slid off her stool and wandered away through the smoky haze, trolling for more profitable prey. The cloudy air swirled visibly around her as she moved. Jonathan thought for just an instant of the mist drifting over Dark Fork after a rain. The smell here was different, though. Stale tobacco smoke, day-old sweat, rancid cooking oil and cheap perfume.

A chemically rendered blonde perched just down the bar, who had come in with Dark Hair, whose name Jonathan had already forgotten if she'd ever told him, apparently was still enraptured by Jason Ember's extended exposition on all his heroic adventures in the building trade. Jonathan suspected she made a concerted effort to appear more interested than she was, and that she would continue doing so as long as Jason kept buying watered-down drinks for her.

Across the room, Dark Hair already sat at a table with another man Jonathan knew from work, bending close, hanging on his every word. Only she knew if she was laughing with him or at him. Jonathan was contemplating if he should have another beer or go back to Mrs. Edgerton's house and finish his letter to his mother, when a womanly voice broke his concentration, "You don't look happy to be where you are, Jonathan Dark."

Jonathan jumped, nearly knocked over his glass, then almost toppled it again when he tried to grab it as it teetered on the verge of shattering disaster. He looked up into the deepest gaze he could recall, and Starblossom Dorn rose clear in his mind, near enough to touch, to smell. Jonathan felt the pieces of his broken soul spill out of him and fall tinkling into his glass, like ice.

"How do you know my name?" when he found his voice.

A slow smile that warmed his heart and chilled his soul. "I listen," said the woman behind the bar. The eyes held him benignly enough, yet harrowing in their intimacy, knowing and oracular. The hair that might have been black in some forgotten day shone in the light like burnished pewter, long and dense, immune to gravity, caressing its owner's face in a luminous cautionary cloud. The face itself, touched but not diminished by time, bespoke mysteries and adventures and secrets and powers. It might have once been a pretty face. Now it was simply beautiful. And for no reason he could name, looking at it made Jonathan afraid.

More accurately, it was the way she looked at him that unsettled. She gave him her attention without reserve, without judgment, without promise or expectation. She was simply and profoundly there, completely present and revealing. Jonathan found himself seen, knew all his secrets were escaped and discovered. If he was fearful then, he was also glad.

The woman behind the bar set two cups between them, took a battered metal coffee pot from someplace he couldn't see, and poured them full. Jonathan watched the

31

steam waft up above the twin darks, thought again of the mist above his river, and lifted his cup to drink. The coffee, rich and spicy, with a hint of bittersweet that might have been cocoa or chicory. Hot to the tongue but not scalding. He took a sip. "But I don't know your name," he said.

"My name is Laurel," the woman answered.

"Is that your real name?" he asked.

"That's what you can call me. Nobody in this place could pronounce my real name." She raised her cup, inhaled the vapor from the ebony brew, gazed at Jonathan over the rim, "Need to talk?"

There was a lot then that Jonathan needed to say, but until this moment, he could never have found the words.

Aunt Margaret piloted her Plymouth away through downtown Asheton, along streets already thronged with tourists and nature pilgrims, between imposing art-deco buildings – survivors from a more illustrious and affluent era when the elite of arts and commerce congregated in the mountain city to enjoy the scenery, the moderate climate, and to hatch their capitalist plots. The writers and movie stars and millionaires had left with the onset of the Great Depression, and found more luxurious hideouts by the time it was over, but Asheton still drew the tourists, who were as enamored of her mountains and rivers as their parents and grandparents before them.

To Star, the town seemed as exotic and foreign as London or Paris or Rome.

What on God's green Earth am I doing here. Aloud, she said, "Why did you come to Asheton, Aunt Margaret?"

Margaret stopped at a cross walk as a flock of uniformed Cub Scouts swarmed past, herded with small success by two frazzled den mothers. She laughed. Star wasn't sure if at the spectacle before them or the memories in Margaret's head.

"I'd have gone anywhere to get away from the Fork," Margaret said, "Asheton was just the first stop on the way. But the bright lights caught my eye, and there were interesting people here in those days. Before I knew it, I'd caught the eye of one of them, and Asheton became the last stop on my journey."

"Did he catch your eye, then?" asked Star.

Margaret laughed again. "It wasn't a he, Dear. Robert came along later. By then, I'd become more pragmatic in my outlook. He didn't catch my eye so much as his money, but there was more to him than I could see at first." Star sat silent, gazing at the shop fronts passing by, the people clustered to them like bees to blossoms.

"Do I shock you? I hope you're not disillusioned with your old aunt."

"No," said Star, "I haven't had enough money to know much about it, but I've had enough love to realize it can't be counted on for sustenance."

Margaret laughed again. "A woman after my own heart. If you stay, we'll try to find you enough of both to satisfy."

Jason Embers hung his head over the edge of the roof and vomited. "Watch it up there, man," a voice shouted from below. "Hey, that's nasty."

"Feel better now?" Jonathan said without looking up from the shingle he was nailing down.

Jason didn't answer, just crawled across the slant of tar paper, picked up a shingle from his bundle, and added it to his row. After he'd secured three more, he muttered, "Damn, I'm hot."

Jonathan swallowed his laugh. "That's what you kept saying to that girl at the bar last night. She might believe you now." He regretted the impulse as soon as the words were out. Jason didn't like to be teased about anything, and

Jonathan knew from experience that he could carry a grudge for days.

Jason swiped his crimson face with a soggy sleeve. "I didn't spend the whole night confessing my sins to an old lady," he said dryly.

"I didn't confess anything. We were just talking." Jonathan kept working as he spoke. "Besides, Laurel isn't that old, but she is a grown woman."

"Laurel is old enough to be your grandmother," Jason said, with a snicker, apparently feeling better now that he could focus his innate anger on someone in particular. "Did she give you milk and cookies?"

"She didn't give me a hangover," murmured Jonathan, "but she did offer me a job."

Jason stopped his work, stared at Jonathan. "She need somebody to sweep floors?"

"She might. I don't know. But she asked if I'd be interested in tending bar."

Jason laughed at that, went back to his shingles. "What do you know about keeping bar? You won't hardly even drink a beer."

"Laurel said that anybody who likes to drink shouldn't be keeping bar."

Jason's voice began gathering an edge, "Missy Laurel was just pumping you full of wisdom, she was. Did she offer you some lessons in bed?"

Jonathan's face reddened in the shade of his hat brim. The thought had not occurred to him, but now that Jason had put it in his head, it seemed like a not unpleasant prospect. He answered, more loud and sharp than he intended, "She's not that kind. I'm not sure she even likes men that way."

Jason snorted. "Maybe she prefers little boys."

"We were just talking business, mostly," Jonathan said, ignoring his friend's baiting.

"Well, you be careful of Laurel," Jason said, sounding all at once sincere, almost sympathetic. "Things I hear, she's been in some pretty strange business along the way."

They worked silently for a while, then Jason said, "Jon boy, you going to take her job?"

Jonathan smiled to himself then, "Well, I tell you, I'm starting to think about it."

"Drink your juice," Aunt Margaret said, "and eat your eggs."

"I'm not really hungry," Star murmured, "but it does look delicious."

"It is delicious," Margaret affirmed. "Helen made it just for you, and you are hungry; your stomach is just still asleep."

"Maybe a biscuit," said Star, picking one up, weighing it in her hand. It might have been a feather. Then she broke the biscuit open with her fork. The moisture steamed in the cool air until she laid a pat of butter into it. Star watched it melt away, turning the white insides the color of dandelion. She tasted. She was hungry after all. She took a sip of her juice, decided she might be up to Helen's omelet.

"This is good, Aunt Margaret. Really good. I've never tasted eggs like this. What is the green stuff?"

"Cilantro," Margaret informed. Helen makes the lightest biscuits and the best omelets on earth. That's why she works for me. She'll be happy you approve."

A telephone rang in the hall just beyond the door. Margaret went to answer it while Star communed with her groceries. She couldn't hear what her aunt was saying, but she caught the tone, not harsh but quietly commanding. Helen brought in a pot from the kitchen and without asking filled Star's cup. She expected coffee, but the dark liquid proved to be some sort of tea, the taste unfamiliar but not unpleasant, vaguely nutty.

"Maté," said Helen, "it'll settle your stomach and make

you hungry. You need to eat." Before Star could compliment her omelet and biscuit, Helen turned and glided swiftly away into her kitchen.

Margaret returned from her phone, sat down at her place, looking decidedly pleased with herself.

"You have a phone," Star said, not sure that was at all what she'd meant to say.

"I have three in the house," said Margaret, managing to look amused without appearing patronizing. "I also have a brand new television receiver."

Star didn't try to hide her surprise. She'd only seen pictures of television consoles in magazines, tiny screens and knobs set in massive wooden cabinets begging large rooms. Her family had only had electricity in their house for two years. There still weren't enough people on Dark Fork to convince Summit Utility Cooperative to run a phone line into their corner of the county.

"I didn't know there was a television station in Asheton," she said.

Margaret nodded. "There will be soon, and we'll be ready for it."

"How do you know?" asked Star. "I haven't seen anything about it in the news."

"You will." Aunt Margaret beamed, as if announcing a birth. "We're about ready to make it public."

"We?" said Star around her biscuit bite.

"Wallace Hoover, Robert and I own the station."

When Jonathan Dark came down the steps at Falls Street Room and Board, Charlene Edgerton stood in her front hall in conversation with a young man he'd talked to enough at breakfast to know his name was James Smeltzer. They'd had brief conversations over eggs and biscuits about James' work and ambitions as a photographer, and about Jonathan's momentary satisfactions and continual frustrations as a carpenter. Jason didn't like Smeltzer, called him Pictureman.

When Jonathan hesitated before going out the door, Charlene looked at him, flashed her smile reserved for boarders who paid their rent on time, and lilted, "Can I help you, Jonny?"

"When you have time, Miz Edgerton," Jonathan said, a little embarrassed to interrupt a conversation, "I'd like to talk to you about getting a room of my own, if you have one open."

Charlene glowed with delight. "Just happens I do, Jonny. Jim's running off from us to work for the newspaper over in Knox. If you're ready to move right in, I can refund his deposit. It's a really nice room. Gets the morning light. Let me clean, and I'll show it to you after supper."

"Thanks. Don't let it go. I want it for sure," said Jonathan.

"You and Embers parting ways?" asked Smeltzer. He didn't sound surprised.

"I'm changing jobs," answered Jonathan. "Different hours."

James had apparently finished his business with Mrs. Edgerton, as he started out the door with Jonathan. "Can I give you a lift, Jon? I have to go gas up my car."

"No thanks. I'm just going down to The Dreadful Dram to accept my new job."

"You going to tend bar for Laurel Charon, are you?"

"I hope so."

Smeltzer laughed as he opened the door to his black coupe. "You'll still be seeing your old roommate every day then, won't you?"

"I'll try to keep the bar between us," Jonathan said.

"You really want to be a barkeep, then?" Smeltzer queried.

"It's a job I can do well, I think," Jonathan said. "Can't everybody be a photographer like you."

"You could come with me to Knox," Smeltzer said. "Plenty of jobs there, that pay better than this. I could teach you photography, if that's what interests you. You see things as they are. I think you might have a talent to suit the newspaper business."

"Well, that's a notion," Jonathan said. "When would I need to let you know."

Smeltzer laughed. "If you want a ride to Asheton, now would be the right time."

"What are your plans now, Star?" Margaret queried over her morning coffee.

"I'm going to keep the child," Star said, rubbing her belly, rounding now to the life inside. "He's all I have left of Jonny."

"You're sure of that?" said her aunt with a glint of a smile.

"Sure as I can be. He's gone. I don't see him back for the likes of me."

"I meant, are you sure he's left you a boy?" Margaret said with her little laugh that could serve either merriment or distress.

Star took it for merriment, smiled despite herself. "Feels like a boy. Feels like Jonny there inside me."

Margaret shed her laugh, spoke with a stern edge, "But you never told him. Don't you think he would want to know, has a right to know?"

Star answered solemnly, but not sad, with calm acceptance, "I about spoiled his life once. This isn't his burden. I invited him. Wherever he is now, I want him free to choose his own way."

Margaret shook her head. "I don't think you give your Dark man enough credit. One day, your child will ask about his father, and what will you tell him?"

"I'll tell him his father was a fine man, a splendid man,

38

and I hope he'll grow up to be just like him and find someone to share his life who will have more sense than his mother."

Margaret's laugh sprinkled the air between them again. "And assuming this child is a boy, what will you name him?"

Star didn't hesitate. "I'll name him after his father, of course. I'll name my son Jonathan."

"And if you're wrong, and it's a girl?"

Star laughed now, sounding just like her aunt. "I'm not wrong, but If I were, I'd name her Margaret."

Jonathan wasn't sure if he was on his way to find his life or if he was running from one he had lost. Either way, he reckoned he would remember Laurel Charon for the rest of his tenure on earth. She had heard his story, as best he could tell it, and trusted him to be what he said he could be. Jonathan's last night tending bar, Jason Embers came in spoiling for a fight with anybody who might give it to him. He tried to conjure an argument with several he knew from work, who had the good sense to laugh him off and bribe him quiet with a drink. Late in the evening, drink had pretty much gained his full attention, Jason ordered a whiskey, then accused Jonathan of watering it, though he'd seen it poured straight from the bottle.

"If you don't like it, Mister Embers, you don't have to pay for it, but that's the last drink you'll get here tonight. You've had enough," Jonathan said, his voice quiet and steady.

Jason roared like a wounded bear and tried to crawl over the bar. Jonathan stood his ground, not sure what he would or could do about the escalating situation. The other patrons simply stared, either afraid to intervene or not wanting to spoil the show. Jason, atop the bar now on hands and knees, too enraged or too drunk to speak, spat into Jonathan's face and reached for his throat.

Jonathan had not seen Laurel come in from her office, but suddenly, there she was behind Jason. She reached up, laid her palm between his shoulder blades, and whispered, just loud enough for Jonathan to hear, "Sleep."

Jason whimpered like a puppy, crumpled and folded, his face flat against the polished wet, his eyes open and staring at nothing. His glass rolled off the bar and shattered on the floor. Laurel patted his face tenderly, beckoned to one of the regular customers sitting across the room. "Willis," she said, "come help Jon carry this boy to his bed and your next drink is on the house."

Willis' prompt response testified to his thirst, and it only took a few minutes for them to hoist unresisting Jason down the street and deposit him in his bed at Charlene Edgerton's boarding house. On their way out, Jonathan paused to turn out the light, and heard Jason's slurred voice in the dark, "Jonboy? You still here?"

"Yup, Jason, I'm here."

Jason's next words sounded sober as a judge. "She's a witch, Jon. Laurel Charon is a witch. Get away from her and save your soul."

"Good night, Jason." Jonathan closed the door. As he started down the hall after Willis, he heard the muffled sound of a man weeping.

Midnight came and, in accordance with the city ordinance, Jonathan and Laurel ushered the die-hard drunks out into the fog-bound street. Jonathan began turning off lights. He and Felix, the chief cook and bottle washer, would stay and put the place to bed. Laurel began putting on her coat. Jonathan held it as she slipped her arms into the sleeves.

"Tomorrow's Sunday. We'll be closed." She said, as if Jonathan didn't know that. "What are your plans for the weekend?"

"I'll write a letter home, I imagine." Jonathan said.

"You're fired, Jon." Laurel said softly, as if comforting a mourner.

Stunned, Jonathan prayed he'd misheard. When he found his voice, "I thought you liked my work."

"You do good work and you are a good man, Jonathon Dark. That's why I'm firing you. You have an interesting life ahead and it isn't here." She handed him an envelope too weighty for a letter. "Here's your severance. Before you leave tonight, borrow the phone in my office and call your friend James Smeltzer. Come Monday morning, buy a train ticket and get yourself to Knox."

Laurel turned then and walked away into the night, leaving Jonathan standing open-mouthed in the doorway. Whatever happened to him now, Jonathan reckoned Laurel Charon would be the second woman in his life he would always wish he had known better and longer.

Charlene Edgerton was disappointed her favorite boarder would be departing so precipitously. Since he was leaving without notice, Jonathan offered to pay an extra week's rent, which he could do, thanks to Laurel Charon's generosity.

Charlene pretended to be offended. "Keep your money, young man, she snapped. "You'll need every penny to stay afloat in that big city." Then she sent him off with a kiss on his forehead, and a motherly hug, and before he could feel embarrassed, or notice the tears in her eyes, turned and disappeared inside her door.

Jonathan had not made the phone call to Smeltzer, as Laurel Charon instructed, but he did buy a train ticket to Knox, and once again found himself being jostled through the night to some strange place he never hoped nor feared to be. Lights passed through the dark beyond the windows, some bright and

41

near, some dim and far. Occasionally, he caught a glimpse of the moon riding down the current of the Long Broad as it flowed on, skirting the railbed toward the Shaconage, and beyond into Tennessee. Stars winked in and out of clouds, and once, one streaked across the sky, gone almost before it startled. Jonathan wondered if it was a sign that his life had some plan and purpose after all, or if it was a portent of one more incompletion. Or if it was just a flash in the night, God's little joke on Jonathan Dark.

Over the grumbling mutter and rattle of the train, faint conversations filtered through the dark, voices that didn't quite jell into words, conveying varying intonations of weary anticipations and half-hearted forebodings. Jonathan tried to listen, wanted for some distraction and escape from his own thoughts, which after all that had happened, still dragged him back, only half unwillingly, to Starblossom Dorn. He'd asked about her in letters to his mother. *Is she well? Have you seen her, by chance?* He tried to disguise his veiled inquiries as idle curiosities, though there was no reason anyone who had known them both would think so. His mother's responses were all in the same vein. *No. I never see the Dorn's. Mr. Dorn told your father that his daughter had gone off to care for his sister-in-law who was ill. How is your work? Do you have any friends there? Your Father would never say so, but he would welcome a visit if there is ever a time for you that you can come to us.*

"How was your lesson with Peter Murphy?" Margaret asked over supper.

Star put down her spoon a bit too abruptly. Robert flinched at the clash, glanced at Margaret, shook his head in silent disapproval before he wiped his mustache.

"Terrible," blurted Star. "I can't sing a measure without making a mistake and Mister Perfection makes me do it over."

"That isn't what Peter told me," Robert put in. "He says you have a fine voice but are afraid to use it."

"You have a beautiful and powerful voice," Margaret agreed. This fall, we'll arrange a recital."

"I can't sing in front of other people," Star protested, her face pouted like a child.

"You sing in your room. You sing in the bath. You sing in the garden. You can sing anywhere you want," Margaret insisted.

"Why can't I just sing for myself, then?" Star said, her voice clipped and sharp, not at all musical.

"You should sing for yourself, no matter who else is listening," Margaret said, like a teacher addressing a recalcitrant pupil. "But understand this, Starblossom Dorn, you do not live just for yourself, but for the life that is growing inside you. You must make a way in the world for you both. You are a lovely woman, but it is your voice that will sway men to your will. Your looks render you a fine ornament to any social occasion, but this town is full of decorative females. Your voice is your power. It is your weapon. Murphy will train you to hone it and use it to effect."

"Aunt Margaret, you make me sound dangerous," Star said, intrigued and vaguely flattered despite her protestations.

"Yes, Miss, you certainly are that," murmured Robert, as if he believed it, and rose from the table to fetch their desserts.

The train burrowed through the night like a mole through spring soil. Jonathan slept and woke and slept again. Sometimes lights sparked the dark, lonely and solitary, occasionally paired, never more than a few. Where there were no lights, the mountains rose up steep and close against a barely less dark sky, for one mile leaden with cloud and over the next aswarm with stars. At Shelton Crossing, the train stopped on a siding, while a fast freight roared past in the opposite direction, rattling whatever and all that was not tightly fastened down. Freight was more profitable for Transmountain Rail Lines than were passengers, so freight claimed the right-of-way.

While the train waited at Shelton Crossing, the kitchen crew must have taken on provisions, because when the sun emerged above mist-shrouded heights, an aroma of coffee permeated the dining car, where Jonathan ordered a cup to go with his eggs and biscuit. He ate, readied himself for a big day in a strange place, and sat watching buildings emerge from the wider morning beyond the tracks until the train swung on a high bridge across the Long Broad. It descended in a slow and slowing crawl before coming to rest with clanks and groans between two long platforms, where people and baggage waited to be carried away deeper into the wilds of Tennessee.

Jonathan retrieved his bag, said a polite farewell to the pleasant lady in the seat opposite, and emerged into the bright morning air filled with the unaccustomed music of a genuine city already intently pursuing the brand-new day. Before Jonathan had time to consider immediate possibilities, a familiar voice called out of the transient crowd, "Jonathan Dark, there you are, only ten minutes late." It was Smeltzer. Jonathan's surprise wrestled with his delight at finding a friendly and familiar soul in this alien city. Small, as cities go, but to Jonathan it appeared and sounded like a metropolis.

"James Smeltzer, you leaving town already?" he said as they shook hands. "What are you doing here, waiting to catch a picture?"

"Believe it or not, old salt, I've been waiting for you," the photographer said cheerfully, clapping Jonathan's shoulder hard enough that he almost dropped his luggage. James made a mild attempt to take the suitcase, which Jonathan refused to relinquish.

"How did you know I'd be on this train?" Jonathan queried, encouraged and irritated in roughly equal measure.

"Laurel Charon phoned me, because she knew you wouldn't," Smeltzer confided smugly.

"Wherever I go," Jonathan muttered, "people are trying to plan my life for me."

Smeltzer laughed. "Don't knock it. Being on your own can get lonely. Take it from one who knows." He waved his arm like opening a door and led the way through the aggregate commotion.

"I have a car," he confided in a whisper, almost as if he were ashamed to admit it.

Days passed, added up into weeks, became a month, then some more. Starblossom Dorn watched her belly grow, developed strange tastes for vinegar and dill, as well as marked aversion toward anything that smelled or tasted like fried fish or fresh-brewed coffee. Her awareness that she did not inhabit her body alone became constant and intense. Finally, one day the expected happened unexpectedly, in the middle of a song she was practicing – pain, immediate and hungry for release. Margaret wasn't there. Robert, unruffled and efficient as ever he was, drove her to the hospital.

Margaret was there afterward, when a nurse brought the baby to Star's room, and as the two women looked on, Star brought him to her breast and murmured, softly, like a summer breeze, as she held his head to her, "Jonny, oh, Jonny, my beautiful, beautiful boy."

What would have been scandal in the rigid, stratified moral matrix of Drovers Gap, in the wider and wilder cultural climate of Asheton was regarded as delicious spice for the social stew. Dawn Starr, the professional name Robert had concocted, had evolved into a singer of talent,

45

an artist of growing repute, thus not expected to abide by the sensibilities of more mundane mortals for whom respectability meant survival. The wags and witches of that wicked town speculated endlessly about who the father might be, since the singer seemed to cultivate a vast indifference toward any local male that might be deemed worthy of her affections. The more inventive among the gossiping elites suggested that Jonathan Dorn might not be the singer's son by birth, but a servant's or an unseen relative's offspring, or even, as one or two extremely imaginative tale-spinners insinuated, Margaret's. After all, everyone agreed she was younger than her years, ripe as a summer peach ready for peeling, and even more generous with her affections than she was with her money.

As for her money, several local grand causes had basked from time to time in her benevolence, rendering the movers and shakers of Asheton tolerant of her personal vices and desirous of her esteem. Margaret Boone was an institution. She could do no real wrong and actually accomplished a lot of good in their fine town, so all whose opinion was important agreed. All anyone knew for a fact was that she and her musical niece had gone off to an exclusive inn in the High Balsams on a spring retreat and returned before winter with a wee babe among their luggage. This was not deemed anything extraordinary, for everybody said Margaret had always exhibited a penchant for bringing home strays.

As for young Jonathan Dorn, if he was doted upon and spoiled, he was also loved and guided. If his faults were generally ignored, his best tendencies were consistently encouraged and praised. He was an intelligent child, like his father of whom no one other than his mother rarely spoke. And in answer to his childish inquisitions, she seldom answered more than, "Your father was a fine and wonderful man. You're growing up to be just like him."

It didn't bother Jonathan in the slightest that his friends had resident fathers. He had Uncle Robert, and in that privileged household, where all affairs were discussed and debated freely in his presence, as if he were a miniature adult, he grew to know about all the foolish cruelties loosed in the community around him without being personally wounded by them. By the time he was seven years old, he was as worldly-wise, or perhaps wiser than many human males of seventy.

The course of Jonathan's life would take a drastic change in direction when his mother announced that to celebrate his seventh birthday, Jonathan and Aunt Margaret would accompany her to her next concert in Knox. Although Jonathan had heard his mother singing since before he was born, he had never seen her perform on stage before an audience. As they boarded the train to Tennessee, in Jonathan's mind, another world entirely, he was feeling very grown-up indeed.

Jonathan Dark had no ambitions to be a music critic. He had not spent the past several years convincing the Editor-in-Chief of the Knox Record that he was a hard news writer just so he could spend two hours sitting among rich strangers listening to a woman he didn't know singing in languages he couldn't understand; not the sort of music he was accustomed to at all.

Normally, Ed Long, chief editor and self-proclaimed opera fan, would have covered the event himself, but Ed was in bed with the influenza that had been wracking the city of late, and Jonathan had not been able to invent a convincing excuse in time to avoid being tagged for the assignment.

"And behave yourself," Ed had commanded. "You'll be sharing a box with one of the major broadcast people in Asheton, television, no less. Convince her the Record is a real newspaper, that their little screens will never be able to compete with timely print for a news audience."

As he drove his almost new car to the theater, Jonathan marveled at the unlikely turns in his life since he stepped off the train in Knox into James Smeltzer's custody. He recalled the unsettling ride across town to Smeltzer's apartment, with James driving one-handed, waving the other out the window as he said blithely, as if they had discussed it already, "There's an opening on the Record for a feature writer. I told Ed Longstreet – he's our chief editor – that you're just the man for it. He's willing to give you a trial. Part time, you understand, but show him your good and he'll make a proper place for you on staff."

When Jonathan could get a word in edgewise, he said, "I don't know anything about writing for a newspaper."

Smeltzer went on, unfazed, "You have a good eye for details. You don't use big words, and you can spell. Just fake it until you make it. Pretend you are writing letters to your mother."

That was essentially what Jonathan had done, finally, after two weeks of trying to find "normal" work and feeling guilty because his friend wouldn't let him pay rent. "When you're working," Smeltzer would say, "you can buy me a steak dinner at Riverside Inn and we'll call it even."

Jonathan's job search was hindered by his having no idea what he wanted to do. He knew he didn't want to tend bar which accounted for most of the work experience in his brief employment history. He might have accepted an offer to join a logging crew up in the High Balsams, had not Smeltzer told him horror stories about the short and risky lives of timbermen and insisted one more time, "Go talk to Longstreet. What can you lose by it? If he hires you, he might buy your lunch."

Although the Editor-in-Chief of the Knox Record immediately grasped that Smeltzer's recommendation was not based on the applicant's experience, he led Jonathan to a vacant desk in the newsroom and queried, "How did you get to this town, Pilgrim?"

"I rode a train all night from Poplar Spring, Mister Longstreet," Jonathan confessed.

Longstreet gave no sign he was impressed, but said, "Sit down here and write me a story about your train ride. Six hundred words. You have thirty minutes." He turned and walked back to his office. Thirty-eight minutes later Jonathan knocked on the office door and handed over as many words as he'd been able to write. Longstreet read them while Jonathan stood in front of his desk, hat in hand, coat folded across his arm, ready to leave upon hearing the inevitable verdict.

Finally, the Editor looked up, appeared surprised, as if he had forgotten Jonathan was there, handed back the pages.

Only Longstreet's eyes were smiling when he said, "That's your desk out there." He pointed through the glass door. "Get Doris over yonder to show you how to type. She will if you offer to buy her lunch."

Doris turned out to be a good teacher of typing and other things pleasurable and interesting, and Jonathan proved himself to be a quick learner, and now, seven years down his road, he was in a theater box introducing himself to a tastefully-dressed and handsome woman of indeterminate years from Asheton, accompanied by a male child lively and quick, who for no reason Jonathan could discern, seemed startlingly familiar.

The boy introduced himself, "My name is Jonathan. My mother says I was named for a prince."

"So was I," Jonathan Dark said. "Our parents must have read the same book."

The lights in the hall dimmed. The crowd below quietened. The boy reached up to take the hand of the woman in charge of

49

him. "Aunt Margaret and I came to hear my mother sing tonight," he said. Little Jonathan pointed at the stage. "There she is," he whispered, and the curtains began to part as the audience applauded.

Parts of "An Unaccustomed Music" originally appeared under the title "Dark Fork" in the anthology, *Fall*, published 2018 by Dark Ink Press.

PÚCA

"The Blood of Christ, the cup of salvation." Ward heard the words, stared at the wafer in his hands, dipped it into the chalice held out to him, placed the Host into his mouth, felt it melt away on his tongue before he stood. He wandered away from the rail, avoiding the supplicants shuffling forward. An usher took his hand, as he stepped down from the chancel. Ward grasped the hand with firm intention, as would a Quaker breaking meeting. It was a conscious gesture. The usher, who knew him from a former life, returned the intention.

The dispersing congregants, densely packed and still winter-wrapped in the first week of spring, nudged Ward slowly toward daylight. Nobody hurried to leave, not even Ward. It was cold outside, and now released from constraining liturgy, folk were eager to raise their voices and drown out whatever seeds of piety the rector's sermon had planted within them. Ward did his part. He smiled when smiled upon, answered when spoken to, shared his opinion of the weather, and when one or two made inquiry, informed in the vaguest possible terms about how his new book was coming along. He didn't make anything up. Neither did he tell everything he knew.

Eventually, only Father Daniel stood between Ward and the door. The priestly silhouette bled into the bright March morning beyond.

"I quoted from your blog in Adult Study this morning." He said it with a smile, a thinly veiled accusation.

"Then I became infamous before I arrived," Ward answered with a straight face.

"You certainly did," said the woman behind him, adjusting her scarf before descending into the real world. She and the priest laughed, as if she had made a joke. Ward decided it was safe for him to laugh, too.

51

He emerged at last into sunlight more cheerful than warm.

"Watch out for angels," he heard behind him. The priest again.

"I'll keep my head down," Ward shouted back, without turning around, hoping he sounded light and sociable.

He could not quite say to anyone that he believed in God, although he could not tell himself that he did not believe. He felt no ambivalence at all toward angels, however. His mind allowed no possibility for them at all. Nothing in Ward's experience encouraged in him any notion that benevolent spirits were hovering over his days, guarding him against hurt and making his paths straight. He knew he didn't deserve his life and figured only incredibly good luck accounted for his present transient comforts and illusions of safety and control.

Ward would have been astounded to know that, despite his shallow faith, angels believed in him. He had been totally unaware of their meddling in his life for some time now, and had no premonition of the drastic turn his life was about to take.

Ward was not an insensitive soul. All through the past week as he tried to work about his place, he felt as if he were being watched by some unseen presence. Once, he asked Oren Taylor, who had been hired for the day to plow Ward's garden plot and set out some onions, "Mister Oren, have you seen anyone hanging around here today?"

Oren laughed at the serious question. "Nobody our old eyes could see, Mister Ward, but that don't mean we ain't been seen, now, don't you know. There's many been here afore our time, and this is a good old place. Who mought blame any if they was wont to stay past their years?"

Ward knew about Drovers Gap's reputation for being the most haunted town in the Southern Appalachians.

Ghostly tales were recited to all the tourists and flaunted in books and brochures at every shop and inn. "Do you believe the stories then, Mister Oren?"

Oren's face turned deadly stern. "I don't believe onliest in things, I see, Mister Ward."

Ward had not set foot under a steeple since Emma died, but that Sunday was Emma's birthday, and that is why Ward decided to go to church. He had first met the priest, Father Daniel Jamison, down at Mountain Brew, where Ward went on Monday nights when the crowd was mostly local. He went not to drink but to eat a pretty good stew, hear human voices, watch the people and maybe even glean an idea for a story. Dan was also a regular. "Recovering from my sermon, like the rest of the congregation," he explained with a laugh. Ward told the priest that his wife had been a church person, but he wasn't, and though they talked about many things on succeeding Mondays, Dan never hinted that Ward might be missing something on his secular wander. By now, Ward reckoned, they were almost friends.

Emma had been his third wife, and his last wife, he was certain. Emma was the best, spoiled him for the rest. Ward's first wife had left him as soon as she discovered what an arrogant selfish jerk lurked beneath his public amiability. The second wife, whom he loved better, severed ties when after a few years she discovered she liked their lawyer's wife better than she liked Ward. The jilted husbands never exchanged speculations about what happened to the absconded spouses.

By then, Ward's first novel had been published and sold enough copies that his publisher had contracted for a second. Writing and alcohol consumed his days in an alternating cycle until he met Emma. His real life began and ended with Emma. For the first and last time in his existence, he belonged to another. Emma grounded him and filled him and gave him wings to fly into a sober life. Under her watchful care, he found a modest career as an academic, and to his surprise, discovered teaching made him a better writer.

After Emma died, Ward didn't take up drinking again, because he had promised her. That promise was all he had left of their shared life. He sold their condo, moved out into the mountains west of town and bought an abandoned twenty-three acres of tilted woodland and a sad and sagging house with a roof like a sieve. Making the house fit to live in, clearing a garden space and building a shed for chickens left him time enough for writing but not enough time to tend a bottle. The arrangement worked well enough to keep him sober and productive.

Emma had grown up on a farm. Ward hoped he might find her there somewhere on the land, and sometimes he did glimpse her in his dreams or in the shadows among trees, and sometimes she whispered to him in wind stirred leaves or laughed with him in the tumbling waters of a rowdy little creek in the woods behind his garden. When he wasn't gardening or tending his chickens, Ward wrote another novel. Emma spoke to him out of every page. He promised his publisher one more. By now, though, he thought that one might take longer to write than he had in the world.

On his way home from church Ward didn't see any angels. As he turned into his drive, he did notice the U-Haul parked in front of the dilapidated house on the old Longley place across the road. He wouldn't have thought the house fit for anyone to move into or that anything left in it would be worth hauling out. He wondered which was happening.

Next morning, when Ward walked down his drive to check his mail, the U-Haul had gone. He didn't see any people about the place, but along the road, beside his own, stood a shiny new mailbox, neatly lettered on the side, *T. Stone.* The morning after that, he found the usual assortment of flyers and ads in his box and a book he had ordered. He was scanning his mail when a woman stepped up beside him and opened her mailbox, startling him. He hadn't seen her when he came out or heard her walk up behind him.

They stood there for a moment, smiling at one another like new neighbors do, their hands full of paper freshly arrived from other places.

"Ward Bryant," Ward said, "how did you find things over there?"

"Tsula Stone," the woman said, "I'm right at home." Her long white hair under the sun half-blinded Ward but he noted a willowy frame, deeply tanned arms, adequately muscled, a pair of hands, strong and lean, long fingers grasping packages and what appeared to be a newspaper.

"Glad you're my neighbor, Ward Bryant," added a low musical voice that sounded like a smile Ward couldn't see for the sun in his eyes. Then she turned from him, crossed the road and walked away toward her house. He watched her go, her smooth steps more flow than gait. *Tsula,* he let the name rest in his mind, at once strange and familiar, then turned to go back to his own world. Halfway to his house, Ward Bryant stopped and looked back. Tsula Stone was not to be seen.

So began their series of daily exchanges at the mailbox, too brief to qualify as conversations, but with each occurrence leaving Ward knowing nothing more about his mysterious neighbor, only with a vague and unacknowledged hunger to be known by her. Over the weeks that followed, Ward became more observant of the scene beyond the road. He seldom saw Tsula out and about her place, or any workers at all, but one day he would notice the house had a new roof and, a week or so later, a fresh coat of paint. May arrived, and her tumbledown barn lay flat, dismembered and stacked for salvage in its lot. Ward would intend to question or comment on his neighbor's doings next he saw her, but whenever they met at their mailboxes, Tsula would steer the conversation away in some other direction and be gone again before Ward could bring their talk back around to where he meant to start.

Something was at his chickens again. The hens' terrified gabbling hauled Ward Bryant out of a dream deeper than recalling. He emerged abruptly from that inner darkness into the opaque black of a pre-dawn mountain morning, stumbled and floundered into his clothes, fumbled after his light and gun, and with a roar and a yell that didn't quite belong to him, plunged out his back door.

By the time he reached the hen house his birds were all quiet and settled, as if Ward had only dreamed the entire ruckus.

"What's going on in here, girls?" he asked them. The Speckled Sussex kept their secrets. Ward counted his chickens. They were all still there, apparently unscathed. He checked their nest boxes, reckoned there should have been more eggs. The hens had not been laying well for weeks, ever since the almost nightly incursions into their space began, not long after the Sunday he attended church, also, he recalled, about the same time that strange Tsula Stone moved in across the road. As far as he knew, though, she didn't keep a dog that might be the guilty raider. Next time he saw her he would make a point to ask about her animals.

A thorough inspection turned up no damage or opening where any animal bigger than a mouse might have gained access to the hens. Whatever was terrorizing Ward's chickens couldn't get to them without coming through the door, and he always found it securely latched when he arrived at the scene. He had seen bears open a barn door on occasion, but he'd never known one to lock up behind himself. Only humans did that. Maybe, Ward speculated, the interloper was not after chickens, but their eggs. Maybe his hens were laying just fine.

Before dark that evening, soon as he finished his supper, Ward sprinkled cornmeal liberally all around his chicken shed. Whoever or whatever was visiting his fowls at night would leave tracks. If he couldn't catch the interloper, at least he might be able to identify its species. Of course, on second thought, some night-flying owl wouldn't leave tracks behind, but he'd never heard of owls stealing eggs or opening doors.

The next morning revealed the tracks Ward anticipated. He thought they might have been left by a dog or coyote. When he showed them to Oren Taylor, the old man knelt and adjusted his spectacles, stared intently at the ground, then looked up and wheezed, "Nossir, she's the Fox."

"The Fox?" Ward said. "You thinking of one fox in particular here?"

Oren lurched toward upright. Ward reached out a hand to help.

"Yup," said Oren, when he found his feet, "the White Fox. See, she's missing a toe on her right hind foot. That's where Deac Roberts almost caught her in a trap. That must be ten years ago. Haven't seen her since. Deac's dead now."

"Foxes live that long?" Ward said, skeptical of the tale.

Oren's snort sounded to Ward like annoyance. "White Fox ain't an ordinary soul." The old man erased the track with the toe of his boot. "They's púca. Shapeshifters. They can be anything or anybody. She ain't really interested in your chickens or your eggs, Ward Bryant, she's just trying to find out about you. Careful she don't come to fancy atter ye."

57

Ward tried mightily not to laugh in the old man's face. "That would be a bad thing, Mister Oren?"

Oren aimed his chew at a drooping milkweed and spat. "Ganny nobody's told you about Deac. Once he got her attention, the Fox fixed on him. A púca can love a man to death in no time."

A week went by after that, and Ward Bryant and his chickens slept peaceful and unmolested. Day by day, he went about his usual routine, tending his garden, plowing his current novel manuscript, explaining to his publisher via email why he missed her last deadline, gossiping with his mysterious new neighbor when they met beside the road at their mailboxes. He did ask her if she had a dog or any sort of livestock.

"I don't fancy being leashed, caged or fenced in myself," she said, "so I wouldn't dream of doing that to any other creature."

Ward went to fair pains cultivating his reputation as a loner, but he found himself watching the road, timing his trips to his mailbox to coincide with sightings of Tsula Stone walking down her drive. Their roadside conversations tended toward brief, not because Tsula ever seemed in a hurry, but because Ward found his spoken words to her even more reluctant to emerge into the outer world than the words he splashed across his computer screen during the darks before dawn. Much of the time he should have been writing his novel, he spent trying to think of questions to ask his neighbor, that without prying into none of his business, might extend their fleeting exchanges at the mailbox.

Ward was beyond curious about the woman. He felt a bone-deep need to know more about her. The Longley place, as all his neighbors called the twelve acres opposite his, had been vacant and abandoned when he moved in five years before. He never saw a sale sign go up, but suddenly, three months ago, this woman appeared, commanding the ground like it had been hers forever.

Ward judged Tsula a true beauty, not pretty at all in any conventional sense, but possessed of a lean clean elegance, like some creature born from the forest and the hills, as much the soul of her place as a soul in a place. Her speech made a music that hung in a man's head long after she gathered her mail and walked away toward her own house. *Smitten*. That was the only label Ward could paste on his mirror in his most honest moments. Yet, he hardly knew the woman. They had never entered each other's door. Had never talked for more than five minutes at a time. They had never shared any history or confidence or even stood close enough to touch. How could this near stranger be so familiar to him? Ward had been ruffled in his space as much as his hens. Tsula Stone had rendered him a troubled man. He realized that if she disappeared tomorrow his life would be somehow smalled by her absence.

Ward forgot all his conjectures about Tsula Stone, when he began reading the third email he opened one evening after supper. It was from the dean at the university where Ward had taught for sixteen years. He shot back a quick and resounding *Yes*, promptly arranged his airline reservations then texted Oren Taylor to ask if he would look after Ward's chickens while he was away from home.

Ten days later, a few minutes past noon, a loquacious cab driver deposited Ward on the State University campus where, in a couple of hours, he would receive a Distinguished Alumnus Award. A reading from his latest book was scheduled for the evening. He had lunch with the head of the English department and his publisher, Augusta Shucker, who flew into town from her lair in Chicago just for the occasion. Ward was surprised she accepted, and he wondered if she had come to thwart his self-destruction, or if she, like him, suspected *Under the Mountain* would be his last book. Maybe she just wanted to see for herself if his promised new work-in-progress was progressing on schedule. It wasn't.

He was fond of Shucker, affectionately addressed her as Gus. She liked his work when nobody else did, published his first book. It sold well enough that she was willing to take on the second. The last one had been their sixth, a collection of stories mostly stolen from the lives of his mountain neighbors. During the intervening years, Ward's story books, as he called them, had brought in enough money to sustain their friendship through all the ensuing editorial conflicts and missed deadlines on his part.

Over the course of the afternoon, he renounced sobriety and downed several calming libations, knowing that Oren would scold him like a worried mother when he got home. That evening Gus spoke some elucidating and eloquent words about his novel, by which time Ward had gathered himself just enough to slur his way through a brief reading he knew by heart and offer nearly coherent mumbles in response to questions from the audience.

The affair was moderately attended. A couple of adjunct professors, several unpublished authors, the manager of the campus books store, one or two feature writers from the local papers, and a dozen or so students. Someone had the idea to induce a trio of string students to provide *Eine Kleine Nachtmusik*. They played in tune most of the notes as written.

After the questions, the assembly converged on a table by the door to receive their reward of bland cheese and mediocre wine. A young woman, garbed in a scholarly style lifted straight from a zine ad, came up to Ward, removed her glasses before she spoke, so that he could see her intelligent brown eyes. Even through his customary haze now augmented by alcohol, she made an impact.

"Why do you write so much about old men?" she asked.

"Because I'm old," Ward answered, "and I'm male. So are most of my friends. I tend to write about whatever's in front of me." He was close enough to sober to recognize the child was posing for him, trying to arouse at least a vague unease. At the moment, his mind was more occupied by a growing insistence from his distended bladder that he needed to search out a restroom.

He was about to make some socially appropriate excuse to cut the conversation short when she bludgeoned Ward with a question he would have never seen coming.

"Do you miss being married?"

The words stung like an accusation. He realized that for the past few weeks his new neighbor had occupied his thoughts more than his dead wife. Ward fired back, "What is your name?"

"Grace," through a brilliant smile. "Grace Tenshi."

"Japanese?" The question essentially constituted an effort to steer conversation away from Grace's query.

"My Father," answered Grace patiently. "Now my question?"

"I can't allow myself to miss what is forever gone," Ward said. "I don't miss people. I just write them."

"But you still love her," Grace said with a smile quite lost on Ward whose mind was suddenly years away.

"It isn't your place to question my loves or my losses," Ward said, sharp just beyond pleasant. "You haven't suffered enough to undertake such an investigation."

"It wasn't a question, really," Grace insisted. "Just saying what I see." When Ward opened his mouth, bereft of words to fill it, she added, "Have mercy on the fox when you get back to Drovers Gap."

Ward by now had assembled in his head a scathing indictment of undergraduate hubris and callous ignorance,

61

but before he could spew it between his lips, Grace Tenshi walked away and became a blur in the herd.

Her impertinent probing into his bereavement still rankled, but his mind stuck on another question. *How did she know about the fox?*

He turned to look for a quick exit and came face to face with the chair of the English Department, who had been observing the exchange. "I see, Bryant, that you still attract the impressionable young minds. We'll have to do a headcount in the dorm when you leave."

"You give me too much credit, Professor," Ward snapped. "Your impressionable young minds have less to fear from me than from your predatory and opportunistic faculty." He didn't add that he was the one who'd been impressed, not to mention unsettled, and it had nothing at all to do with sexual attraction. Ward fled Chair's academic smirk and reached the men's necessary just ahead of embarrassment.

After the Occasion, Ward and Gus and the American Literature Professor, his successor in the post, shared a light supper at a quiet restaurant more expensive than it had any right to be. Then Gus whisked away to catch her plane. The professor went home to bed after depositing Ward at his hotel room. Ward's last conscious thought before he fell asleep was that he wished he'd stayed home where he didn't have to go to so much trouble to get drunk.

That night he dreamed vivid dreams about his white fox, always watching him from shadows and edges, eluding his approach, ever just beyond reach of his retribution. At some point in his dreaming, White Fox became his dear lost forever Emma, and before dawn, Ward dreamed about Tsula Stone.

He woke next morning and without opening his eyes, thinking he was still back in the cramped apartment where he and Emma had first known one another as the Bible says, he reached out to touch Emma who wasn't there. Ward hadn't done that since he moved to the farm. That arrogant child, Tenshi, had brought it all back to him. He didn't speak of that time in his previous life to anyone who knew him now. He wondered how much of his history was public knowledge, was glad he wasn't famous enough to have a biographer to dwell on his trivia.

Despite his headache, Ward was hungry by the time he carried his bags down to the lobby. As he sat sipping his coffee and munching on his second complimentary croissant while he waited on the shuttle van that would take him to the airport, Ward thought about the times he'd shared with Emma in the rented room over the bakery, where the wheaty-yeasty smells wafting up the stairwell always assured that he woke hungry and wrote hungry. In those days he imagined he was already the great novelist that he never quite became in all the years that followed.

In Ward's honest moments he would admit to himself that his hunger to be known as a writer tended in those early days to be greater than his hunger to write. When Emma Blair came up the stair the first time and he opened the door to her smile, a deeper hunger consumed him. He felt like he might have encountered an angel. Suddenly it struck him, the girl last night at the reading, Grace, she said her name was Tenshi. Ward knew just enough Japanese to recognize the word translated into English as *Angel*.

On the van from the airport at the other end of his flight, there were only two other passengers, neither more inclined to conversation than Ward. He gazed vacantly at the lights and shadows sliding by the window. He didn't think about Emma. He didn't think about Tsula Stone or the white fox. His head hurt, his stomach churned, and he was tired. As soon as he was home, he vowed he would sleep and when

63

he woke, he would be back on the rails again. He had no desire to resume his disastrous career as a drunk.

Ward didn't sleep long before his hens roused him with their cacophonous cackle. Still only half awake, he ejected himself from his back door just in time to see a white blur dart away from his chickenyard toward the line of trees beyond his vegetable garden. Oren had been right about the fox tracks at least. Without taking time to really aim, he raised his rifle and fired in the general direction of the fleeing animal. It was more an attempt to intimidate than to kill, and Ward was as surprised as the fox when he heard it yelp and saw the animal cartwheel to the ground. The fox struggled to its feet and began limping off toward the woods. Ward took careful aim to fire again, but when he saw the pale vulpine ghost standing still under the moon, watching him with eyes that, even in the night, shone golden and bright like candleflame, he could not muster intention to pull the trigger.

He remembered the words somebody had told him. He couldn't quite remember who. *Have mercy on the fox.*

"I'm sorry," Ward whispered to the fox, to himself, to the moon, perhaps to God.

"I'm so sorry," he said again, louder, as Fox melted away into a shadow among trees.

Ward couldn't find his sleep again after that. He pretended to write until it was time for breakfast, even though he knew most of the words he scrolled across the screen of his Dell would be deleted after his second cup of morning coffee. Over his scrambled egg sandwich, he watched the road for some sign of Tsula Stone. Jane McCarson, the mail carrier came and went, and when he went out to check his box, Ward stood there some minutes, alone in the wind, pretending to read his mail, without anyone to talk to.

The next day, Ward was waiting beside his mailbox when Jane arrived. She handed over his mail and was preparing to drive away when Ward said, "My neighbor didn't get any mail today?"

Jane gave him a look that said his neighbor's mail was none of his business, then relented. "Tsula called in to hold her mail for a week. Said she's gone to visit her sick sister."

"I didn't know she had a sister," Ward said, wondering why he did.

"She keeps herself close," Jane said. "She only tells us what we need to know."

As the carrier's old jeep pulled away, Ward felt like he had just been accused of something.

The chickens were quiet for a week, and the next time they set up a great ruckus in the night, Ward got out his door too late to catch sight of the fox. Later that morning, when he went to fetch his mail, he was quietly joyous to see Tsula Stone walking out her drive. He dawdled by the mailboxes, until she crossed the road.

"How's your sister?" Ward asked, wanting too badly to say something, anything, to her to consider if the question was appropriate.

"She's mending," Tsula said. "You're kind to ask."

They were both several steps back homeward when Ward, not knowing he was about to, stopped and turned, called, "Miss Tsula?"

She looked around at him, as if she'd been expecting it. "Yes, Ward?" saying it more like an answer than a question.

"Would you like me to fix supper for you tonight, after all your traveling?" As he spoke, Ward was trying to remember what he might have on hand to cook for a guest.

Tsula bestowed a smile, rare and radiant. "I'd love that, Ward Bryant. What time?"

Ward calculated in his head how long it might take to make a quick run to Tom's Grocery, clean his house and cook. "About seven? That okay?" he said.

"I'll bring dessert," Tsula said, and carried her smile away to her house.

That afternoon was the longest Ward could remember. Fortunately, he had more than enough to keep him busy. But all was ready when he looked out into the remains of the day and saw a crepuscular Tsula Stone walking into his yard, a vague, shifting glimmer in the twilight. He managed to wait for her knock before he opened the door.

Their supper that evening was a resounding success, as far as Ward could judge. Tsula deemed his stew that he called Highland Perloo delicious, praised the bread he had baked, and when he exulted over the poundcake with carob icing she brought for dessert, she just smiled and said, "Blame it on the eggs."

Ward had bought a bottle of wine to serve her, although he didn't intend to drink any himself. It went unopened when Tsula presented a concoction she had infused with herbs from her garden and the woods around. "No spirits about it," she informed, "but you'll find it heady enough." In Ward's estimation, it was indeed.

Over the course of the summer, supper with Tsula became the high point of Ward's weekly routine. Sometimes at his house, on occasion at hers, and in good weather, under the holly trees in the surrounding woods. They ate and talked and laughed and listened together, and gradually across the weeks, Ward ceased to think of his life as something he did alone.

Almost to October, when the air carried a gentle prophecy of frosts to come, leaving for what he suspected might be their last picnic of the season, Ward went out his door carrying an extra blanket under his arm and met Tsula doing the same. Ward built a little fire before their favorite holly tree, and after they had eaten the food they brought and liberated the last drop of Tsula's herbal elixir from its green bottle and said all the words they had to say, the fire was needy and Ward turned to lay on more wood.

Not for the first time, Tsula leaned across to plant a kiss long and slow and deep, and for the first time, as Ward gazed into those eyes gleaming golden as candleflame in the light from the fire, she began unbuttoning his shirt. The dance that followed was unchoreographed and unrehearsed and unfolded naturally and freely as a breath and ended with them both outside all their clothes.

For the first time, he saw the scar above Tsula's right wrist. He had served in the military for four years and seen enough combat to recognize it for what it was.

"That's a gunshot wound," he said, a tremor in his voice he couldn't suppress. Who did this to you, Tsula?"

She laughed, as if God had told a big joke on them. "Oh, Love, after all our time together, don't you know me? You did."

Ward had a thousand questions then that he forgot to ask.

Oren Taylor hadn't heard anything from Ward in more than a week. He'd texted and phoned but got no response to any of his messages. After he finished his chores, he walked down to the writer's house to see if he was still in the world. It was nearly dark when Oren came into the yard to find the gate ajar and the chickens running loose. As soon as he got the hens rounded up and penned, he went to the house, all dark inside with the back door open to the night.

Oren leaned through the door and called loud enough to scare the chickens, "Ward Bryant, airyeaboot?" Except for the crickets in the woods, silence. A search through the house turned up no Ward, dead or alive. "Bet he's took up with that woman ayonder," Oren said to the chickens. He closed the door, figured he might walk across the road and ask Tsula Stone what she knew of his friend. As he stepped down to go, Oren heard a soft yip from among the trees beyond the yard and looked up just in time to see the ghostly forms of two white foxes flow soundlessly away into shadows.

———————————

"Púca" originally appeared in the anthology *Happily Ever Never*, published 2022 by Creative James Media.

HEPHAESTUS BY ANY OTHER NAME

Festus watched a solitary cloud brighten and silver as it swallowed the moon. He held his breath and counted the seconds until the gleaming honey-hued disk emerged again among a scatter of stars populating his open window. He sighed, almost a groan, threw back the quilt and lurched to his feet, letting his sound leg bear most of his substantial weight. His other leg, the twisted aching one, had stolen his sleep from him one more night.

Festus shrugged his robe over beefy shoulders and cinched it tight across his ample belly. Everybody in Drovers Gap had remarked at one time or another on his size and marveled at his prodigious strength, which most who knew him agreed was not quite natural for a mere human. His only evident weakness was that warped leg of his, broken at a time he couldn't remember, that had never been properly set and pained him his every waking hour.

He fumbled the dark, found his cane, and hobbled off toward the kitchen. Sunrise was hours away, but Festus was hungry. An early breakfast now and he could have the forge fired and ready for work at first light. A full day's work awaited his attention. While his barley tea steeped, he catalogued the current projects in his mind. He needed to finish the flowery gate for Homer Priapus. Homer was threatening not to pay if he didn't get it in time for the Drover's Gap garden festival. Charlie Charon down at the crossing was after him every day for the gearbox for his ferry. Charlie had been a good customer over the years. He also ran a gristmill, and Festus had made the waterwheel as well as half the fittings for the machinery inside.

Festus knew he had neglected his clients of late. It wasn't that he hadn't been working. He blamed it on that damned chair Hera Guice commissioned. He'd been at it obsessively nearly a year now, and it had eaten up all his time. He couldn't tell himself why the formidable old hag had such a hold on him. She lived all alone in her little hovel across the river, away up in the woods on Warrior Knob. Nobody in town knew how old she was or how long she had been up there. Some of the elders claimed she had been living on that mountain when they were born, maybe before there was even a town. It was rumored that she had a husband once, but that her tongue had proven too sharp for him to live with. A few times, somebody mentioned to Festus that Hera had a child way back in the dim past, maybe a girl, but most agreed a boy. If she had a son, he never in anyone's memory came to see his old mama.

Festus pondered the irony of their situation; an old woman who never saw her child, and an old man, not as old as her, but old enough to count, who couldn't remember his mother. They were both orphans of a kind, all alone, she among the trees of the mountain, he among the people of the town, both unburdened and unblessed by any bonds of affection or expectation. At least, Festus had his work entailing obligations and promises that gave him occasional and temporary respite from the loneliness that pervaded his days.

He supposed old Hera must get lonely, too. Why else would she have come into town one spring day and walked into his shop to order that fantastically fancy chair? He relived the scene in his head every time his thought turned to it. He hadn't heard her come in. He was dousing a bit of steel into his water bucket to temper it for a knife blade. As the steam lifted and the water stilled, he saw another face beside his own, so alike about the eyes that for an instant he thought his reflection had doubled. Startled, he nearly dropped the blade from his tongs.

He looked up and there she stood. He knew instantly

who she was though he had never seen her before. He laid the steel against his anvil and between hammer blows, said, "Miss Hera, you must be. Nobody else in this town would steal up behind a smithy when he's working."

"No man's fire nor iron can touch me, Festus Smith. I want you to make me a chair wrought of silvered iron," she said with the same tone one might ask for a spade or a pair of shears.

She pulled from her shawl a roll of paper and spread it on the worktable. Festus laid aside his hammer and bent over to look at the drawing of a chair drawn in precise and intricate detail. Delicate enough to be tedious but not impossible, the artifact was ornamented all around with leaves and vines and flowers and grapes that looked almost alive on paper but would require unaccustomed skill and care to render convincingly in drawn and beaten metal born in the forge's fire and shaped between hammer and anvil.

"This is a mighty fancy chair," Miss Hera," he murmured, tracing the fine lines but not quite touching the paper with his blackened fingertip. "You expecting high company are ye then?"

"I don't have company, neither high nor low, Smithy," she said, so softly that he had to lean toward her to hear. "None sit at my table that I don't hold close to heart."

You must need only a short table then. Aloud, Festus said, "It must be somebody closer than close to warrant such an extravagant chair."

"Close enough," Hera said. "That chair's for me. Will you make it then?"

"Will you pay me?" Festus said, thinking as soon as he spoke it that he was being rude to a customer.

Hera did not appear offended by his bluntness. "If you can finish it by the next spring, exactly as I have drawn it for you, I will pay whatever you ask."

"I can and I will," Festus said quietly.

Hera took out a leather bag and set it on the table between them. "For your materials, my Smithy," she said, looking at him with eyes that made him feel like he was looking at himself and flashing an instant of smile that broke his heart.

Festus looked down at the bag, picked it up, loosed the drawstring, spilled the contents onto the table. Silver coins. He counted half of them before he judged there were at least a hundred there. "This is too much," he whispered. Festus looked up to find Hera no longer with him. He knew then that he would never spend Hera's silver. He would melt it down and mold it into ornaments for her chair.

Hastily Festus scooped the coins back into their bag and dropped it into the pocket of his apron. He rushed outside and nearly collided with Charlie Charon come to inquire about his gearbox. "Where did she go?" Festus shouted at the startled ferryman.

"I saw nought any," protested Charlie. "Who ye atter?"

"Old Hera Guice. She was here."

"That witch," Charlie snorted. "What did she tell ye?"

"She didn't come to talk," Festus said. "She just wanted to order a piece of work."

"You don't have to tell me your secret then," Charlie allowed a wide grin. "That's the main dealings people have with Hera. She knows people. She knows what's in their hearts. She knows what's close to them and far away. People go up there on the mountain to hear her tell them where's their lost money, or if their sick child will live, or be their lover true or false. Questions of the heart and dire necessity. Tell me now, friend, how answered she your query?"

"With a thousand other questions," murmured Festus, gazing up the street after an old woman who wasn't there.

Then coming to himself, said, "Your gearbox, Charlie. Almost done. I'll bring it down to the Crossing in the morning."

Now, in the last week of winter, Hera's chair was finally finished. What began a year past as a challenge ended as a consuming passion. To say he was proud of what he had wrought was an understatement. He thought it the best work he had ever made. He doubted he would ever be able to fashion anything so fine again. It was his masterpiece.

Festus checked the mechanism he had built into the arms of the chair. That was the only thing about it that varied from Hera's specifications. Satisfied all was working properly, he spent the rest of the morning carefully wrapping the chair against the untoward touches of a callous world. The chair was heavy and especially awkward to manage with his twisted leg uncertain beneath the weight, but after much sweat and strain and a few words he would never say to a friend, he got it loaded onto his cart. Festus hitched up Molly Dear, as he named his mule, and they hauled the chair through the luminous afternoon down to the landing on the Long Broad to wait for Charon's ferry. He could see the ferry on the other side of the river taking on a loaded wagon with driver and a pair of horses, and a couple of passengers. His wait wouldn't be long. Downstream, a bank of dense fog crept slowly up the river, as often happened this time of year. By the time the ferry cast off on that farther shore, the fog had come between, veiling everything across the water and hanging over the river like a vast curtain masking the edge of the world.

Festus watched the fog thinking about his upcoming delivery. He didn't doubt that Hera would be pleased. He knew no critic of his work more demanding than himself. He recalled they had never named a price beyond the silver

Hera had given him "for materials" as she put it. He was bringing her coins, all but three, back to her in her chair. By his reckoning, she still owed him. Hera said if he finished the work by spring, she would give him whatever he wanted, and Hera, as many had told him and he had no reason to doubt, always told the truth. As the ferry emerged from the fog like a vessel from another realm, now nearer this shore than the other, Festus thought to himself, *Old Hera, you who give answers to every man's question, even the unanswerable, you will answer me mine when you have your chair.*

Festus watched as the ferry approached the landing, the ancient engine, repurposed from some long dead farmer's tractor, chuffing like a bad cough, the flywheel chattering insanely on its loose axle until the craft nudged the dock and Charon made fast his lines and lowered the gate. Festus waited as the horses towed their driver and wagon onshore, and two passengers, apparently traveling afoot, debarked. They appeared mildly unnerved by their brief voyage, nodded without speaking to Festus on their way toward town.

When the deck was clear, he took up the reins to urge Molly Dear aboard, but Charlie, who probably weighed as much as the mule, stood in the way, arms spread, his weathered brow crinkled to a scowl. "Did you bring my gearbox?" he demanded.

"It's ready, Charon," Festus lied, "but I didn't have room on my cart for it what with this other delivery. I'll bring yours tomorrow."

The ferryman smiled like a true friend, stretched out his hand. "Then today, you'll have to pay to cross over."

Charlie's unfaltering grin convinced Festus that he could not be persuaded. Remembering the three coins left from Hera's chair, Festus pulled the leather bag from his jacket pocket and mutely handed it to the ferryman. Charlie dumped the contents into a broad and calloused palm and gazed fondly at the three silvers, then held one up to the light, squinting at it as if he doubted its provenance.

"That's for my crossing over and coming back," Festus said.

Charlie dropped the coins back into the bag and tucked it into his vest. He nodded at the cart. "That the chair ye done made for Hera all wropped up there?"

"It is that," Festus confirmed. "That chair's why I didn't get your gearbox done more timely. She said if I got it to her by spring, I could name my price."

Charlie shook his head, chuckled deep in his big chest, murmured as if to himself, "I didn't know the old witch was so generous." Then he directed a serious gaze at Festus. "You taking it up there all by yourself, then?"

"I am so," Festus declared. "I mean to put a private question to her and not leave without the answer I desire."

Charlie exploded into a laugh. "Then you've likely paid me double and I hope this mule can find its way back down the mountain without a driver."

"I'm not afraid of one old woman," Festus affirmed.

"Old Hera always tells the truth," Charlie said, all serious again, "and truth is almost never what a body desires. You'll be a disappointed man coming back, if at all you do."

Festus shrugged, carefully led Molly Dear onto the ferry. Charlie double chocked all four wheels. He said the river flowed high that morning, and the water ran rough mid-stream. Although the sun still shone strong upon the landing, the encroaching fog bank hung dense over the middle of the river allowing no sight nor sign of the far shore. As he listened to the water's rush, Festus doubted Charon had exaggerated caution.

Charlie motioned to his passenger to cast off the moorings, then fastened up the gate, and pulled on the big lever set into the deck. The engine below came alive with a great whump. A cloud of black smoke billowed from the stack, the flywheel moaned into motion and the faltering gearbox screamed and shrieked. Charon put his hands over his ears, shot a reproachful glance at the smithy who hadn't delivered, and by some miracle of grace, the ferry began to pull away toward the wall of fog appearing now to Festus as great and solid as any mountain of earth and stone.

The landing slipped away across a shine of sparkling water. Ahead, the fog overshadowed the river rendering it murky and opaque. Festus had crossed the Long Broad hundreds of times on this and other craft, but as the sun began to dim and festoons of mist commenced twining about the ferry, he felt an unaccustomed sense of foreboding. Charon, who had been watching him, perhaps sensed his passenger's unease, or felt some unsettlement within himself, for he sought to ignite a distracting conversation.

"Your mule there's a good one, Festus," he ventured. "Calm on the water like most of her kind are not." In fact, the animal did stand placid and content munching the bit of grain Festus had given her when they came aboard.

He pulled his gaze from the encompassing fog and looked at the ferryman as if he had forgotten Charlie was there. "Charon, not much perturbs my Molly Dear short of an empty feed bag. She's used to all manner of comings and goings by now. Would that her owner shared her equanimous nature."

Charlie spat a wad of something dark and viscous over the side. "Well, no offence to Molly Dear, but ever ye wished we was back in the Old Time, when they put engines in carts and wagons, just like on this ferry, and you'd only need feed 'em whilst they was going for ye?"

"I don't think that engine would fit on my cart," Festus said, afraid Charlie was about to revive the subject of the tardy gearbox.

"Not like this'n," Charlie said. "They could make smaller ones then, no bigger'n a cabbage crate, and they didn't burn wood nor corn spirits, neither. They ran on dragon blood, I've been told."

Festus didn't try to hide his incredulity. "I believe, Charon, that somebody told you a joke and you forgot to laugh. Ever you see such a thing with your own eyes?"

"So did I see," Charlie huffed. "But never a one that was still working."

"Where was that?" Festus queried.

"Way off down river, all to Sunkentown. They dredge such things up from the mudflats and melt them down for good metal to forge."

Festus didn't respond, stared off into the foggy dim. Charlie murmured, as much to himself as to his passenger. "It must have been a marvel to live in such a time."

Festus shifted his weight. A soft groan escaped him as he leaned more heavily on his cane. "It is a wonder to be alive in any time at all, Charlie," he said softly, as the fog closed around them weighty as a blanket, damping the sound of the water to a distant murmur. The engine boomed and echoed against the silence like a war drum. Charlie, standing a few feet away, rendered pale and vague as a ghost. When Festus peered over the side, he couldn't see the water. The ferry, for all he could tell, might be floating in a cloud miles above any river or world.

Without warning, a surge of vertigo twisted his gut. Festus clung to the wheel of his cart to keep from falling. Molly Dear nickered softly and stamped a foot. Even she seemed to feel their displacement, the unrighting of their world, as horizontal shifted to a vertical plane between nothingness and nothingness. The ferry chugged on. Festus couldn't decide if they were being delivered up to Heaven or down to Hell.

The fog obliterated all form and space and time. It might have been minutes or years before a pale disk of sun began to brighten overhead and green water rippled again in the ferry's wake and Festus saw, faintly at first, then with sudden clarity under a true blue sky, the landing on the opposite shore. He looked for the familiar details he remembered from his many previous crossings and recognized nothing.

"Charon, is this the right place?" he queried.

"It is, if you're going to see old Hera," the ferryman assured.

The landing appeared seldom used, a narrow, rickety dock in need of drastic maintenance, accessed by a single rutted and muddy track. This side of the fog the day remained clear, much warmer than across the river. Maple trees along the road were red with buds. Wherever they were, they had arrived on the brink of spring.

"I don't know when I'll be back to meet you here," Festus said, once they had Molly Dear and the cart safely ashore.

"Worry naught," Charon said, "I took your fare and I'll be here to take you over if ever you need to go."

"Sure this my right road, then?" Festus asked.

"It is the only road to where you're going," Charon said with a cheerless laugh. "Follow it to the end, and you'll be there, right or wrong." With that, he cast off his moorings and never looked back as the ferry creaked and groaned and shrieked and coughed and wheezed and sighed out and away from land, until the fog mid-river swallowed it whole. With a grimace, Festus hauled his aching leg after him onto the cart, propped his cane on the seat beside him and spoke to Molly Dear. The cart commenced to clatter after her on the rising road, where at the end, so Charlie Charon had promised, Hera Guice waited for her silver chair.

The road wound promptly over a ridge and through a wood, up and down and around, crossed several small streams and skirted a great tumble of boulders on its way up the face of Hera Guice's mountain. Unseen creatures scurried deeper into the brush as the cart noised past. Strange birds called from the trees. Festus recognized none of their songs, tried to catch a glimpse of beak or feather, but, like the beasts, the birds kept invisible to inquiring eyes. It seemed to Festus that the miles went on forever, though the sun did not swing perceptibly in his arc, and Molly Dear seemed not to tire at all. Festus himself felt no thirst nor hunger and was no more wearied than if they'd been on the road half an hour. Although, apparently seldom used, and grown with grass, the road higher up lay free of ruts and uncluttered with hindering stones, as if it had been freshly graded just for their passage.

Festus was still puzzling about these things when they rounded a bend and there in a little glen tucked into the mountain's face just below the summit, stood the most peculiar house Festus had ever seen. Yet there was something indefinably familiar about the scene. He couldn't shed the sense that he had been here before sometime lost to his memory; that he was known here, and though he could not recall his association with this place, the place had not forgotten him and embraced him now with something akin to welcome.

Festus had no doubt they had reached their destination. He pulled gently on the reins and called Molly Dear to halt. She obeyed promptly as always she did. The silence fell around them like a lid on a pot. No wind. Not a leaf stirred. No birdsong. No rustle or thump of life anywhere. The immovable sun shone down from a cloudless azure sky. Festus stretched out a hand to the light and felt neither warmth nor chill. It was as if time didn't exist, as if he had arrived at a changeless unchangeable forever.

He sat for a long moment on the cart, listening to the pervasive quiet; the only sounds Molly Dear's slow breathing, his own heartbeat, and the occasional creak and pop of the cart settling into stillness. Across a yard already hinting of spring green, a house most strange, taller by far than wide. It looked more like a tree than a dwelling. In fact, it was a tree, or perhaps several, a holly grove, growing in a tight circle, the gaps between their intertwining limbs walled up with stone. Other than a narrow door of stout timber bound with iron bands, the only opening into the house was a row of close-set windows high up, shaded and nearly obscured by the spiny green canopy of the constituent trees. The stone apparently had been salvaged from the ruins of what must have once been a castle or even a small village, that arrayed tilted and tumbled in the surrounding wood.

Festus didn't realize he had been holding his breath, until the narrow door opened with a grating rasp and Hera Guice stood before her house like a goddess in her sacred grove. His first impression was that she was much younger than he recalled from her visit to his shop a year past, but the longer he gazed the more uncertain he became of her age. Her long hair gleamed in the sun like burnished pewter and streamed down around her like a waterfall, flowing and caressing her shoulders and hips. Festus felt a breeze lifting, heard birds calling from the woods about. He pulled his gaze from Hera, looked up and saw trees greening, buds swelling, leaves unfurling as if days had become seconds.

When he lowered his sight and Hera's golden eyes fastened on him again, she said, "Smithy, so you brought my chair after all."

"I have done it," he said, and for no reason except it was at the center of his astonishment, he added, "You are younger here."

Hera laughed. It sounded like water splashing over stones. "My time rules here," she said. "I can be as young or old as I like, a spindly girl or a wrinkled crone, a ripe juicy woman or the ageless wind. And never you fear, Smithy, I would have kept spring for your arrival however long your journey." She gestured toward her open door. "Now bring in my chair and let us see if it is worth your price."

Festus directed Molly Dear to pull the cart up by the door. Hera held the reins but made no move to assist, as he climbed down and with much tug and struggle and unuttered profanity, managed to ease the chair intact and unmarred to the ground. Getting it inside the house proved no easier. He feared the door was too narrow, but when he was there, found it just wide enough.

Hera followed him inside, brandishing his cane which she had taken from the cart and pointed to the center of the room. "Put it there, Smithy," she commanded.

And though every step was agony, Festus did as he was bid. Hera handed him his cane. "Unwrap it. Let me see what you have wrought," she said.

In a few minutes the chair gleamed before them in all its intricate and meticulous splendor with the grand presence of a monarch's throne. Totally spent, Festus collapsed onto the pile of wrappings and sat there rubbing his throbbing leg.

"It will do nicely," he heard Hera say. "I expected no less from you."

Festus looked up, watched her sit regally upon her chair hands in her lap, looking younger yet than when he arrived. "Now name your price," she said. "I've more silver or gold to offer than your cart could bear to carry."

"I have not need for your treasure," Festus said, struggling painfully to his feet and leaning with both hands on his cane while he found his breath. "I need but answer to one question that has troubled my sleep through my life."

"I know the answers to all questions, and I know what secrets to keep," Hera murmured cryptically. "Let me hear yours."

"Who are my parents?" Festus queried.

"You know that as well as I, Smithy," she said, lifting a brow, her tone faintly mocking. "Your father was a Smithy, and so are you. Your mother was his wife, Lena. The milk of her breast was your first drink."

"If you know that," Festus said, "you know that their own boy died an hour after birth, and my mother gave them me, like a changeling, to fill their loss."

"They told you that?" Hera barked, a flash of displeasure in her face.

"Yes, but had promised they would not tell who she was. They are long dead now, and I cannot ask them again. So, I ask you, who knows all secrets and all answers. Who is my mother?"

"I will tell you anything but that," Hera said, resting her palms against the arms of the chair. The clever mechanism Festus had built into it whirred and the vines of silvered steel swiveled and twined about Hera's arms and locked, holding her fast to her throne.

"You will not leave that chair until you tell." Festus said softly.

"You will age and die and be dust on my floor before I tell you," Hera replied, quiet-voiced but adamant.

"Then you will sit in that chair longer than that," Festus retorted, unshaken.

Hera's golden eyes locked onto his. She looked deep into his soul and saw that he was content to die in his ignorance rather than live with it. After an hour or a day or a year, she whispered, "I am your mother, Hephaestus, for that is the name I gave you."

"And my father, who is he?" Festus demanded.

Hera roused, strained against the restraining vines, but the chair would not let her go. "My husband had no part in you," she said, angry now. "I made you for myself."

"Then why render me broken like this?" Festus raged back, slapping his thigh. "Did you hate your own so much?"

"I loved you then and I love you now," Hera confessed, her voice low, almost soft. "It was my husband who left you broken, who, because he was jealous of you, because I had done for me what he could not, seized you by the leg and flung you through yonder door. He would have ground you into the earth with his armored heel had I not taken you away beyond his sight." Hera was weeping now; her tears bounced on the floor and lay there gleaming like drops of molten silver.

Festus hobbled behind her chair and pressed the lever hidden in the back that released her bonds. "Tell me who he is," he said, "and I will kill him for us both."

"You can't find him," she said, "he's gone."

"Dead?"

"Worse than dead," Hera said quietly, "just forgotten. Nobody fears him now. Nobody speaks his name. Nobody remembers Zeus anymore."

BEARSKIN
(with apologies to Jacob and Wilhelm)

Ben leaned back in the old wicker chair, felt it creak under his shifting weight. Millie insisted that one day he would do this and the chair would collapse, dumping him onto the floor. At his age, he reckoned he'd be lucky if only his pride suffered from the fall. All the adults in his life called him Bear, except for Millie, who addressed him as Ben when she was pleased with him or Benjamin when she wasn't.

He watched her now under the lowering afternoon sun, tending her herbs in the garden, their two grandchildren frolicking around her, "helping" as they called it. Ben marveled at his wife's patience which he had tried often enough himself, and for all his faults and failings, come to this late chapter in his life forgiven and well-loved.

Ben pretended to be absorbed in his book, as Millie stood, pointed toward the house, handed her basket to the boy and girl who carried it between them as they scampered toward the porch. "Slow down, you'll spill it all," Millie called through her laughter. The children managed to reach the porch steps with their load intact, Millie right behind them. She took back her basket and the children descended on Ben like crows on a cornfield.

"Tell these children a story, Ben," she said as she passed his chair, "and I may be able to get our supper ready."

"I'll help," he said, struggling to stand as the children clung to his arms.

"Sometimes the best help is not to. Tell your story," she said, and disappeared into the house.

Ben sighed, closed his book, and surrendered to the chair and the children. Lisa settled into his lap. Horace, a year older and none taller, perched on his knee. The knee protested silently. Ben knew the boy would not stay in one place more than three minutes, so gave no voice to his discomfort.

"Tell us about when you were a soldier," commanded Horace.

"That was a very long time ago. I've quite forgotten being a soldier," Ben said, although he remembered it too well to talk about.

"Then tell us about when you became a bear," pleaded Lisa.

"I'm not a bear," Ben answered, tousling her honey golden hair. "People just call me that."

"Why do people call you Bear, Grampa?" asked Horace, as if he'd never heard the story before.

"Well," Ben said, his voice settling into what Millie called his story tone, "it happened the summer after I'd just come home from the war." He wouldn't tell the children that he became a bear on a summer long before that, before he knew about wars and weapons and how damning it felt to kill a stranger just because he wore a different uniform.

He never told anyone, not even Millie, but Ben reckoned he became a bear the summer after his twelfth birthday. He was staying, as he did every summer, with his crazy Aunt Mary and her family up in the Wilderness, as his parents referred to the remote Appalachian cove where his father's sister lived. His father delivered him to Mary as soon as school was out and returned to collect him in the Fall just before the next term began. Ben guessed either his parents were at a loss as to what to do with a resident child or they just needed a break from the constant disappointment their son had proven to be. That he was a disappointment to them he had no doubt.

To his father, Ben pretended to hate his annual exile in the mountains. Harry Drum assumed that any experience distasteful to the boy would surely improve his character. Ben went to lengths to maintain his father's illusion, for fear that if Harry sensed the liberation and elation his son felt during his seasons with Mary, they would be promptly denied.

Mary was an avid gardener. From the day of his arrival, the garden became Ben's school when he wasn't out on the mountain learning wilder and deeper lessons. By the way she did things, as much as by her words, Mary taught him how to read the map of his life, to know not just who he was, but what was more important at his age, to know what he might become. One morning, while on his way out to the garden to help weed Mary's many and varied herbs, with his nose, as usual, in his book, his unguided foot came down amidst a fine clump of wormwood.

"Mind your way, Nephew," Mary commanded sharply, then, with a smile. "That was mighty careless. I should turn you into a bear or a tree."

"If it be the same to you, I'd as soon be a bear," Ben answered brightly. "Being a tree would get awfully same-ish after a spell."

"You be a bear, then," she said, "but I will leave you a man's flesh and brain. You will go off to live in a town amongst humans and spend your days grubbing after things other people want you to have, but all your years, your soul will ache for the mountain and the woods."

Ben remembered Mary and her hillside garden while he had been watching Millie in hers. It had been just a game. Some of Mary's neighbors put about that she was a witch. She delighted in playing the role for them when they came to her for remedies and potions. But Ben reckoned now that Mary's pretend spell had power after all. Most of his life he had spent as the discontented bear, being very good at things he'd just as soon not be doing in places he'd rather not be.

"Tell us about the bear, Grampa." It was Lisa, calling him back to his present.

86

"I will do that, children. I was just trying to remember it all," Ben said. "You know that bear skin on the floor in my den."

"Yup," piped Horace. "Gramma told us not to play on it. She says it's nasty."

"She said the same thing about me the first time she saw me," Ben said, "but I've had plenty of time since to change her mind. Anyway, that is the bear that almost ate Colonel Flagg."

"And you killed him," the children chorused.

"No, I did not kill the Colonel," Ben said, laughing, as if he'd misunderstood.

"Not him," shrilled Lisa.

"The Bear," Horace said. "You killed the bear."

"Actually," Ben corrected, "the Colonel shot the bear. I just hit him with a chair."

"And you saved the Colonel's life," Lisa said, having heard the tale many times before, and embracing each telling with all the excitement of the first.

"That's what he said," Ben confirmed. "Flagg kept this little cabin way up on the mountain, and he would go up there to hunt. He took me with him to be his guide, he said, although I think he just wanted somebody along to carry stuff. The plan was to hunt bear, but when we got to the cabin, the door was wide open."

"And the bear was inside," shouted Horace, clapping his hands.

"Yes, he was," Ben nodded, "and the instant the Colonel stepped through the door the bear was on top of him. The Colonel's gun was underneath him on the floor. My rifle was in the pack I'd left on the porch, so I picked up a chair and hit the bear across the back of his head with it. It ruined the chair, but it got the bear's attention."

"Then the bear tried to eat you up," gleed Lisa.

"I think that was his intent," Ben said. "He grabbed my arm in his mouth, and I believe he would have bitten it right off, but Flagg got to his gun and shot him dead."

Ransom Flagg. Nobody who ever knew the man would have said he was good or kind. A fair portion of his acquaintances would have called him a devil. But the Colonel had two virtues, he was loyal to his allies, and he kept his promises. Ben had served under him in the war. Served well, as witnessed by a couple of medals he kept secreted in a desk drawer. So, when Flagg had found Ben drunk in a local bar, he recognized his former sergeant. When Ben slurred through the sad tale of how he had come home a hero to find his parents dead and his older brothers in charge of the family lumber business where they had no place for Ben, Flagg offered him a job with American Flagg Mining and Timber Company.

By the time Ben sobered up, he had signed a seven-year contract to serve as Flagg's Operations Assistant which translated as personal bodyguard and enforcer. None of this Ben was about to tell his grandchildren. Most of his seven years in Flagg's hell he had never told Millie, who knew more of his secrets than any other soul on earth.

"And you skinned the bear and ate him up." Horace said, smacking his lips as if he could taste something delicious.

Ben blinked, regained his moment, nodded and said, "Yes, we licked our wounds, then we skinned the bear and chopped him up into steaks and cutlets, and we dined on bear stew that very night."

"You licked your wounds?" whispered Lisa. "Did they taste awful."

"That's a figure of speech," Ben clarified. "We washed our hurts and wrapped them in bandages and then we skinned the bear."

"And after you ate the bear, the Colonel gave you the whole forest," Horace said.

"Well, he put me in charge of it," Ben corrected. "When we got back to town, he promoted me to Chief Forester."

"With a uniform," declared Lisa.

"Yes, a green one," Ben agreed. "All of us foresters wore green uniforms."

"What does a forester do?" asked Horace, for maybe the hundredth time.

"A forester takes care of the forest," Ben said.

"You plant trees," ventured Lisa.

"Yes, we planted lots of trees," Ben acknowledged.

"And you put out fires," Horace affirmed.

"More of them than I wish to remember," Ben said.

And he did a lot of other things too, while in Flagg's service. Things not fit to assault children's ears. He shot timber thieves and game poachers on sight. He evicted tenants on newly acquired tracts of lands who could not pay their increased rents to their new landlord. He stripped innocent trespassers of their gear and equipment, extorting inflated fines to restore their possessions. Those deemed malicious or guilty he simply beat to a bloody wreck and left to the mercy of the mountain.

Flagg ruled his domain with an iron fist like some feudal grand duke and paid Ben a pirate's share to be that fist. There were countless times over the seven-year term of his contract that Ben wished he had never signed his name on Flagg's paper, but he had agreed to serve and so long as Flagg kept his end of the thieves' bargain, Ben did his brutal part.

"And while you were taking care of the forest, you found Gramma," Lisa said, reaching up to tug Ben's beard so that he looked at her eye to eye.

"It's more like she found me, I think," Ben said.

From the kitchen, Millie called, "Children, come set the table for me, please."

With a leap and a bound the children were gone into the house, abandoning Ben to the tyranny of his remembrances. Shadows stretched out across the yard and down the garden rows beyond, the air cooling noticeably. A chill shuddered Ben's shoulders, as he sat on the shaded porch listening to the muted babble of happy voices inside the house. In his mind, he heard the sound of an icy wind, sharp as a knife, feeling the sting of the snow it drove against his face. The memory took hold of him, and he was back there in the middle of a day gone bad.

It had begun well enough. He set out with a satchel full of eviction notices to deliver to tenants of Flagg who had not paid their rent, or to those who had borrowed against their properties and fallen behind on their loan payments. Ben's instructions were to collect or remove. Flagg's consuming ambition was to stand before his big house above the valley and behold no land that wasn't his. Over the years Ben had been in his employ, the tyrant had added field to field and farm to farm and hill to hill toward that end and was no more content holding half the county in his possession.

A light flurry swirled about him as Ben mounted his horse that morning, but the sky to west looked to be clearing. He anticipated a day bright and warming to cheer him in his heartless task, but he was hardly out of sight of Flagg's compound, when the wind shifted and brought down serious snow. His first visit yielded moneys due. His second found a family in hopeless debt. Ben did his duty, but found pity enough to help them load their meager belongings onto their wagon and give them a few coins that would buy them food for a day.

By then, the road was buried in snow. Ben watched the high-boned mule and wagon out of sight, the man and his wife trudging beside to spare the mule their weight, then he mounted his horse and rode on into what was fast becoming a blizzard. He could hardly see the road before him. The horse stumbled on some hidden obstacle and went down hard. Ben rolled free, bruised but unbroken. The gelding was not so fortunate. When Ben wiped the snow out of his eyes, he saw his mount standing, one foreleg lifted, unable to bear weight. A closer inspection confirmed the worst. Ben pulled his rifle from its scabbard, assured the barrel was clear of snow and mud, and shot the horse without warning or apology. He aimed well and the animal crumpled without a twitch.

Wet from his tumble in the drifts, shaking with the cold, Ben pulled from his pack the bearskin he used as a bedroll on his forays, and cinched it about him. He hoped it would keep him from freezing until he found shelter. He hoisted his pack, slung the satchel over a shoulder and hefted his rifle. The horse was already just a white mound beside the road. There was nothing left to do but walk away while he was still able.

Ben walked a mile that seemed to him like ten and then walked more through frequent drifts past his knees. When the whole world was snow and he himself covered with it and his beard a forest of icicles and he looked more a bear than a man, he saw the house. He knew the place, had passed by it on occasion. Not on his list, it was one of the few remaining freeholds within Flagg's expanding territory. Flagg was not popular among the lesser landowners, as he pressured them incessantly to sell out to him, but Ben hoped now that mountain hospitality would prevail. Another mile in this weather and he would not be a living man, just a cold one.

Approaching the door, he knocked with a hand already half-frozen. It was still poised in the air to knock again when the door opened, and a young woman peered out at him with an expression mingling alarm and pity.

"I lost my horse out there," Ben mumbled through his icy whiskers, gesturing vaguely behind him at the storm. "Can you spare me shelter, Miss?"

The woman, Ben decided she was not much beyond a girl, seemed on the verge of inviting him in, when her eye lit on the collar of his green uniform, not quite concealed by his bearskin. That face, which he still considered the most beautiful on earth, hardened as he watched. He could sense her inner conflict until finally she said. "In the barn, Forester. You won't freeze there. I'll bring you out some food when you've settled."

There among the animals Ben settled, grateful for their nearness and their warmth. When he finally quit shivering and could stop his teeth from chattering, he watched the snow falling out of the gathering night. Near dark, he saw a man afoot, coming in from the woods, a bundle on his back. The man went to the house and entered without knocking.

Fatigue took Ben then. He was asleep in a shock of hay, when the man woke him, held out a steaming bowl of venison stew and a spoon.

"Thank you," Ben muttered, carefully wrapping his stiff fingers around the offered bowl. The man nodded and watched silently as he ate. "That was good," Ben said when he was done, handing back the bowl.

"Millie was half a mind to turn you back out, don't you know? She afeard you were on Flagg's business," the man said.

"You're not on my list," Ben answered. "Don't you own this place?"

"I do, but I borrowed from the bank agin' it," the man said. "We got a letter from the bank telling us Colonel Flagg bought up the loan and likely would demand full and immediate payment. We been expecting one of you to come for it."

92

"And you can't pay?" Flag asked, sure already of the answer.

"Everything I have is in this place," Millie's father said. "It's all the home my daughter has ever known, and all I have to leave her."

"How much do you owe Flagg?" Ben queried.

The man told him an amount equal to a year of Ben's wages, almost all the money he had saved over the past four years, and since he trusted bankers even less than he trusted Ransom Flagg, carried strapped around his waist beneath his shirt. Ben didn't think about what he did next. If he had, he mightn't have done it. He acted on what his heart showed him in that instant, the homeless family following their hopeless mule through the snow, the lovely face in the doorway, suddenly turned cold and hard by what he had become. He undid his tunic and pulled out the leather purse beneath and handed it to Millie's father. "Take this and pay off your loan," he said, "and keep free of Flagg."

"What about you?" the man asked.

"Three more years and I'm my own man again," Ben said.

"The man nodded, held up the purse. "You sure about this?"

Ben laughed. "If you're sure I can come back in three years and apologize to your daughter."

ROSE VALIANT

Rose never thought herself brave or strong, or even smart or clever. Her ambition from childhood was to live an ordinary life, to dress in some style without ostentation, and to be surrounded by objects of quality, things comfortable and durable. She married Samuel Valiant because her father advised that Sam was just the man to provide and sustain for her the life she wanted. He judged his prospective son-in-law industrious and intelligent and propertied more than most young men his age; religious enough to likely avoid many of the sins by which some men rendered their wives miserable, but not so religious that his charity would extend too far beyond his own household. It would be a safe marriage and tolerably pleasurable, Rose's father, Colonel Ellis Graves said, or at least as safe as such an insane arrangement as marriage could ever be.

"Were you and Mother happy together?" Rose asked her father.

"Only your mother could tell you that," the Colonel replied. Rose heard his deep voice suddenly going hoarse, as he went on, "Men are not put into this world to be happy. We are here only to please the women in our lives, and most of us fail at it miserably."

Rose would have asked her mother, but Georgiana Graves died giving birth to her only daughter. Rose supposed she loved the mother she couldn't remember. She did at least love the photographs and the stories her assorted aunts told her about their sister. Rose's father seldom spoke of his wife, answered any question about her as briefly as was civil, hoarded the details of their together life to himself, as if her spirit might fly away from him with his words.

"Too painful," the aunts would say, when Rose asked

why her father was so reticent to speak of the past. "Some hearts break too deep to ever heal," remarked Aunt Margaret, sounding as if she might know from her own experience.

Rose worshiped her father. The grief that might have hardened the heart and meaned the temper of a lesser male had only served to make him tender, kind, generous to those he cherished. Of his charity, or lack of it, toward those who did not merit his esteem, Rose had no knowledge. She regarded her father's every word as gospel. When he said Sam Valiant would be a suitable husband for his daughter, she never expected it might ever turn out otherwise.

All her friends told her Sam was handsome, and Rose agreed. Her honest acquaintances said to one another, though not to Rose, that it was a mystery to them how a man like Sam Valiant would want to marry her, of all people. Rose knew why he'd wanted to marry her, of all people. Colonel Ellis Graves had promised to finance Sam's latest business venture if he did. Rose was not by any measure ugly, but she knew she was plain. She expected other women to be attracted to her husband, and she was not greatly surprised when he was attracted to more than one of them. She pretended to be without suspicion, and Sam, for his part, maintained careful discretion. He was adept as a lover and seemed genuinely gratified to give her pleasure at every opportunity. In those moments when he did, Rose forgot that she was not the sole object of his desire.

After a few years of marriage, when there were still just the two of them in Sam's big house, Rose consulted her doctor. When he couldn't offer much hope of her ever becoming a parent, she told her husband. He took the news quietly, with cool and polite disappointment, and went off to work. In the weeks and months following, he was at work more than he was at home, and many nights Rose had their bed to herself. They never discussed this change in their relationship, but Rose realized that Sam's interest in intimacy between them had sprung more from a desire for an heir than for the comfort of her touch. Sam immersed himself in his business. Together, they went to an occasional party or concert, as much because Sam said it was expected of them as for any enjoyment they might derive. Rose lived for her garden while servants cleaned her husband's house and cooked their meals. She won prizes for her roses.

One evening, after dinner out with several couples who had more money than the Valiants, Sam poured an unaccustomed late whiskey for himself and sat staring at the fire while Rose read from *Great Expectations*, which she'd read once every year since she was fourteen.

"That is a lovely dress you wore at dinner tonight," he said, banishing the quiet that had settled between them.

Rose looked up from her book, closed it on the mark, her smile in her voice. "Why thank you, Samuel. I'd forgotten you notice such things."

Sam dropped his gaze to the fire again. "How much did it cost?"

Rose lost her smile. "Why, you've never asked me anything like that before and I've never abused your generosity. You know that?"

Sam looked at her again, his expression not angry so much as pained, as if he'd been physically hurt. "We'll have to start keeping track of our spending, Rose. The shipping firm is not doing well since the railroad finished their branch line."

"I'm sorry Sam." Rose meant it. She would have crossed the room and given him her hand, but for knowing he'd shrug it off. Sam could not abide being mothered, as he called it, when he was distressed or upset. "Do you want me to take it back?"

"No," he said, pausing for another sip of his single-malt. "But your allowance will have to be less now. I'm…" Sam left the last word hanging in the dead air, finished his glass in one swallow, barely shy of a gulp, coughed, stood and left the room.

After he'd gone, Rose remembered she'd never answered her husband's question about how much she'd spent for her new dress.

After that evening, Sam's late-night whiskey became a regular feature. It never went beyond one drink, and Rose was grateful for that. She had no trouble staying within her clothes budget, because they quit going out at all. She went to church alone and would awake alone next morning to find Sam asleep on his chair at his desk, his head and arms draped over his ledger, as if by his presence he might alter the figures on the pages. When she realized she could do nothing to bring her husband rest or pleasure or comfort, she gave up trying. Meanwhile, her roses thrived.

The shipping business continued to falter. Once she asked him, "How are you coping?"

"Please don't ask me that," he said. The plea in his voice was genuine, ringing more of despair than annoyance. "I do the best I can, but wagons carry less than trains and trains are faster than wagons."

Rose had resigned herself to sharing a house while they lived their separate lives, when Sam came home one day, kissed her at the door, handed her a bouquet of flowers not roses, and said, "We're having company for dinner Thursday. Could you plan something special?"

Sam was happy, so she was happy, but she asked, "Who are we having?"

"James Holloway and his wife, from Asheton."

Rose cataloged their friends and acquaintances in her

head. None of them lived in Asheton. "Do we know them?" she asked.

Sam reached out and gathered her into a waltz. "We will soon enough. Holloway is buying into the business. He's going to help me save it."

Breathless and bewildered, Rose let her husband sweep and spin her through all the downstairs rooms of their house. They sent the cook home and made their own supper that night. Afterward, she rediscovered the landscape of her love, and at the height of her exultant exploration was almost derailed, ambushed by a sudden recognition, *He's lost so much weight.*

Rose revived her dormant culinary talents, and with Martha the cook's help and reassuring counsel, prepared a venison roast that turned out, according to the cook, "well-nigh perfect, Miz Rose." The rest of the meal, Rose left to Martha's more capable hands. Sam felt they might relax their austerity budget enough to allow a new dress for the occasion. Rose went shopping, spent hours trying to accommodate herself to the finery, then chose one she had already, convinced the new dress was too daringly grand for her.

Wendel, their part-time handyman was recruited, garbed in his Sunday best, for butlering and table service. Wendel, a largely self-taught but avid reader, was addicted to Victorian novels, and played his part with appropriate flourish and reserve. When he opened the front door and ushered James Holloway and his wife Lena into the foyer, Rose felt her plainness like an accusation and wished herself invisible. She thought she'd never met such a splendid couple. They looked, they smelled, they moved like royalty. Rose stood mute and lost before them. When Sam stepped up and introduced her to their guests, Rose resisted an impulse to curtsy. James reached out to take her hand and

Rose felt something like an electric shock. His voice enveloped her as he spoke her name. She said something in response but later couldn't remember what.

Lena's touch calmed her. Thrilled her like an angel might. The woman exuded a power that healed and frightened at the same time. Rose thought they would have to be friends, for she could never hold her own against such ferocious beauty.

When they settled down to dinner and James complimented the venison, Sam said, "That is all Rose's."

She blushed like a schoolgirl, embarrassed as much as she was pleased.

Barely a week after, Rose was in her garden facilitating with Wendel the placement of a new specimen, her gloves muddy, her apron asplatter with earth, a chocolate-hued smudge at the tip of her nose where she'd unconsciously wiped it with the back of her hand, when Wendel looked up, and she heard behind her a voice terrifyingly familiar.

"So, there you are, Rose Valiant," called Lena Holloway, her words riding on her laughter. "Martha said I would find you here. The garden should be the first place I'd seek a rose."

Rose lurched to her feet. Lena stepped forward, held out a hand to steady her. Rose swiped at her unruly hair to neaten it, only succeeded in daubing her cheek with fresh dirt. She frantically brushed at her apron, smeared more soil than she removed.

"I'm such a mess. You must think me quite unrefined," she stammered.

Lena only laughed some more., With her handkerchief, she cleaned the tip of Rose's nose. "I think you're beautiful," she said, losing her smile, her tone serious. "A beauty among all these beauties," gesturing at the roses blooming all around. "You look very much at home."

It seemed to Rose an honest moment. "I can be myself here, and none will judge me for it," she confessed, wishing as she spoke that she hadn't.

"I've come unannounced," said Lena, more a declaration than an apology. "Can you spare time from your roses to have tea with me?"

Rose blushed at that, her neat round face looking something very like a flower. "Of course," she murmured, taking off her gloves as she led the way toward the house. "I'll ask Martha to fix something for us."

She felt Lena's hand on her back. "I thought we might go to Nordlic's and spare the trouble."

Rose felt an inexplicable urge to slow her step, prolong the contact. Instead, she walked faster. "Oh, no. I can't go out like this. Martha won't mind at all. It will be easier for us just to sit here." Lena's stride was longer, and she came up alongside Rose now and gazed at her with an expression that could denote either affection or amusement. "If that's alright with you, of course," Rose amended.

"Just we two," replied Lena, leaning close now. "How lovely is that?"

James Holloway had become enamored of motorized trucks during his service in the Great War. He provided the funding to replace the wagons in Sam's business with trucks, thus Valiant Cartage became overnight Holloway Valiant Transport. If Sam's pride suffered being relegated to second partner, his improved financial status soothed the pain. He ceased quibbling about Rose's expenditures, increased her allowance. She considered her situation somewhat improved by Sam's business merger with her now best friend's husband. The expansion of the business meant the partners found even less occasion to be at home attending to their wives. Rose once mentioned to Lena that Sam nowadays spent more of his time with James than with her.

Lena just laughed and said, "I know. It gives me more time for my own life. But they do seem to crave their own company, don't they? Perhaps they are in love."

Taken aback, Rose blushed like a rose, blurted, "Lena Holloway, what an odd thing for you to say."

Lena smiled her enigmatic smile and replied, "Only odd for those who think it so. Not at all strange for me." While Rose tried to parse the meaning of this declaration, Lena added, "Besides, don't you crave my company just the wee bit?"

Impulsively, Rose reached out and took Lena's hand. "You have become my dearest friend," she murmured, looking up into a face she was convinced more beautiful than her own. "I have never had enough of your company." Later, alone, reflecting on the exchange, Rose, unsettled by the conversation, decided it was true. She did crave Lena Holloway's proximity.

A new year arrived, bringing more promise for Holloway Valiant Transport to expand and prosper. A deal with Mountain Rail gave the company an inside track on local deliveries where tracks didn't reach. Sam Valiant bought a new automobile. A Ford. Although the weather was mild for the season, and the party at the Holloway home was near enough to walk, as Rose and Lena did often, Sam insisted on driving his new car. He was in an expansive mood, frequented the punch bowl between dances where he partnered with Lena and a couple of other wives of their acquaintance more than with his own. When his business partner invited several of the males, potential investors or customers, to join him in his study and sample his old and expensive whiskey, Sam disappeared, leaving Rose to dance with men who looked to her like boys, or to converse with her friends, which translated mainly to Lena Holloway.

"We could dance, I suppose," Lena murmured as they waited with their cups of punch for their husbands to surface.

Rose blushed, not because she found the notion unappealing but because she did. "We're too old for such cavorts, Lena," she replied. "Only children and the young do that in public."

Lena trailed a finger lightly down Rose's arm. "Still, we might cavort in private, don't you think?"

Rose had no time to think, as the influential men of Drovers Gap emerged from their sequester and began gathering up their women to herd them homeward. Sam seemed not entirely sure of his bearings as he ambled more-or-less in Rose's direction. She took his arm and discreetly guided him to collect their coats.

In the yard before the Holloway's impressive townhouse, Rose said brightly, "It's a lovely night, Sam. Why don't we just walk home, pretend we're young lovers again. You can collect your Ford in the morning."

"I'm tired," Sam slurred. "Why don't we just ride home in our new car and pretend we're young lovers in the morning?"

As they were barely out of earshot of the other departing guests, Rose whispered not so brightly, "Sam Valiant, you're in no condition to drive and you know it."

"I intend to drive," Sam snapped, sounding almost sober.

"Well, I'm not riding with you in your state," Rose said, for once following Lena's admonitions to assert herself in the face of male obstinance.

"Walk by yourself, then," Sam growled as he shambled off toward his vehicle. Rose heard him mutter something else at her as he turned away. She wasn't sure what he said but hoped it might be *witch*, which though entirely unpleasant, remained preferable to any alternative epithet she could surmise.

A misty rain commenced as Rose watched Sam's Ford weave away down the street and around the corner. She pulled her coat close about her neck, suppressed a shiver. Too embarrassed to turn back to pitying shelter, she walked faster toward no place she wanted to go. She didn't hear James Holloway striding up behind her until he came close, opened his big black umbrella over them both, and spoke, "Rose, let me walk you home. Did you and Sam have a falling out?"

"My husband is drunk, James," she murmured, her voice a thin and brittle barrier against her tears. "I didn't trust him to drive us safely." Rose's father had always taught her that an inconvenient truth will invariably serve better than an insupportable falsehood.

"Watch that puddle," James said, resting his arm about her shoulders to guide her around. Once they passed the puddle James let his arm remain as they walked on, and Rose allowed it so. She was cold and on the brink of weeping and the calm and warming support of a responsible and capable male answered her moment of need. She thought of her father for no reason she could name. She thought of her friend Lena, assured and commanding, like a man would be. She thought of James Holloway's arms wrapped around his wife, as they likely would be before the night was out, and Rose stepped away, gave an involuntary little cry as the cold rain ran down inside her collar. James took her arm and drew her back beneath the sheltering umbrella. They both laughed softly, as if to themselves, and walked on. James continued to grip her elbow lightly, holding her close and dry.

Rounding the corner, they saw her house ahead, and Sam's Ford shining in the rain in front of the garage, one front tire off the drive, sunken in the lawn. The porch was dark, though a light showed through the parlor window. At the door, James folded his umbrella, and before Rose could register his intention, he leaned close and kissed her full on her lips.

Rose drew back, alarmed, wondering what she had done to bring this on herself. "I'm so sorry," she whispered.

James Holloway smiled. "You're safe now," he said, and without bothering to open his umbrella, strode away into the rain and the night.

"Lena, dear," murmured Rose Valiant as they sat sipping their tea in the garden among her roses. "There is something I fear I should tell you and I don't know how to begin."

Lena didn't try to contain her amusement at her friend's discomfort. "One usually begins at the beginning." She laughed. "But I think I am there before you, Little One."

"Really?" stammered Rose. "So, you know?" It irritated Rose mildly whenever Lena called her that, as if she were Rose's big sister, though that was, after all, how she had come to think of Lena Holloway.

Lena laughed again. "I know James walked you home after our party. I know James and I know you, Rose, so I know all that happened."

"Why did you let him walk me home then?" Rose blurted, entirely flustered now, her secret misadventure no secret at all.

Lena apparently deemed their conversation hilarious. "Let him? Dear, I sent him after you. Didn't you enjoy your encounter?"

Rose blushed red as one of her roses. "I was mortified, Lena. How could you?" She didn't mention that beyond mortification, she had experienced an unsettling thrill and satisfaction that other men than Sam might find her desirable.

Lena reached out, touched her fingers beneath Rose's chin and lifted her face until their eyes met. "If there is anything about my husband's attentions you don't find unattractive, my darling Rose, perhaps you should encourage him, discreetly, of course. Your Sam has been neglecting you of late."

"Oh, Lena, I could not allow myself even a mild dalliance. What if it should lead to...?"

Lena leaned forward, kissed Rose on her forehead, then stepped back, laughing. "Sex, Rose? What else is any man good for?"

"But James is your husband, Lena," Rose said, standing suddenly, stepping away, her voice all atremor with confusion and frustration. Then another thought. "How do you know about Sam and me? I don't speak of how things are between us. Not to anyone. Not even to you."

Lena sat smiling up at her. "Why Little One. Can't you guess?"

Rose spent a lot of time in her garden as spring came on. Her visits with Lena became shorter and less frequent. Whenever the Holloways had a party, she made excuse that she wasn't feeling well. Twice, Sam went off alone and returned home next morning. Rose never summoned courage to tell her husband what she knew of his involvement with her erstwhile friend Lena, but his increasing caution in their conversations convinced her that he knew that she knew. Sam came home one morning in May to find Rose had moved her things into a guest bedroom. After that they slept apart and cultivated a polite distance during their days.

Over breakfast on a sunny Monday in June, Sam announced, "We're going to host a Fourth-of-July picnic, Rose. Our friends expect us to be sociable, and it will be good for the business."

"I'm not up to a party, Sam," Rose demurred. "Couldn't James and Lena do it?"

"James and I are partners. I need to do my part," Sam tried to keep his tone even. "Customers will get the idea that James runs the company if his hospitality is all they see."

"I'll need some help. I'm not practiced with these things," Rose admitted.

"That isn't a problem," Sam said. "Ask Lena to help you. She would enjoy it and be hurt if you didn't."

"You seem to assume a lot about her tastes and feelings. How well do you know your partner's wife, Sam?" Rose murmured.

Sam folded his napkin slowly and precisely, stood from the table. "I know Lena Holloway is a capable woman," he said quietly, "not like…" He stopped, stood with his back to the table, looking out the window over Rose's garden.

"Not like me?" Rose whispered.

"Not like any other woman I've ever met," Sam said, and without turning to look at his wife, left the room.

"Oh, Lena, I don't know where to begin," Rose said in frustration. "There's so much to do, where to start?"

Lena Holloway smiled benignly and said, "Start with invitations. How many? Make it RSVP so we'll know who we need prepare for. Then we'll think about a menu. Take it step by step and it's simple. Don't worry, Little One. I'll show you."

And she did. Through June, the two women hardly saw their husbands at all. The men were consumed with their burgeoning shipping business, and their wives spent their days in their own close company inviting, planning, gathering staff, overseeing preparations for the big July Fourth Picnic.

On the final day of June, Lena turned to Rose and said, "Well, all's ready. You've done it, Little One."

Rose said curtly, almost sharply. "We've done it. Mostly, you've done it. I wish you wouldn't call me Little One, Lena."

"I'm sorry," Lena said. "I only do it because I'm fond of you. We're friends aren't we?"

"You are my closest friend, Lena, but when you address me in such a way, it makes me uncomfortable."

"Whyever for?" Lena said.

For a moment, Rose was silent, searching out her answer. Lena just stood with her quizzical smile, until Rose whispered, "It's what one would say to a child... or to a lover."

"Have you ever had a lover?" Lena asked.

"I have a husband, Lena Holloway, and so do you," Rose said, sounding like a scolding parent.

"They're not the same at all," Lena retorted.

"I could never be intimate with another man than Sam," Rose said.

Lena reached out and brushed her cheek lightly with the tips of two fingers. "We don't need men, you and I," she whispered, her eyes searching Rose's face, her gaze probing. "We can please ourselves."

The fourth-of-July picnic was a rousing success, impressing their few friends and many acquaintances and luring new customers for Holloway Valiant Transport. Over the summer, Sam put in more of his time at the business, often sleeping there overnight, so he told Rose. When, over an infrequent shared breakfast, she complained for want of his company, he confided that he intended to increase his stake in the shipping enterprise until he could buy out his partner's share. "It's for our future, Rose," he said. "For our children's future."

"But we haven't children, Sam," Rose said.

"That's your fault, not mine," snapped Sam Valiant, and he disappeared into his day.

Over the weeks that followed, as Rose saw less of her husband, she saw more of Lena Holloway. Rose, being remarkably shy, made few friends. Lena filled that void in her experience, being, if not quite Rose's only friend, her best and far the closest one, her sole confidant and confessor. If Rose went out for tea or a luncheon, she went with Lena. Sam and James usually spent Sunday mornings going over the company's books, so when Rose went to church, she sat with Lena. While the husbands made money, their wives made a life together. Over time, Rose came to agree with Lena's proposition that "we don't need men", an impression augmented when Lena revealed that many of the ideas James had implemented to turn the shipping business toward success had originated with her. "Poor James tells me all his problems," she said, "and I tell him what to do about them," her tone that of a mother talking about her inept child.

On a Monday when Martha had the afternoon off, Rose heard a knock at the front door. Thinking it might be Lena she ran to open it, only to find James Holloway standing outside. She didn't recognize him for a moment, for she had never seen the man looking so stern and serious.

"James?" she said, "Sam isn't here. I thought he was at work."

"Sam's been hurt," James said softly, taking her small cool hand in his large warm one.

"How did it happen, James?" Rose asked on the way to the hospital in Sam's car. James didn't answer at first, concentrating on mastering the unfamiliar machine. Rose, fearing he was trying to shield her from worse news, repeated, "Please, James. I need to know."

"Sorry," James said. "I'm not used to piloting this damned thing. Sam was supervising a loading crew, as they were transferring a shipment from a railway car. A stanchion broke and a pile of lumber fell on him. We got him free and carried him straight to the hospital. The doctor says his vital organs are spared."

"But…?" Rose whispered, not daring to even think the question.

"He's broken up pretty badly," James said, trying to coerce the Ford around a corner. "The Doctor says he should survive if there are no complications. Time will tell. We'll just have to wait and see how he heals."

As soon as they reached the hospital, Rose demanded to see her husband. "Not now," the surgeon said. "We've given Sam something for pain. He wouldn't be able to talk to you. Tomorrow morning perhaps."

Rose refused to leave the hospital, settled in a chair outside the intensive care room, determined to maintain her vigil until Sam was able to assure her personally that he was not destroyed. James Holloway left her there reluctantly. "I must get back to the business, Rose. Someone has to run things. I'll send Lena to check on you."

In less than an hour, Lena Holloway came down the hall in a white summery dress. To Rose, she looked like a ministering angel. She fell into her friend's arms and held close like a child, wept until she slept.

Lena was still there when the doctor came to tell Rose that Sam's legs were ruined, that he would live, but would probably never walk again unassisted, and would need some degree of care likely for the rest of his life. "I'm sorry I haven't better news, Mrs. Valiant, but Sam is very lucky to have survived at all," the doctor said, and left.

"Oh, Lena, what shall I do?" Rose said when they were alone again.

Lena held Rose's hands and kissed her forehead. "You

will take care of your husband and manage his affairs. You are capable and I will help you live your life."

It was Lena's idea to convert the parlor next to Sam's office into a downstairs bedroom. James sent around workers from the shipping company to move furniture and in a day it was done. Rose discovered she was able to tell strangers what to do and they would obey, that she could change her mind and they would undo and redo according to her instructions. And if she faltered, she could defer to Lena who seemed to know precisely what was required of any situation. Rose found her new and sudden responsibilities stimulating but was comforted to know she was still sheltered and shielded by souls more able and worldly-wise than herself.

Sam Valiant could not abide his frailty. He resisted the exercises prescribed for him, though Rose chided and pleaded, often through frustrated tears. Lena Holloway would come to the house then and bully and badger him into going through the motions. Although the doctor forbade him spirits, as often as he could gain unsupervised access, Sam drank without restraint.

Weeks passed as his body regained incremental function while his mind sank into bleak and unremitting depression. James Holloway visited frequently, trying to discuss details of their company's projects, until he became disgusted with his partner's apathy and disinterest and turned to Rose, who discovered she had an aptitude for business and soon was more deeply involved in the affairs of Holloway Valiant Transport than Sam had ever been. James was generally receptive regarding Rose's ideas, especially as they usually agreed with advice he received from his wife, who, as he often remarked solely to himself, *is as good in the head as she is in bed.*

"Rose, if Sam doesn't quit drinking his poison, he'll be dead within a year," Dr. Wayne Smathers informed her on his way out their door.

110

"Doctor, I'm at wit's end," Rose said, broken-voiced. "I locked our spirits away, and he broke into the cabinets. I removed all hard drink from the house, but still he manages to bribe somebody among the workers to bring him some. I've told them all they're killing him to do what he wants. I think Sam wants to die, Doctor. I really do."

"It's a hard place to be in, I know," Smathers said. "You're essentially running the company now with James Holloway. Can you afford to hire someone to stay with Sam and ward him when you must be away?"

"Has it come to that now?" Rose queried, although she knew the answer.

"That, or you must consign him to a facility where he can be controlled."

"Tell me truly, Doctor. Will my husband get better over time?" It was a desperate question. Rose trembled to ask it.

"If Sam had cooperated with his therapy, he might have had more improvement in his legs," the doctor said, "but as things are now, he is unlikely ever to walk again unaided. His mental state is what worries me at this point. That is what fuels his life-threatening behaviors."

"He says he is a cripple, that he has nothing to look forward to but pain," Rose lamented.

"I have other patients who are impaired," Smathers said, "who live full lives. Remind him of what he has, a devoted wife, a successful business, and the comforts that can buy. Sam Valiant is not a man to be pitied. Tell him he should live up to his name."

"I try and I try and I will try again," Rose said. "Thank you for coming, Doctor."

The door closed behind the medic and a strident male voice came from deeper within the house, "Rose. Rose. Where the hell did you go?"

Rose leaned against the jamb, sighed, wiped away a

threatening tear with the back of her hand, managed to inject something that might pass for affection into her voice as she called, "I'm here, Sam. I'm coming."

Rose sat in her garden on a warm and sunny afternoon, sipping tea with Lena Holloway. Underneath their pleasant conversation, Rose carried a troubled mind. She felt she needed to tell Lena what she wanted to forget. "Lena," she said at last, when an awkward silence loomed between them, "I'm afraid we have a problem."

Lena only looked amused. "You're talking about my husband James, I presume," she said.

"You know?" Rose blurted.

"I know that when women talk about their problems, they're usually talking about the men in their lives. Sam is your problem, not mine, thank God, so the only problem we share is James." One of the things Rose found as much irritating as endearing about Lena Holloway was that she always seemed to know what Rose was about to say. She could think of no occasion where she had been able to surprise her friend.

"James has made advances, Lena. Yesterday he tried again to… to touch me."

"And did you let him?"

"Lena Holloway, you are wicked to even suggest such a thing," Rose countered. "Of course not. I never encouraged him in any way. I wouldn't."

"Don't you find my husband attractive?" Lena asked, arching a brow.

Rose blushed like her namesake. "James is a handsome man, and I am a married woman."

"So am I," Lena said, but I am happy to share my husband with friends. His performance improves with practice. You shouldn't frustrate his desire for you."

"I can't believe you are saying these things to me." Rose

pretended to be more shocked than she was, for her friend often said scandalously outrageous things to her when there was no one else to hear. "You can't be serious, Lena," she added.

"I'm never serious," Lena confessed with a laugh, "but I am sincere. Be honest now, dear one. With Sam the way he is, don't you ever long for a lover's touch?"

"Well," stammered Rose, feeling herself totally out of her conversational depth, "yes, I still have a woman's needs."

Lena laid a hand against Rose's breast, leaned close enough to kiss. "I can help you with that now, dear Rose," she whispered.

Sam Valiant wheeled his chair to the window where he could watch the street. He sat staring through the glass though the light hurt his eyes. He was out of his "medicine", as he euphemistically termed it to his supplier. "Medicine" was not to be confused with the laudanum that sawbones Smathers had prescribed for his pain. He watched as the woman turned up his walk. She wouldn't bother with the bell. Rose had gone to the office early this morning to confer with James Holloway, and Martha was shopping groceries today. Sam turned his chair to face the door.

"It's about time you got here," he growled as she came in. "I've been by myself here for an hour already."

"Should I open this for you?" Lena Holloway said, taking the bottle from her bag.

"Please," Sam said. It came out almost as a plea. "And pour that glass on the table, if you will."

"This doesn't mix well with your prescription, you know," Lena said as she handed him the filled glass."

"It keeps me from wanting to kill myself," Sam said after taking a deep swallow of the contents.

"That's what you're doing," Lena said quietly. "Don't say I didn't warn you."

"Well, you brought it to me," Sam said. "Does that make you my murderer, then?"

"I am your facilitator, Sam." Lena smiled, not quite sadly, rather ironic. "I've only done what any good friend would do. No more than what you asked of me."

"At least we are still friends," Sam muttered between swallows of his whiskey. "I preferred it when we were lovers."

"But you're not able to do your part now, are you Sam?" A question answered before it was spoken.

"I'm tired. I need to go back to bed," Sam said, his speech already slurred by the drug enhanced effect of the alcohol.

"Let me help you, dear." Lena said, pulling the blanket from his lap.

"James, could you teach me to drive Sam's car?" Rose said in the middle of their discussion about sixty acres of woodland James wanted the company to purchase.

James continued his monologue as if he hadn't heard. "We've made some money, Rose, hauling other people's logs. We'd make a lot more milling and hauling our own."

Rose knew who had planted the notion. "Have you discussed this with Sam?" she asked, knowing it was a moot question. "He's your partner."

James sighed, pointed a finger at Rose as if accusing her of something. "Your husband is hardly coherent for business discussion these days," he said, exasperation in his voice. "He's too consumed with pursuing his addictions and voicing his boundless self-pity to think about growing our firm." James continued in a calmer tone. "You're effectively my partner now, Rose. Sam will sign any paper you put in front of him."

"I think you have a good idea, James," Rose said. "Forested land is underpriced right now. We could sell off the timber, then develop the properties."

"That's what Lena said," James murmured, immediately looking as if he wished his words back.

"You've discussed this with Lena?" Rose said, feigning surprise, although she knew he had. She and Lena had discussed the subject between themselves already.

"I run all my ideas past my wife," James said, somewhat subdued. "She has a good head for business."

"She does, indeed," Rose agreed. "Now, about Sam's car…"

"I can teach you to drive," James said, "but why bother? You can hire a driver now."

"I wouldn't trust a man to take me where I want to go," Rose responded, smiling sweetly.

"That doesn't sound like the Rose I know," James said.

Rose laughed a laugh that reminded James Holloway of his wife. "Maybe you haven't been paying attention," she said.

Driving lessons went well. Rose found she had an affinity for the machine, and soon she was driving her business partner beyond the confines of Drovers Gap to inspect prospective tracts for Holloway and Valiant Transport and Timber to acquire. James was a perceptive soul, willing to forego his pride if there was profit in it and quickly realized a mountain farmer was more likely to lower his asking price if Rose were leading the bargaining. He thought her powers of persuasion were based on more than her looks, and he did consider her a handsome woman, but she exhibited an indefinable quality he couldn't name, that made a man want to trust and please her. He reckoned he was not entirely immune to her spell himself.

Once, when they stood in the mud on a secluded mountainside, holding a topographical map between them, trying to estimate how much lumber might be in the trees on the slope below, James turned suddenly, kissed Rose passionately on her mouth and tried to slip a hand inside her blouse. Rose didn't shriek with fright or slap his face, but firmly pushed his hand away and said, "Not here, James. Don't come at me like some moonstruck boy."

James didn't apologize, but kept a respectful distance the rest of the day while he considered how he might arrange a suitable location for manly seduction. Rose duly reported the incident to James's wife.

"I'm surprised it's taking him so long," Lena said when she heard it. "Make him beg, won't you?"

Rose promised her friend that she would so do, but being deprived of her own husband's attentions, reckoned she wouldn't make James Holloway beg for too long. Lena had introduced her to a plethora of exciting pleasures new to her experience, but Rose had spent her life cultivating attachments to males and was by now conditioned to find her deepest comforts in their company.

Summer passed and autumn began to look and feel like winter. The wind rattled naked branches against the window, as Rose sat with her whiskey glass perusing a trade journal. Sam always said Bourbon was a man's drink, at least he said so back in the days when he still talked much about anything at all. Now, he mostly slept, except when he woke to mumble that he was thirsty or wanted his medicine or to be cleaned. Since James Holloway recommended Rose hire Wendel Truelight to care for such necessaries, she sometimes went a whole day without seeing her husband at all.

She saw considerably more of Sam's business partner, however. Lena Holloway, having other interests of her own, never seemed reluctant to share her husband's affections. She never told him she knew of his affair with his partner's wife. She confessed to Rose one day that his ardor in their bedroom seemed heightened since he'd become Rose's lover. "Guilt does that to a male," she said. "How is he with you now? Is he better than…"

"Better than Sam?" Rose said. "It's been so long now, I scarcely remember enough to make a comparison."

Lena's smile faltered for a second. "I was about to say, better than me."

Rose laughed at that. "We're hardly the same thing at all," she said.

Rose was recalling this conversation, her journal lying folded in her lap, the smoky burn of the whiskey still in her throat, when Martha knocked, put her head through the door, and said, "Mister Holloway is here Miss Rose, to see Mister Sam."

"Wendel just put Sam down after his bath," Rose said. "He'll be asleep. Bring James in here."

Martha pressed her lips, nodded and disappeared. Rose swallowed the last of her drink and put the glass away as James came through the door. "I brought some papers for Sam to sign," he said, brandishing a manilla folder.

"He'll be out for hours, James. Just leave them on the desk and I'll take them in when he wakes."

James did as he was told, stood by the desk, hands in pockets, gazing at Rose. He stood there until they heard the front door close, as Martha left for the day's grocery shopping. Rose watched out the window, as the woman carried her basket away toward town. She turned back to James. "Is that all you came for?" she murmured through a smile that looked like an invitation.

"Actually," James said, "that was just an excuse."

Some minutes after, Rose glanced over James Holloway's bare shoulder to see Sam sitting in his wheelchair in the doorway, holding something in his lap.

"James," she said softly, gripping his arms. James misinterpreted the warning as a summons.

117

"James Holloway," Sam called, sharply and loudly as if he were sober.

James froze for a second, stood and turned to face his future. Instinctively, he reached to conceal his vulnerability, as Sam raised the small pistol and fired. Sam had been a marksman during the war. A sniper. Perhaps some remnant of his whole self guided his drug ravaged body now, or maybe he was just lucky. A small, neat hole, dark and round, appeared at the bridge of James's nose and without word or whimper he folded against the floor.

Rose watched calmly, perfectly still, as if entranced by the spectacle, while Sam put the barrel of the pistol between his lips and fired again. She sat for minutes, listening to the ticking of her little clock. In the still and quiet it seemed to her almost as loud as the pop of Lena Holloway's little pistol she carried in her purse the previous time Rose had seen it. She watched blood trickle down the front of Sam's pajamas. She didn't have to touch the men to know they were dead.

Rose's first thought was that she needed to minimize scandal. She didn't know how long Martha would be gone, but she thought there was time. She picked up her new telephone and called Lena Holloway. "Our husbands are dead," she said without explanation. "You need to come over here right now and help me get yours dressed."

NAOMI

Thunder. It fell resounding like God's hammer into her half-sleep. Naomi opened her eyes to the flash and flare of lightning limning the window at the foot of her bed. She glimpsed a poplar branch scrabbling frantically at the glass. The music of the little creek outside was lost now in the roar of the wind and the deluge drumming against her house. Naomi didn't know quite what had broken her sleep, the cannon of the thunder, the spiky brilliance of the lightning, or the scrape and rattle of the branch against her window. As she listened, another sound registered on her waking ears, not musical, but a deep rumbling growl like a ravening predator. The creek, now a torrent, hurtling down the mountain bearing mud and boulders and trees in its mad riotous plunge toward the Long Broad and Tennessee. The broken top of a disgrounded maple scraped against the house as it rode by on the flood. Naomi heard siding tearing loose, felt the walls around her shudder with the impact as the house began to shift ever so slightly on its foundations.

"It's all coming down on us. We've got to go now," she heard her father shout from her parents' room down the hall.

Her mother's voice, closer, but barely audible over the gathering rush and roar. "Our daughter. I'll get her."

Her father again. "You go, Alice. I'll bring Naomi."

But it was her mother's face illuminated by a flash of lightning in the doorway when it opened. Then a great thump and bang and the house tilted like a ship caught broadside by a tsunami. Her mother vanished, and the door slammed on a splintering darkness. Furniture slid across the room, jamming against Naomi's bed, knocking it against the wall. Books and bottles and mirrors went crashing and smashing through the black and Naomi couldn't hear her own screams.

For a long duration, there was nothing. Not light. Not dark. Nothing. Awareness, yes, but awareness of what? No time. No thought. No passage or movement at all. Not like sleep. Not like death, either, until Naomi knew who she was, tangled in her covers, wedged between her upturned bed and the wall, or was it the floor? Pitch black and silent, until she heard a scrambling and thumping outside, and a voice, an old man, perhaps, dragging something, until a square of brilliance blinded her and a window was open to the sky high up on a crooked plane that was not quite the ceiling that was not quite a wall, tilting acutely overhead like the sides of a tent. Furniture and clothing heaped in jumbles around, impossible to tell what anything was. From somewhere beyond sight, Naomi could hear the hilarity of rowdy water, a waterfall perhaps, or a tumbling creek.

As Naomi stared at the window, a bright square bereft of pane or muntin, a large bird flew past, casting a shadow like the blink of an eye, and the outline of a human head appeared in the opening, dense and flat, the features obliterated by the glare beyond. And a voice, the same voice she heard before. Definitely old, and full of surprise. "Hello? Anybody in there?"

Naomi waved. Somewhat to her surprise, her arm seemed to work just fine albeit a bit sore. "I'm here," she called, her voice rusty with fright and fatigue. She sounded old to herself, like somebody raised from the dead.

"I see you," said the head, inserting itself into the shadow. Yes, an old face, squinting into her darkness. "Evelyn," it yelled to someone Naomi couldn't see. "There's a child in here." Then, not so loudly. "Are you hurt? Can you move?"

Naomi squirmed and wriggled free of the mattress and a

120

tangle of sheet and quilt. Unsteadily, she stood. The window was much closer now than she had thought. "I'm alright," she said, "I think. Have you seen my mom and dad?"

Another head appeared in the window. "There's nobody but you, child," it said. Also old. A woman.

"Reach up to me," said the first head, the old man. Naomi stretched her arms up as far as she could and two hands as strong as they were old gripped her wrists and lifted her off her feet.

"Help me, Evelyn," said the man, and the old woman reached in beside him and took hold of Naomi's arms. Slowly, slowly, it seemed to her, although it was just a few seconds until Naomi rose into the morning and found her feet planted on the side of her house, slanting now almost to horizontal. All around she saw mud and toppled trees and, laughing through the chaos, a sparkling creek tumbled away toward a broad valley beyond.

The old man held on to her as if he feared she might fall and peered into her face, his eyes full of wonder and disbelief. The old woman standing behind her wrapped her arms around Naomi's shoulders and whispered, "Don't be afraid, little one. You're ours now."

Miraculously, except for a bruised elbow and a minor scrape on her left leg, incurred on her way through the broken window, Naomi emerged unmarked by her transit down the mountain in the wrecked house. She was cold and hungry, but not even wet. She had been carried atop the flood as securely, if not as comfortably, as in an ocean liner.

The old man wanted to carry her, but Naomi said, "Put me down, please." She didn't trust a body who appeared so frail to keep his own footing on the tottering heap of debris that had been her home. She compromised by letting the elderly pair hold her hands, as they gingerly made their way to *terra firma*. They kept a tight grip.

The old couple led her up a winding path among rocks and pines above the still-swollen creek until they reached an almost level clearing, where she saw a small cabin walled with square-hewn logs and roofed with wooden shakes. A thin spiral of smoke lifted feebly from the stone chimney to be shredded away by the morning breeze.

A tilting shed that might have sheltered tools or perhaps an animal stood off to one side of the cabin with a neat vegetable garden between.

As they crossed the yard to the porch of the house, the man and woman still clung to Naomi's hands, as if they feared she might disappear. Finally, the old man loosed her to open the door.

"Evelyn," he said, and waited until the old woman led them into a dim that smelled like a hope of breakfast. A fire flickered timidly on the stone hearth. The old man picked up a stick of oak from a stack beside the fireplace and lay it carefully across the coals. Immediately, blue flames lapped hungrily at the dry wood.

The old woman tugged at Naomi's nightgown. "Adam, bring down some clothes for this child."

"My clothes are all back in our house, what's left of it," Naomi said.

"Those will hardly do here," the old woman said, chuckling as Adam disappeared up narrow stairs. "Our granddaughter Lilith was about your size. Hers will be yours now."

"Does your granddaughter live here with you?" Naomi asked.

"Not now," said the grandmother as the grandfather came down the stairs holding a large cardboard box in front of him.

"There's only us here anymore," he said. "Just us two – and now you."

"My mom and dad," Naomi said, "they were in the house with me. Are you sure they aren't there?"

"Like we told you, they weren't there," said the old woman.

"We looked and we listened," Adam added. "They must have gotten away."

"I hope they're alright, Naomi said, verging tears.

"Your parents are just fine, child," the old woman named Evelyn reassured, "otherwise we would have found them when we found you."

"They'll be off living their lives somewhere while you are with us," old Adam said.

"They will be worried about me," Naomi protested. "We need to tell them where I am. Do you have a phone?"

"Phone?" old Evelyn laughed. "We don't have phones here. No screens or gadgets. Nothing of that sort."

Old Adam knelt so they were face to face, and took Naomi's small soft hands in his large and worn ones. "They won't be worried, Naomi. Trust me in this. By now they will know you are with us, safe and sound. They are missing you, and when time comes round, they'll be along to fetch you home."

"Meanwhile, child," Evelyn said in her cheery quavery voice, "let's get you clean and in some proper clothes. Adam," she commanded. "Bring in the tub."

Adam did as he was told and bobbed out the door. A rattle and a clunk later he returned with a round metal tub that had been hanging on the outside wall of the cabin. It was just big enough for a little girl the size of Naomi to take a bath in. Evelyn set several pots of water on the stove and stoked it with wood to get them steaming. Adam set the tub in a corner of the room and hung a big blanket before it as soon as his wife had filled it with hot water, adding enough cold to render it temperate.

Evelyn handed Naomi a towel and a big bar of soap and a soft "scrubbing rag" as she termed it. Naomi slipped behind the blanket and when she ascertained that she was indeed invisible to her hosts, shyly undressed and slipped into her welcoming tub. It was soothing. It was healing. It was heaven. Naomi sudsed and scrubbed a bit, then scrunched down into the blissful bath until only her head and knees were above water. Somewhere beyond the blanket a kettle whistled softly, a warbly music, and the old people murmured warmly to one another. She couldn't catch their conversation, but once, she heard her name and thought about her parents and before she could really shape the thought, she was asleep.

"Wake up, child, and dry. Surely you're clean by now." It was Evelyn. She held out a towel as Naomi stood in the washtub, lukewarm bath water dripping, the air chill on her wet skin. Evelyn wrapped the towel, thick and soft, around her. "Get dressed and we'll eat," she murmured and disappeared into the world beyond the blanket.

Naomi dried and dressed herself in the clean clothes laid out for her. She had been dreaming about somebody while she dozed in the tub, chin deep in water and visions. Perhaps it was her parents. She wondered where they were, if they had survived the storm, if they were alright now. It puzzled her that she couldn't quite remember their faces, as if the flood had separated them a long time ago.

More immediately demanding her senses, the smell of breakfast cooking on old Evelyn's old iron stove. Adam was setting plates on the old table, as Naomi emerged from her sequester.

"Morning, Bright," he said with a morning smile.

"Mercy," Naomi exclaimed, disoriented and abashed. "Did I sleep all night?"

"You slept no longer than you needed," murmured Adam in his gentle grandfatherly tone. "And now we need to eat. We wore the shine off that old day, so now we'll start a new one." He pointed to a cabinet with three small drawers below. "Fetch us some knives and forks, won't you? There's napkins, too, behind the door atop."

Naomi did as she was asked, willingly enough, though she wondered what kind of world she had landed in where times folded so tight together like the pages in a book.

She might have asked the question aloud to Evelyn or Adam, but by the time she finished arranging the napkins and tableware the smells of breakfast filled the little house and the teakettle whistled merrily. Adam and Evelyn sang along to it's strange bubbly tune, which they continued to hum together after Adam took the kettle from the stove to fill the pot. The warm magic of the present moment filled Naomi's mind to the very limits of her awareness.

Somewhere not too far away, there was apparently a town, or at least a village, although Evelyn and Adam never went there. From time to time, maybe every week or so, maybe once a month – Naomi found it impossible to judge the flow of days, or even seasons, in this strange valley – a boy came riding an oversize tricycle with a cart full of stuff attached behind, presumably destined for families Naomi never saw, who lived somewhere up or down the twisty road that looped past the cabin and coiled away between the hills toward or away from places unknown to Naomi.

The boy told her his name the first time he came riding by on his tricycle, and he said his village was named Drovers Gap. "Call me Abe," he said, and so Naomi did whenever he brought flour or sugar or cornmeal or salt for Evelyn or a hoe handle or trowel or whetstone for Adam. Before he peddled away around the bend again, he would always talk to Naomi for a few minutes, not long enough to suit either of them, for he had places yet to go before night, he said.

Abe was just a boy, Naomi reckoned, for although tall as a man, he was still growing into a man's broad shoulders, and his voice was light with a peculiar crack at odd moments in the middle of sentences, so that he tended to measure out his words by the spoonful, as it were, as if he needed to gather and fortify himself for every utterance. Naomi was careful not to laugh at his halting discourses, in part because she liked him, in part because she didn't want to offend, and abbreviate their already too-brief exchanges.

Along with the pantry staples, Abe sometimes delivered a newspaper, presumably recent although never bearing a date. Most of the articles were about misfortunes and disasters, usually resulting in death. Adam would read the news aloud to Evelyn and Naomi by the fire at night after supper, and at the end of each account, he would breathe a sigh as if relieved of a burden, and Evelyn would murmur, "Thanks be, that one is none of ours."

Days passed. Impossible to be more precise than that, for there were no logical progressions of seasons. One day it would be fall and the next day spring. One day Naomi would be stacking the firewood that old Adam split for the hearth, and the next she would be swimming in the cold creek in the shade of green willows. Perhaps years passed, although Evelyn and Adam, who already seemed impossibly ancient to Naomi, never got any older, and she herself, long after she lost all counting of winters and summers, never grew an inch. Her skin paled and tanned to match the complexion of a day, but through all she remained the wee child who had ridden down the mountain in a wrecked house borne upon a torrent of mud and flood.

Abe came and went times past number, but never quite grew into the man he was becoming the first time Naomi saw him. Every day was different, and times were all the same. It was inevitable that eventually Naomi would stop wondering about the strange life she lived with Evelyn and Adam, and though she never quite forgot her parents, she ceased to inquire about them. They might have been dreams, or they might have been dead, but they were no longer precisely real in her mind.

This peculiar state of affairs seemed to go on forever, but of course, nothing does, and one grand summer day Abe came riding his tricycle up the winding brown road, raising a fine red dust which promptly settled behind him in the windless air. Naomi, weeding bean rows in the garden beside the road, stopped, leaned on her hoe, shading her eyes with one hand, and watched him approach. He looked just the same as last time, as every time, and his machine was no more nor less rickety and rusty than ever it had been, but there was something different on this occasion. Perhaps he was peddling a bit faster, as if he were on a mission or in a hurry. As he came near, Naomi saw sweat glistening in the shadow of his hat brim, throwing back the light to the day.

"We are well-stocked today, Abe," Naomi said. "We've flour and meal and sugar and salt. That being, can you spare a moment to stop and talk to me?"

Abe stopped, held out a newspaper. "I've brought news," he said, a bit short of breath. And before Naomi could summon a word in reply, Abe stood on his pedal and propelled his machine onward and away. As Naomi, clutching Adam's newspaper, stared speechless after her Abe, he threw up his hand and without turning around, called, "We'll talk later."

That night after supper, Adam unfolded his newspaper and began to read aloud to Evelyn and Naomi. There were ads about who had honey and eggs to share, who was making shoes or coats or hats to offer. Most of the long articles, as usual, described disasters, deaths and misfortunes in other places far away, "in that other world", as Evelyn termed it. The longest article covered a plane crash on a mountainside in Spain.

"No survivors," Adam read. "Most of the passengers on the flight were pilgrims, planning to walk the Camino de Santiago. What's that?"

Naomi knew. "The Way of Saint James," she said. "It's a long road across Spain to an old church. It takes weeks and weeks to walk. My parents talked a lot about it. They said when I got a bit older, we would go there and walk it together. But the storm came, and we never got to go." Lately, Naomi would sometimes go for whole days at a stretch without thinking of her parents at all, but now, the mention of the Camino brought back their memory to her as fresh as if the storm had wrecked their house yesterday.

Adam began reading the list of passengers on the crashed airliner, names of people they didn't know, until he paused suddenly, and Evelyn asked, "Is there one of ours, Adam?"

"Not ours, dear," he said, his voice not quite his own, "but Naomi will have to go with Abe tonight."

"Leaving us?" whispered, Evelyn. "Mercy. So soon?"

"We always knew she would," Adam said. His eyes glistened in the firelight. He lifted a gnarled hand to wipe his tears.

"Why are you crying, old Adam?" Naomi asked.

"I'm just happy for you, child," he answered softly.

It must have been near midnight, when the cycle of a day was just ending or just begun, and Naomi stood beside the road in front of their cabin. She had a pack slung on her shoulders that Adam and Evelyn had filled with clothes and food, as if she were about to undertake a journey.

"Wait here, child," Adam said when they deemed her ready and brought her out to the road.

"Don't fret, little dear," Evelyn said, patting her head lightly, "Abe will be along presently to take you away." They went back inside their house and left her there in the dark with the owls and frogs for company.

And before Naomi had time to become afraid in the mysterious and voiceful night, she heard the rattle and creak of Abe's contraption, and he was there with a wave and a smile to lighten the dark. He dismounted his tricycle, took his own pack and a walking staff from the basket behind the seat, and reached out to grasp Naomi's small cool hand in his large warm one.

"Let's go," he said, leading her down the road. "We've just time enough."

Naomi looked back at the tricycle. "Shouldn't we ride then?" she said. "It would be faster."

Abe chuckled as if she'd told a joke. "We'd never get those wheels up the mountain. We must walk to where we go." Later, it might occur to Naomi to wonder why she never thought to ask where they were going. In the moment, it didn't seem to matter. Anywhere she went with Abe she figured would be a fine place.

They walked through the dark while night birds queried them on their passage. Naomi wasn't sure when the road became a twisting footpath or when the path began to twine and climb up the side of the mountain. The going wasn't hard, and it didn't tire her. She felt she could have walked on for two forevers. It might have been an hour, or it might have been that last deep dark before dawn's first paling when they stopped and looked out over the scattered lights of a village far away and below. Abe, who had been talking or singing strange little songs the whole way suddenly fell still and silent, and they heard it then, the faint whisper of a jet aircraft in the distance that steadily swelled into a deafening roar as an airliner passed overhead so low and close that Naomi could see the lights in the windows for an instant before the plane disappeared over the ridge ahead. A moment later, the sound of an explosion, and flames and smoke billowed into the dawn.

"Hurry now," Abe said, striding away up the hill, a mild urgency in his voice. "They will be looking for you."

The road rose to meet them and before they were breathing hard, they crested the hill and the sun rose on a grassy swale tucked into the mountain just below the summit. Little fires burned here and there among scattered shards of metal and other debris that might have once been seats or luggage. The plane had apparently disintegrated upon impact or perhaps been blown apart by a bomb. Among the devastation, a crowd of people, maybe forty or fifty, came walking unsteadily toward Naomi. They seemed dazed, confused, but unhurt, miraculously unscathed.

Naomi remembered the storm that wrecked her house and spared her inside. She wanted to ask Abe if there was some connection, but when she looked, he was gone. As the people came closer, a woman and a man who were holding hands looked familiar. They were older than she remembered, but immediately she knew them.

"Naomi?" the woman queried, almost unbelieving, running ahead of the man and kneeling tearfully in front of the girl to take her hands.

"Oh, look, John," Naomi's mother said, looking back to the man behind her, trotting to catch up. "It's our child. Our child. I thought we'd lost her. And now we are all found together."

YAMADORI

Mason Garrett cursed and hauled out another six-pack. The ice in his cooler, all water now, but still cold to his fingers. A dozen empty cans lay scattered around his feet, although he was certain he'd only drunk half that today. On impulse, he snatched one up and flung it out across the sun-shot water to land among other fishers' floating trash.

Mason held the pack in his lap, wrestled a can free, and dangled the rest toward the man at the other end of the boat. "Ken, you want some?

Kenneth Watson, roused from either intense concentration on his fishing line or a semi-conscious drowse, shook his head. "Not thirsty, thankee. Mase, you gonna make yourself sick drinking all that in this heat."

Mason popped his can and dropped the remainders back into the cooler where they landed with a small splash. "I've only had a couple, Ken. You always were prone to exaggeration."

"I've had a couple," Ken retorted, although he could claim almost as many dead soldiers as Mase. "If you've had two you've had ten. I'm driving home."

"A man can't get drunk on beer, Ken. You know that."

Ken's laugh came out like the bark of a startled puppy. "I never knew you drank until one day I met you sober."

If Mase took offense at the remark, he swallowed it and changed the subject. "Ken, you read the County Bulletin this morning?"

"Nothing ever happens in Marshall County, Mase. Why should I read it?"

"Somebody done bought my daddy's house, Ken."

Ken looked genuinely surprised. "I thought the bank was going to sell it back to you."

"They promised they would, then they said I didn't

qualify for a loan. Some foreigner bought it," Mase growled, a quavery rumble that sounded like a bear about to cry.

"Foreigner?" Ken said, looking almost interested.

"Not from around here," Mase confirmed. "Got one of them names nobody can spell."

"What are you going to do about it?" Ken asked.

Mase chugged down the rest of his beer and, before he thought, threw the empty can as far as he was able. Another one he wouldn't be able to sell to the recycle center. "I'm thinking about going up there and burning the place down," he muttered.

Mase, of course, had no intention of setting fire to the house that belonged to his father before it belonged to Mountain Bank. His remark to Ken was just talk. Ken's response unnerved him slightly. "Let me know, Mase, if you need any help at that." Ken was probably talking serious, Mase suspected. Ken was a mean spirit who did almost as many mean things as he said.

Mase's father used to say back when Ken and Mase were boys together, "Ken Watson has a criminal bone. You keep hanging out with that boy, he's going to get you into some significant trouble." On a couple of occasions Ken had done just that. Still, Mase reflected, bad friends beat no friends at all. Had Mase any good friends, he might have thought differently.

Three days later, Mase had more pressing matters weighing on his mind. Jeff Markley's sawmill shut down, and Mase's part-time job suddenly became the job he used to have.

"I ain't been paid yet for last week," Mase reminded his employer when he showed up for work and Jeff told him the establishment was closed indefinitely.

"I ain't been paid, neither," Markley informed. "Soon's I get mine, I'll give you yours."

"It's hard, Jeff, getting cut down like this with no warning at all," Mase complained.

"Yeah," Jeff snorted. "Tell me about it."

No apology. Mase didn't expect one. He would have liked to tell Jeff Markley several things at that point, but held it in, figuring Jeff had some troubles of his own that didn't bear speaking of aloud.

The rent on the trailer where Mase lived was due next week. He'd need to pay at least half of it to keep old Doris Clyburn from throwing his stuff out in the road. Passing the post office, he went inside and scanned the notice board. He found more there wanting work than wanting workers. Piano teachers wanting students. Cleaners wanting dirty houses. Painters wanting walls. Quilts wanting beds to cover. Eggs wanting cooks. Tractors wanting gardens to plow. Stone masons wanting places to stack their stones. A multitude of givers wanting takers and a paucity of takers wanting anything for money, love, or pity's sake.

Mase spat his disgust and was about to turn away to someplace he could spend his last dollars on a cold beer, when his eye caught the corner of a business card almost hidden behind a flyer for the Baptist Church's barbecue fund-raiser to send some unfortunate child to summer camp. It occurred to Mase that when he was an unfortunate child, it might have been nice if somebody had eaten enough barbecue to send him away for a week beyond reach of his father's belt.

Mase lifted the flyer and pulled the tack holding the card to the corkboard. He held the bit of stiff paper in his hand and studied it. He saw a picture of what looked like a tiny scraggly tree on a pie plate and a name he couldn't pronounce and couldn't have spelled from memory. Hand-written neatly across the bottom of the card, *Need help building greenhouse. Pay right.*

Mase was glad he could read. He had helped some licensed carpenters over the years. Figured he knew better himself than some of them did. He gazed at the address on the card. Read it twice, then tucked the card into the pocket of his overalls. He couldn't believe it. He felt sure he'd been given a sign but had no notion of what it might mean.

Mase couldn't get his old pickup to start, so he caught a ride with the mail carrier, Jane Armstrong, as far as the turn-off to what he still thought of as the family farm. Jane said it was against the rules, but she had been close with Mase's father and when Mase said it was an emergency, she chose to believe that it was.

"What you really going back up there for, Mase?" Jane questioned as they bounced and jounced along a twisty upward road more pothole than pavement. After a hard winter, the county road repair crew hadn't yet worked their way out this far from town.

"I got me a job, Miss Jane," Mase stuttered, managing not to bite his tongue as Jane's car plummeted into a precipitous chasm amid the broken asphalt. If Jane suspected he was giving her a highly optimistic prediction based on his present tenuous hope, she gave no sign, just nodded and gripped her wheel while the vehicle lurched around an even larger pothole than the one her machine had just survived.

"Really?" she said when a less treacherous stretch of their way opened before them. "Who with?"

"That guy that's starting a tree nursery up on my Daddy's old place," Mase said, as if he knew it for a fact. What he did know was that the man wanted help building a greenhouse and his business card had a picture of a tree on it.

"Sounds interesting," Jane said, perhaps because it did or maybe she wanted to plumb the depths of Mase's ignorance. "What's his name?"

Mase pulled the card from his overalls and squinted at it, trying to hold it still enough to read. "It's foreign, I can't pronounce them out-lander names with all their wrong spelling."

Jane stopped her intrepid Toyota by a familiar row of tilted mailboxes, reached over the back of her seat and retrieved a bundle of envelopes, held them out toward Mase. "Should I leave Mister Imai's mail in his box, or do you want to take it to him since you're going up there?"

Mase stood gazing at his hand-full of envelopes. He was half-minded to put them in the mailbox and walk on back to town. He also thought about tossing them in the weeds or lighting them afire, but he didn't want to get in trouble with Jane. She was a good soul. She never talked down to him even when she caught him out short. She had trusted him with her mail. Next time he saw her, he wanted her to think he'd told the truth about having a job. He shifted the mail bundle from his right hand to his left and began walking up the drive toward his daddy's house. Only it wasn't his anymore. It wasn't even the bank's. Mase looked at the name on one of the envelopes. Why couldn't foreigners use real names like Americans did? How had Jane said it? The farm belonged to Mister Eye-May-Eye now.

Gravel crunched underfoot as Mase trudged up the hill toward the house. To Mase, the gravel said money. When his dad had owned the place, the dirt drive was rutted deep. Fowler Garrett could never have afforded to have his drive graded and stoned. Their old pickup would drag and scrape in dry weather and in wet, they wouldn't try the way at all short of dire necessity. Mase recalled three times, at least, bringing down their pair of mules to drag the hapless vehicle free of the muck where it had sunk to the axles. A

135

day would be lost to the rescue and Fowler would be fouler than his usual, swiping at everything and everyone he could reach.

The house looked different, too, painted and mended, with a new door and fresh metal roof. The cracked and broken windows had been re-glazed, some of the frames replaced altogether. Mase figured Eye-May-Eye must have spent as much money resurrecting the old shack as the whole farm had cost him.

Mase crossed the yard to the porch, so shiny under new paint he hesitated to walk on it, and knocked on the door. He waited. No one came to answer. He knocked again, heard an engine of some kind hammering the air out back, stepped down into the yard and walked around the house. A big van was parked beside a new barn, bigger and straighter than the old one, which had been torn down and all its potentially useful remains sorted and neatly stacked. Where the feedlot had been, there were rows of long low tables, apparently constructed of material from the barn. A wiry little gnome was directing the moving crew in unloading what looked like little trees growing in pots, which, as they set them out, the old man was fussily arranging on the tables.

"Careful… Slowly… Gently," he kept repeating like a mantra, as if they were handling fragile treasure bound for a museum. Mase reckoned it was about the damnedest thing he'd seen all day.

"He's got all these little trees, Ken. In pots, like they were germaniums or tomato plants. He calls them bones eyes. Says some are older than he is."

Kenneth Watson popped another tab, poured down a swallow, shook his head. "That's what this town needs. One more crazy foreigner. What made you want to take a job like that with some outlander?"

Mase turned on his patient voice that sounded like he was a reasonable adult explaining the obvious to a child who really didn't want to know. "Because, Ken, I need the money and he's paying."

"How you gonna get to work?" Ken snickered. "You sure ain't gonna ride out there with old Jane Armstrong every day."

"He said he'd get me there and back until my pickup's fixed. He brought me back to the trailer last night."

"When he finds out you're no carpenter, he ain't taking you no place. You know that?"

"I can do what he wants," Mase said. "He ain't building a church up there."

Ken opened another can and held it out to Mase. "Drink this down now. You couldn't build a bird house by yourself."

"You're just jealous, Ken Watson, because I got work and you don't," Mase groused, although he accepted Ken's beer. "Besides. I ain't being by myself. I'll be working with Mr. Eye-May-Eye. He's particular."

"Eye-May-Eye?" Ken huffed. "What kind of name is that?

Mase laughed, dribbling beer down his shirt. "Don't you know anything at all Ken?" he said. "That's one of them Japan names. He's 'merican but his grandpap came over from there. He explained that to me."

"Maybe he'll explain to you how to drive a nail," Ken murmured.

Mase already knew how to drive a nail, but over the next few weeks he learned a great deal about joinery from Imai Kosuke, who seemed as adept at carpentry as he was at growing his lilliputian forest. The old man, at least he seemed old to Mase, never made him feel diminished by his ignorance, but would take the tools and say, "Watch." Mase would watch whatever procedure until Imai would smile and hand back the tools. "Now you can do it. You don't need me for this." And over the days they worked together, Mase would need him less and less for one thing or another, but there was always some new thing that needed learning and doing. Mase didn't think of himself as Imai's apprentice, exactly, but that is what he had become. Weeks passed while he began to regard his labor as more than a means to pay for room and beer, but something to enjoy doing well, be proud of, a craft rather than a job. Mase wouldn't have described his situation in quite those words to Ken, or even to himself, but before the last pane of glass was set in the greenhouse frame, he felt he owned the work more than he owed to do it.

Imai remained to Mase a mystery, a riddle, a puzzle, each piece a contradiction. The man was exacting and kind. His silences communicated more than his speech. He shared his space but moved in a different world. Mase soon learned not to pester the old man with questions, but to watch and wait until a thing was made clear to him. Invariably, in due time it was. Often, when Mase looked his question to Imai, a gesture or a glance would tell him that the solution already lay in his own mind.

By the time the greenhouse door was hinged and latched, the two men, one young and local, one old and alien, worked comfortably together, each anticipating the other's moves, sharing common intentions with an ease that often rendered words superfluous. Summer had hardly set in proper, as Mase put it, before the work was finished. Imai paid Mase his last week's wages in cash, for that is how Mase had asked to be paid.

Mase counted the twenties, held them in his hand like they belonged to somebody else. "I still owe you twenty on the money you advanced to fix my truck," he said. "You didn't take it out, Mister Imai."

"You gave me more than you were paid, Mase Garrett," Imai answered. "Thank you."

Mase jammed the wadded bills into the pocket of his jeans, shook Imai's offered hand, wanted to say something but couldn't figure out what it was, got into his now less unreliable pickup, and drove away toward the county road. He was half-way back to Drovers Gap when he slapped the steering wheel with his sore right hand and growled aloud, "Damn! I should have said thanks."

Mase hoped that when he got back to his trailer, Ken wouldn't be there, or that, if he was, he would be mostly sober. Ken had showed up at his door past midnight the week before. Doramae, Ken's girlfriend and principal means of support, had thrown him out of the house. Her house, it turned out, which limited his territorial rights considerably, that, and his own bad behavior. They had argued because Doramae wouldn't give him money that she had earned and he hadn't. Ken had attempted to exercise a bit of manly persuasion, and Doramae proved more forceful than Ken ever imagined she was.

"You ain't my daddy," she told him calmly as she tossed his bag of clothes out the door while he sat on her steps wondering how it had all come down to this, "and I ain't my mama," she went on. "You come around here again and try being smart, I'll break your other arm." Doramae hadn't broken his arm, but it was still sore a week later.

He was rubbing his arm, when Mase, bleary-eyed, barefoot and in his underwear, opened his door.

"Mase, I need somewhere to stay," Ken muttered, trying to conceal his beg behind his growl.

"What's happened to Doramae?" Mase asked, swiping his eyes with his knuckles.

"She don't fight fair," Ken said.

Ken had been in the trailer ever since. In the morning, he drank beer to fuel himself to go out and find a job, and when he didn't, he drank more to ease his disappointment in himself. When the beer was gone, he asked Mase to fund a pint of whiskey.

"I don't get paid until the end of the week," Mase said truthfully.

"You got any of them pills, then?" Ken whined.

Mase didn't have any pills. He had a lot of bad habits, a few of which he'd been trying to break lately, but he didn't do pills. Never had. Stuff like that cost money, which Mase was usually short of, at least until he went to work for Imai. Since then, he'd come home tired at night, and it would be time for bed. Mase considered a man might have time or money for himself, but hardly both at once.

The air conditioning in Mase's pickup had ceased to function a long time before the vintage vehicle was his. He cranked down the window, so the hot air in the cab would at least be in motion. The swelter from outside carried the acrid smell of smoke. Not leaves or brush but the rank raw fragrance of combusting synthetics. Plastics. Fabrics. Like a house burning, or...

He saw the blue haze hovering over Clyburn's Trailer Park. Not quite a park. Old Doris had three used and abused mobile homes parked in the field beside her house that she rented to folk who couldn't afford better. Mase had to stop and let Drovers Gap Fire and Rescue pull out onto the county road before he could enter the driveway. One of the rental units had black stains trailing upward from the glassless windows. An ambulance was parked out front and as Mase stopped beside it, two figures in hazmat gear emerged from the open door of Mase's trailer, of course it had to be his, carrying a stretcher covered with a sheet hiding a human body, judging from the vague shape beneath.

Mase got out of his truck. Sheriff Jolene Bear and one of her deputies Mase didn't know stood beside the ambulance talking with a woman Jolene introduced as the county medical examiner. They had to step aside to allow the EMS crew passage to stow their burden in the back of the ambulance.

"Was Ken Watson living with you now, Mase?" she said, laying out his first name like they were old friends.

"That him there?" Mase murmured, watching the men shoving the stretcher into the ambulance as if it carried bags of flour or a deer carcass.

"Ken Watson," said the deputy whose name tag Mase couldn't read.

"All burnt up?" Mase whispered. The very thought coupled with the smokey stink churned his stomach.

"No, the fire didn't get to him," said the death doctor. Jolene had told him her name, but Mase couldn't remember it. "It was the smoke. He probably was asleep. Just never woke up."

"Like I said, Mase. Was Ken living with you?" Jolene queried again.

"Just for a few days, until he could get a place to stay." *A few days too long*, Mase kept the thought behind his face.

"He was smoking herb, Mase," Jolene said, holding his eyes on her. "Fresh bag. Was that yours?"

"I don't do that anymore, Jolene... Sheriff," Mase stammered, hoping this woman of the law could see the truth in him. "He musta got it somewhere else."

"Where do you think that was?" said the deputy.

"I don't know," Mase said. "Ken was broke, anyway."

"You give him any money?" the deputy again.

141

"Take a fool to trust Ken Watson with money," Mase said. "I had a little cash in there, but it was hid."

"Maybe you didn't hide it good enough, Mase," Jolene said. Mase could tell from the way she said it that she likely believed what he had been telling them.

Somebody knocking on the window dredged Mase up from fitful sleep. For a moment he had no idea where he was. A fine drizzle scrolling down the windshield anchored him. The Sheriff forbade him entering his trailer until the county forensics team went over the scene, supposedly sometime this morning, so Mase had spent the night in a near fetal curl inside the cab of his pickup. He tried to sit up now and banged his head on the dash just hard enough to restore him to full consciousness without doing any permanent damage.

He stared at the driverside window until his eyes focused on the hand knocking again, not so loud this time. He expected to see the face of old Doris, his landlady. As the forces of the constabulary were vacating the site yesterevening, she had tottered by, gazed upon him with the intensity of a harried groundhog.

"You'll have to pay for this, you know," she declared. "I could sue you, you know. It's in the lease, you know. You're not supposed to have anybody else living in there, you know."

Mase didn't think it was in the lease, but instinctively mustered defense. "Ken wasn't living here, Miz Clyburn. He was visiting, just staying for a few days while he looked for a place of his own."

"Well, he wouldn't of found it with me," Doris croaked. "Now you don't have a place either. You can't stay here."

"Jolene won't let me in there, anyway, even to get my stuff, until her people inspect it in the morning," Mase said. "I thought I'd just sleep in my truck tonight."

"Don't be sleeping in my yard, Mase Garrett," Doris said. "I ain't running no refugee camp here, you know."

No ma'am, Mase thought, *You're just a slum-lady*. But his thought didn't quite rise to the level of speech. What he said was, "I won't, Miz Clyburn. I'll sit here and make a few calls around, and then I'll be gone."

"I'll be watching out you do," Doris snipped. "I got a pie in the oven. You still owe me this week's rent, too. I'll have to figure my damages, you know." And with that, she teetered across the yard and disappeared into her neat little brick cottage with lilacs growing by the front door.

Mase hadn't gone. When Doris didn't return to badger him before dark, he just swallowed the ache of his anxious and empty stomach and went to sleep. He didn't even get out of the truck to pee on the grass. Tired as he was, he hoped he could hold it until morning.

Mase expected to be threatened and harassed and banished from the premises now by Doris Clyburn, but the hand that tapped again on the glass, more softly this time, didn't belong to Doris. Neither did the face beyond. Mister Imai stood beside the pickup, smiling against the morning.

Mase rolled down the window, silently gazing at Mister Imai because he didn't know what to say.

"Have you had breakfast?" Mister Imai inquired.

"I need to pee." Mase said, because he desperately did. He got out of the truck and directed a stream against a tire like a stray puppy marking territory. Mister Imai didn't appear startled or offended by this behavior.

"Sheriff Bear and her deputy came up to my place to visit," he said when Mase's bladder was blissfully empty.

Mase nodded. "She wanted to know about me, I reckon."

"Yes," said Mister Imai. "She told me about the fire. I'm sorry for your friend."

143

"Ken wasn't exactly a friend," Mase said, "but he was the kind of trouble I'd gotten used to having. I'll miss him, I reckon."

"Where will you reside now?" Mister Imai asked, sounding like he really cared.

Mase shrugged. "Damned if I know. I can't live here. Old Doris is threatening to sue me. I reckon she might if I had anything worth paying a lawyer to get."

"Do you have another job yet?"

"Hell, I ain't had time to look, even if I knew where." Mase mumbled, getting a little irritated at the old man's interrogation.

"I have a room to spare, and some more work, if you want to learn Niwaki," Mister Imai said.

"What's Knee-Wall-Key?" Mase asked, almost curious.

"Garden Trees," said Mister Imai.

"Them like your Bones Eyes?" Mase said.

"Niwaki grow in the ground, not in pots," Mister Imai said. "They're bigger. That's why I need some help. I'm getting old."

"Where's this room, Mase asked, already reluctantly edging toward a decision. He wondered what he was getting himself into, but his gut told him this was an offer he wasn't allowed to pass.

"In my barn," said Imai. When he saw the expression on Mase's face, he laughed and added, "Don't worry. It's more comfortable than your trailer was."

Mase felt Change grabbing him by the throat, flinched and said, "I reckon if a barn was good enough for Jesus, it's good enough for me."

Mase didn't know where he was when his eyes opened, until he saw the framed photographs on the wall opposite his bed. Several of Imai's tortured little trees, all in a row. He was in his room, of course, in Imai's barn, next to the workshop where the old man worried his trees in bad weather and sometimes conducted classes.

Imai had the room built for guest teachers at his occasional workshops and for special customers from away, who brought their prized centenarian bonsai for repotting, restyling, or sometimes restoration of a half-dead specimen suffering from neglect or incompetence. It boggled Mase's mind that people would pay more to coddle what looked to him like a bedraggled shrub than it might cost to fell and mill a mature white pine or poplar.

He thought there was too much money in the world, or at least that it was mostly in the hands of people who didn't know how to spend it all. Still, he had no complaints. He was getting paid to sleep in the nicest bed he'd ever met, like he was booked at Apple Grove Inn out on Warwoman Mountain. For however long it lasted, he meant to do his part to make Mister Imai happy he was here. If that meant clambering up on a rockface to dig stunted little pines and spruce out of cracks and crannies, which was what Imai wanted them to do today, then so be it. Mase figured he'd done a lot worse for a lot less.

He dressed, walked across the yard to Imai's house, found the kitchen door open, and the old man waved him in. Imai already had their breakfast laid out on the table. Eggs and grits and bacon and slices of toast. Little pans of butter and honey with funny little wooden doodlies to drizzle it out with, and a big bowl of green salad. Imai apparently ate salad at every meal.

"Youns sure eat a lot of green stuff, Mister Imai," Mase said, sitting down and reaching for the toast.

"*Itadakimasu*," Imai said, pouring coffee into their cups and sitting himself. "Green makes the world go around. If there were no green in it, we'd have no air to breathe, no meat to eat. Get as much green as you can inside you and your life will be better."

Mase forked his green stuff, reflecting that since he'd been eating Imai's salads, his life had, in fact, improved markedly.

"Yamadori," Imai said, beaming, rubbing his hands together.

"Yes." Mase said, catching some of the old man's enthusiasm, even in this early hour before the sun cleared the mountain. He wasn't sure about the -*dori* part, but he knew by now that *yama* said *mountain*, and Imai had already explained he wanted to bring home some of the stunted conifers that grew out of the rock seams along the crest of the high ridge above the farm.

"Why do you want them scrawny things?" Mase had queried. "There's plenty healthy seedlings closer in and easier to get to."

"Them scrawny things are survivors," Imai replied, imitating Mase's Appalachian twang before he caught himself and continued in his own voice. "They have endured and survived on little. Little soil. Little water, little protection from winter wind and ice. They have been shaped by storm and duress, and each one has its own bitter story to show us. Yamadori rest as much at home in a pot as among their crags. The life we give them will be an improvement to their health."

"All the same," Mase said, "I think I'd rather live up on the mountain."

"Then, this will be a good day for both of us," Imai said, gesturing at the tools he wanted Mase to carry. He hoisted his own pack containing assorted supplies and instruments of his craft. Mase hoped their lunch was in there too, and something to drink besides water.

146

The old man set off up-slope through the trees, apparently certain of his destination, and Mase, to his surprise, was hard put to keep up. Either Imai's pack was a lot lighter than it looked, or he was more fit than he appeared. Mase was thoroughly winded by the time they had passed through the close-ranked grove of hemlocks and oaks, and they could see the stone shanks of the mountain above them.

Imai stopped to let him catch up, held out a canteen of water. Mase nodded, A whisper was as much voice as he could find for thanks. He drank, slow and deep, thinking there was nothing better in the whole wide world than water from the mountain.

Over the course of the afternoon, Mase and Imai collected several scraggly and arthritic conifers across the fractured face of the ridge. Although Imai would lop off large portions of limb and branch with alarming alacrity, he was painstaking to gather all the roots intact, directing Mase's digging with watchful eye, and digging himself when he didn't trust his helper to exercise proper care and caution. Toward evening, as they started home, Mase could see the farm down below, already dim and purpled in the mountain's shadow. They were so burdened with their bundled trees that they left all the tools stashed at the foot of a twisted pine, too large and deep-rooted to capture. Mase would come back up in the morning and collect the implements.

Dense clouds slid low across the ridge as they descended, thunder grumbled and rumbled threateningly, and before they reached the lower forest near the farm, a drenching downpour hurried them home, slipping and sliding, soaked and shivering.

The next morning, Imai had a rattling cough that persisted for weeks before he seemed fully himself again.

Nevertheless, he sent Mase up the mountain to fetch their tools, and by the time he returned, the old man had two of the new yamadori already pruned and wired into their pots. Two others, Mase was told to watch carefully, as Imai, with patient explanation, secured them in their training pots and prepared the planting media. The last one, a battered twist of Fraser fir, Imai set in front of Mase and said, "You belong to this one."

Mase proceeded to try to follow Imai's process, and with frequent cautions and interventions from the old man, eventually had his fir situated in its container.

"It don't look right. Not like yourn." Mase said, shaking his head.

"Right takes time." Imai said. "You will grow together. The tree will tell you how it wants to grow, and you will know then what to do with it."

Mase nodded as if that made sense to him, and they went into Imai's house to make their supper.

The season passed. Days became weeks and weeks turned into months. A shining stainless-steel clad travel trailer appeared in the yard one day.

"You going on a trip?" Mase asked the old man.

"No, Imai said, "but you can, if you want to."

"I'll have to get a new truck first," Mase said. "I don't think that old crate of mine could pull this thing."

Mase moved his stuff into the trailer as soon as they got it hooked up. It was new and it was comfortable, if a bit tight, and he could look out the window and see all the little trees, including the one Imai insisted Mase belonged to. They cleaned the room in the barn and Imai unrolled a new bed. Mase discovered he missed sleeping on the floor. There wasn't room to lay out a futon in the trailer.

A woman arrived in a van to spend four nights sleeping

148

in the room in the barn, while Imai pruned the little trees she brought, wrapped wires around the limbs he didn't chop off, bent them at crazy angles, then cut off half the trees' roots. It looked to Mase like Imai was intent on killing them, but the woman didn't seem to object to the brutalities he inflicted on her trees, and when they were installed in new pots, a bit smaller, even, than the ones they arrived in, she seemed delighted.

The woman's name was Maria. She was a lot younger than Imai. Mase figured she was about his own age. She didn't look much like a foreigner, but she could talk to Imai in his private language. Mase had picked up a few words of it by now but not enough to follow their conversations. Whenever they thought he was listening, they would converse in English.

Maria worked for an ad agency in Chicago, where she designed ads for electric cars. Two of the trees she brought with her had belonged to her father, she said, and one, with a trunk as wide as the tree was tall, had been handed down from a great-grandmother who told that it had belonged to her father.

"It must be around two hundred years old," Maria said.

"Pines don't live that long around here," Mase said.

Maria smiled. "Not unless they're cared for."

The third day of her stay, when Imai had finished the restyling and repotting of the trees she'd brought, he sent her off up the mountain with Mase to scout for yamadori. The weather held fair, and they had a pleasant time of it, bringing down a couple of small fir that Maria deemed held possibilities. By next morning Imai already had them secured in their training pots and Maria packed one of them with her other trees in the back of her van and drove away north. Mase wished he might have been going with her, even if she stashed him in back with the trees.

When the van passed out of sight down the county road, Imai handed Mase a hundred-dollar bill. Mase stared at it for a moment before he dared take it. "What's this for?" he said.

Imai smiled. "Maria wanted you to have this. She thought you might be embarrassed to take it from her hand, so she asked me to give it to you."

"I wouldn't have taken her money," Mase said. "I don't work for her."

"Yes," Imai said. "It isn't payment for your work. Maria holds you in some esteem."

There were days after that when Imai didn't seem entirely himself. Customers came and went. So did the little trees, not bones eyes anymore. Bonsai, Mase knew now. And niwaki, destined for gardens in distant cities. Tending the niwaki required lots of ladder work, which increasingly Imai relinquished to Mase, directing him from *terra firma*. During the year there were a couple of classes, seminars, Imai called them. One he facilitated himself, and the other was taught by a man from Oregon. People came from as far away as Atlanta and St. Louis for that one, stayed overnight at the Apple Grove Inn and rode out to the farm every morning in a chartered van. Imai projected his customary enthusiasm throughout, but when it was over, seemed glad to have them all gone, told Mase he was tired and needed a quiet spell.

A few days after that second event, Mase found Imai one morning sitting in his workshop, head bowed, arms folded across his chest. He turned his sweaty face up to Mase and whispered, "It's time I saw a doctor."

Mase drove on their trips to the doctor. The doctor did repeated tests, finally announced that Imai's heart was worn out. "A pacemaker will give you some good time yet," he told his patient.

"No pacemaker," Imai said. "I'll take my own time and not be greedy."

Mase, who had learned about trees mostly by watching, now learned by doing, as more and more Imai sat by and instructed him as he worked. "You're a real Niwashi now," he told Mase. "A gardener by nature," he added.

The day came when Mase found Imai lying pale and unresponsive among his trees. Mase called EMS, thinking this was a scene he had lived before. He rode in the ambulance with Imai to the hospital. Before they wheeled him through the emergency entrance, Imai's eyes focused, he reached out and grabbed Mase's hand, mumbled through his mask, "Yamadori."

"Don't worry," Mase said. "I'll take care of the trees, Imai sensei."

"Not the trees," Imai gasped, "you. You're my Yamadori." And he was gone.

Imai had made all the arrangements for his return to earth. Mase didn't know what would happen to the farm now. He was already packed and ready to go, when the lawyer came not to evict him but to tell him Imai, having no living relatives, had willed the farm to him. Maria came from Chicago and spoke a eulogy at Atkins Funeral Home before a small gathering of Imai's tree people, mostly from places far away that Mase had never heard of. Afterward, she and Mase climbed up the ridge to scatter Imai's ashes across the stones.

As they stood looking down over the little farm, she said, "Mase, what will you do with all this now?"

Mase didn't need to think on it to answer, "I'll take care of the trees."

Maria reached across to take his hand. "I'll come as often as I can and help you," she whispered. Mase could tell by the way she said it that she believed what he had told her.

THE OLD WOMAN UPSTAIRS

They wouldn't have believed her even if she told them. She was just the old woman who lived upstairs over the bakery. If she died, nobody would come to check on her until Oscar Ossenkopf, the baker who owned the building, might climb the stairs to see why she had not been down to pay her rent.

He might wonder as he climbed if she were all right, because she always paid her rent on time, in cash. If he found her dead up there, he might prowl through her apartment before he called the authorities, hoping to find any money or valuables she might have squirreled away, for the old woman had no visible means of support. No social security check arrived in the mail each month. No bank statement. Utilities were included in her rent, so there were no bills.

Nobody but her ever saw the boy, Abner, who delivered her groceries. Outside her upstairs window in the post-midnight dark, in the shadow of the north wall of the building never lit by sun nor moon, hovering on his peculiar tricycle with a basket a thousand times bigger inside than out, he would hand her her rations through the window, and she would pay him with old coins from her box, sometimes silver but more often gold. Abner was like her, one of her kind. He would forever be the boy about to blossom into manhood, and she would always be the old woman, born in a time that no one, not even her, could remember.

Ossenkopf, down in his bakery at four in the morning, might have wondered some time or other just how old his upstairs tenant really was. She had been the old woman seldom seen when he was a boy helping his father in the bakery after school, and she had been the same old woman when the father died behind the counter of a heart attack, and his son left college to come home and run the family business.

152

"Just until we find somebody," Nora Ossenkopf had said. "We can't afford to shut down the bakery." They never found anybody, though, and her son was still the baker, and the old woman was still resident upstairs when Nora joined her husband in their plot under the ginkgo tree in the cemetery behind the Lutheran church on Grace Street. The baker married late in life and his wife never bore offspring. He feared he might have to sell the building to some stranger who would turn it into luxury apartments, for he had no one to inherit it when his baking days were over. And the old woman still lived upstairs over the bakery.

Unlike him, she never grew older than she was. He wouldn't have worried so much if he had known, but of course, she couldn't tell him. He wouldn't have believed her if she had.

Rent day arrived, and the old woman took some crisp new bills from her box and made her careful way down the stairs to Oscar's Bread, Cakes and Pastries. After his father died, the baker had changed the name to Oscar's because some of his customers could never be sure how to pronounce *Ossenkopf's*.

"You're looking sad, today, Mister Ossenkopf," the old woman said, as he wrote out the receipt for her month's rent. "Is everything all right?"

"It is what it is." Oscar said it almost like a sigh, as if he spoke with a final breath. "For a baker, one day is like every other day. Up early and late to bed. I'm too old for this stuff, and I'd be lost without it. I'm a baker or I'm nobody at all."

"Maybe you need to hire some help," the old woman suggested.

Oscar shook his head. "Business is never that good," he said with another mighty sigh. "What I need is a child to take over the bakery, so I can retire before I'm dead."

"And what would you do with your retirement?" the old woman queried.

The baker handed over her receipt, stared through the reversed *O* of *Oscar's* on the storefront glass, as if the solution to his life's dilemma had suddenly appeared in the street outside, and realizing it hadn't, came to himself and looked the old woman in the eye, having arrived at a sudden and disturbing honesty. "I don't know anything but this. I suppose I would hang around and criticize every bun and loaf and recipe and pretend that in my time I could have done it better. I might do that until they got sick of me and told me to stay at home all day."

"And what would you do at home all day?" the old woman persisted.

Oscar stood mute for a moment. The prospect terrified him. Finally, he said, "I suppose I could bake some bread. If the weather was good, I could take a walk in the park, feed crumbs to the swans on the pond there. That's what old men who have outlived their purpose do, I suppose."

"Truly?" said the old woman. "That is all?"

"Well," said Oscar, "truly, I've fantasized for years about taking a really long walk, like the Camino or the Highland Way, but I'm already too old and soft for such as that."

"It's almost lunch-time. You could take a walk with me right now," the old woman said. "In the park, of course."

"I don't close for lunch," Oscar said.

"But it's Wednesday," the old woman said brightly.

Oscar was stunned. He'd never seen her smile before. Not ever. He was also embarrassed. All this chatter made him forget the day. The bakery always closed for Wednesday afternoons. It was Oscar's only time off. He spent it buying supplies for the bakery. With an unaccustomed blend of reluctance and anticipation, he came around the counter and flipped the sign on his door.

"You sure you're up to this?" he said. He'd always thought of the old woman upstairs as frail, although she didn't look frail. She just looked old.

"Let's go," she said, slaying him with the ageless music of her laugh.

A lot of trees grew in the park. It was more than a grove, a small forest really. A few minutes through the gate and they could no longer see the street, or the buildings opposite. Traffic sounds became so faint, one might pretend they didn't exist. The breeze in the branches, birdsong, the occasional laughter of a child hidden by the foliage. That was the whole world.

The baker, well on his way to being old, and the woman from upstairs over the bakery, who was well beyond old, walked for a while in silence, counting their own footfalls, until the man spoke softly, as if at a play or concert, "Miss Chloe, how long have you been living upstairs over the bakery?"

She didn't answer for two and a half steps, then, "A long time. Didn't your grandfather tell you about me?"

Oscar shook his head, stuffed his hands deep in his jacket pockets and kicked a stone in the path, just as a little boy would. "Grandfather died the year I was born. I don't remember him at all. Whatever he might have told me, I wouldn't have understood anyway."

Old Chloe laughed softly, a small sound that made her shoulders shiver, as if she had kept most of her mirth deep inside herself where it couldn't present a danger. "He would have told you that I was there when he opened the bakery," she said casually, as if commenting on the weather.

"You can't be that old, Miss Chloe. You're joking me," Oscar said.

"Just call me Chloe," she said. "Truly, I was just as old then as ever I've been. Time stands still if you don't count."

155

"So how long?" Oscar said rather abruptly, being not exactly in the mood for jokes and riddles. "How long have you lived over the bakery?"

Chloe turned her eyes upon him, bright and blue as if there were two holes in her face and a sunny sky behind. "A forever that seems like a day," she said, "and no time at all, so the mirror tells me."

"You're not going to tell me anything, are you Chloe?" Oscar said, somewhat put out by her evasions, but laughing despite himself.

"Sit down with me on that bench yonder," she said, mischief in her bright blue eyes and in her voice that suddenly seemed younger, "and I will tell you everything."

"I had a husband," the old woman began as soon as they were settled in the shade of a spreading oak. "He was a good man, my Roger. We had two daughters, Rose and Violet. Lovely girls. Bright. Roger said they took after their mother. They were prettier than me, though. Smarter, too."

The old woman was silent for a moment, staring up into the branches of the oak, where a bird, hidden in the leaves, sang a single note over and over, like the striking of a clock. Oscar had never heard such a bird before, but he didn't hear many birds singing in the bakery, where he spent most of his waking hours. Now he listened, sitting next to the old woman, his fingers gripping his knees, watching the dappled sun and shadow playing across the back of his hands, waiting for the story to continue. And after a stillness that might have lasted a minute, or maybe several, it did.

"We had the sort of life that everyone might want to have, that most people pretend to have, but almost nobody ever achieves. We were very happy."

"You were incredibly fortunate, Chloe," Oscar said, trying to remember if there had ever been a time in his own life when he had been truly happy.

156

"Yes, we were indeed, until the war came," the old woman said, so softly that Oscar had to lean close to catch the words.

"Which war was that?" He asked, trying to name to himself the ones he could remember.

"They are all the same war, aren't they?" The old woman said. "Started by the greedy and rich for poor people's children to die in. Each war sows the seed for the next one. Peace never really comes. The warriors just get too tired and broken to fight for a while. They bury the dead, erect monuments to the slain, and when they have recovered sufficient strength, they start again."

"But some wars are for a just cause, don't you think?" Oscar ventured, because the truth in the old woman's words was too strong to drink down straight.

"My Roger went away to a just war," the old woman answered, "and when the war was over, he never came back. What he left behind they sent home in a jar. It's still in my room upstairs. I can show it to you sometime if you'd like to see."

"But you still had your daughters," Oscar said, thinking he would have been happy to settle for two lovely daughters.

"Life goes hard for the lovely," the old woman said, with just the slightest hint of bitterness in her tone. "One died slow and the other quick, but before I learned to properly love them, they were gone by no choice of their own. Nothing I could have done would have made a difference. Before they had a chance to fulfill their promise, they were no more, and I, having given my years to make a way for them to claim their lives, was alone all over again."

"Have you been by yourself ever since?" Oscar asked, captured now by the old woman's tragic narrative.

"Yes, except for Laurus," Chloe said, as if reciting a script she had committed to memory and told a thousand times. "That was long ago now, before your time, Oscar."

"Laurus?" Oscar said.

"Yes," said the old woman, laughing, sounding like it was still a great surprise to her, "the angel."

"I don't believe in angels," Oscar said. "I need to get back to the bakery." He braced his hands on his knees, tilted forward to stand.

"Angels believe in you, Oscar," the old woman said. "It isn't up to you, you know." Oscar paused in a half-crouch because his tricky back had caught, looked like a puppet left dangling after the show. Chloe spoke a touch sharply, "You asked for my story. Do you want to hear it or not?"

Oscar didn't remember he had exactly asked for her story, and he wasn't sure at this point he wanted to hear the rest of it, but he sat back down because that was less painful than continuing his striving toward vertical.

"I was in a state you wouldn't believe," the old woman went on, interpreting Oscar's collapse as a gesture of assent. "I couldn't eat. I couldn't sleep. I couldn't rest and I couldn't work. All that I loved and lived for was lost to me. I had nothing left to sustain myself. The bank sent some people to take the house. I had no place to move the furnishings, which strangers came and carried away a piece at a time as I sat on the curb and watched. When I could bear it no more and came here to the park and sat down on this very bench, intending not to rise again until I was dead." She looked over at Oscar who was rubbing his back and looking at nothing. "Laurus found me right here where we are sitting now." She said it with the solemnity of a priest reciting liturgy.

"The angel," Oscar said, just to be sure he was getting the story straight.

"My angel," Chloe confirmed. "Everybody has one, Oscar," she said, as if she knew it was so.

Oscar had to laugh at the notion. He couldn't help himself. Laughing made his back hurt.

"Even you, Oscar Ossenkopf," Chloe repeated. "Even you."

"Where was my angel when I needed him?" Oscar said. It was a rhetorical question.

"Closer than you think," said the old woman who lived upstairs over the bakery. "I felt just like you at the time. I was sitting here on this bench, mourning the lives that had been taken from me untimely. Grieving the gone life I had never lived for myself. And I felt a stirring in the air, a chill and a thrill, and I looked up, and there was Laurus sitting right beside me."

"And the angel fixed everything, and you lived happily ever after. Is that what you are about to tell me?" Oscar said. He wasn't going to sit still for an uplifting pep talk.

"He didn't fix anything," Chloe said. "He just asked me what I planned to do with my life now."

"And what did you tell him?" Oscar let his sarcasm show. "Did the angel give you three wishes then?"

The old woman laughed. "Don't be silly. Laurus isn't a genie in a bottle. I got only one wish. I told the angel, 'I've lived too long already. I don't want to get any older,' and Laurus said, 'Don't worry, you won't', and I haven't."

"You mean…?" Oscar didn't complete the question. Just shook his head in disbelief. "You're putting me on, Chloe," he said.

The old woman nodded. "I thought Laurus was putting me on. But months went by, then years. I was still old, but never any older."

"So how have you lived?" Oscar queried. "I mean, you said you lost everything. You were already old. How have you survived all this time?"

"I've lived out of the box," Chloe said. "That's how it works if you are, well, like me."

"Must be a mighty big box," Oscar observed.

"Small enough to carry in my bag," Chloe held her palms a few inches apart to illustrate. "But Laurus said it would hold everything I needed for a day, and so far, every day that has come, it has."

"So how did you wind up in my building?" Oscar asked. Which was all he'd really wanted to know at the beginning of their conversation.

"As I told you, I was homeless," Chloe said. "Laurus took me to the new building that had just been finished across the street from the park. There was a vacant apartment upstairs and Laurus' box held just enough money to pay a month's rent. And on the first day of every month ever since, it has again."

"I need a box like that," Oscar said. He tried again to stand up and this time his back allowed it.

"You wanting to go back to the bakery now, Oscar?" old Chloe said, looking up at him, not looking like an old woman at all, nor like a young one, either. Ageless, somehow, more like a – Oscar couldn't decide what, exactly.

"I suppose I must," Oscar said, heaving another of his soulful sighs, "but on a day like this, I wish I could just keep on walking down this path forever."

"Don't worry, Oscar. You will," Chloe said, her blue eyes brighter and bluer than the bright blue sky. She took a small wooden box from her bag and held it out to Oscar. "You'll need this," she said.

SEED MAN

Levi Ashe handed over the bag of barley grains to the farmer. "Treat these right and they'll give back to you. Only two pounds, but that's all the Congregation is allotting this year."

"It'll have to do then, I reckon," the farmer said, weighing the bag in her hands. "Pray us some right weather, Seedman."

"I pray for all," Levi said. "There's plenty time for it on the road." He fastened the straps on Molly's satchel and turned to his horse.

"Anna says you have been considerate," the farmer said as Levi settled into his saddle. "Some aren't," she added.

Levi nodded. "I try my best," he said. "What we must do for the future ought be pleasant as we can make it." He spoke softly to his mount and with no farewell, they departed into the gathering day.

The morning weighed close and hot with the sun barely above the trees. Levi pulled his bandana over his face to mask the dust. Toward noon he began to look for some shade where he might rest and water his animals. What he saw first were the vultures circling low above the ridge ahead. He hoped whatever they were feeding on had walked on four legs rather than two.

Coming around the rise, he found a scraggly grove of dying pines. Among them, a half-dozen of the big birds strutting about, tearing at a bloody mess that might have been anything, but the remnants of fabric strewn about the carcass confirmed his apprehension. "Not another," he muttered behind his bandana, pulled his shotgun from its scabbard and fired a shot to disperse the wake. They kettled upward noisily into the putrid air. They wouldn't go far, and they would be back soon.

161

Levi couldn't ignore the stench as he dug a hole, not as deep as he would have wished, in the baked ground. He retched as he gathered what remained into the cavity and covered it over. He found a few stones to crown the grave but not enough to deter a determined scavenger. It was the best he could do. He raked through the scattering of matted rags, found nothing to identify the deceased apart from a bit of metal pinned to the remnant of a vest. Levi pocketed the badge, recited to the pines the prayer for the dead and as the spring here was dry, he rode on toward hope of water.

Levi Ashe patted Artemis on her neck. "I see rest in our future, dear one," he murmured. The mare flicked her ears, either in response to her rider's prediction or to dislodge the persistent black fly that had been pestering her for the past half mile. Behind them plodded Molly, their mule, laden with their food and supplies, numerous bags bulging with grain and vegetable seeds. Levi supplied most of the varieties that sprouted into the spring air each year in fields and gardens ahead of them along the Long Broad. The more perishable seed he carried close and tight above his saddle.

These days, most farmers saved their seed as they were able, but Nature was indifferent to human need. Often as not, due to disease, untimely wet or prolonged dry, a crop stunted or failed and left insufficient seed to replant, and the farmers waited for the Seed Man to assure continuance for their crops and families.

This world is not what she was and will never be again, Levi whispered to himself or to his horse or maybe to the heavy air, as they picked their path along the broken pavement, laced with weeds and an occasional small tree. No living human now could remember the Way as it had been when the great lumbering self-propelled wagons and carriages thronged it like an endless parade. The Wisdomkeepers still recited the songs and stories of the Falling, and Levi had seen the rusted hulks, the few that had not yet been dismembered and melted down for tools and pots and implements. Even so, his imagination would not stretch so far that he could really envision the ghostly past conveyed in rondelles and rumors.

Few traveled the Way now apart from traders, herders, and seed men, those rare ones like himself. There were fewer travelers every year, for the Way was weedier and more tree-pocked each spring when Levi set out on his annual round. He thought it likely that he might live to see the forest retake it, reduce the broad highroad to a footpath. The Wisdomkeepers said the Race was dying, that in a few more generations there would be no humans among the bears and wolves and deer. Levi Ashe suspected this might be true. Today had not been the first occasion he'd seen the big birds swoop down, harried them away, and buried the bones they left behind.

He did his part to preserve the present and restore the future. Every year, the Congregation for Agriculture sent out the seedmen to the farms and towns, settlements and isolated homesteads to replenish the land, so that homes and fields might be filled and flourishing. Every year, it seemed to Levi, there were fewer stops to make along his circuit.

Levi dismounted in front of the Station Agent's office, a building re-built and re-purposed from some earlier derelict structure. He draped his reins over the horse's neck. Artemis would stand for hours if need be until he returned. Molly would stay put as long as Artemis did. The agent looked up as Levi came through the door, smiled. The same agent as last year. In these uncertain times, one never knew.

"Hello, Levi. You're the first man I've seen since before winter. About forgotten what a male looks like."

"Those who have one are keeping them close, I reckon,"

Levi said, returning the agent's smile. Then, intensely sober, he laid the metal insignia on the Agent's counter. "I did a burial today," he said quietly.

The Agent picked up the artifact, turned it in her hands, looked her question at Levi.

"No ID I could find," he said, "but an Enforcer will be missed. When some come looking for him, give them that."

"You staying the night?" the Agent said.

"This night, I will," Levi answered. "It's been a long and interrupted road, and my animals are tired."

"But not you, then?" the agent said, mischief in her voice.

"Of course I am," Levi said. "A Seed Man is always tired, loses something of himself at every stop."

"That's an old joke, but I reckon it must be true," the agent said. Her sympathy sounded almost genuine. "Take the cot up at the end. You'll have a couple of woolies for neighbors. That's their sheep in the stock pens."

"Got any room there for my horse and mule?" Levi asked.

"All we got tonight is the few sheep," the agent said. "Take your pick of the vacant pens. There's some fodder in the shed and a place to store your load in the dry. The woolies don't strike me as thievers, otherwise they'd have horses." The agent paused a second, and as Levi turned to go, she added, "They might take a free sample, though. From the looks of them, their stock is running low."

"I'm only licensed to serve farmers this trip," Levi said, because it was true.

"Woolies don't qualify?" The agent queried.

Levi almost laughed. "I speak of dirt farmers," he said. "The Congregation was very specific about my commission this round. No livestock people. I can show you my papers if you like."

The agent did laugh. "Just show me the Congregation's coin and that will do for now, although, if you're feeling generous tonight, I'm open to an off-the-books exchange."

"Waste not, want not," Levi said with mock seriousness, handed over his silver, took his key and returned to his animals outside.

Levi left his horse and mule in a vacant pen where a lean-to could provide a modicum of shelter in event of a thunderstorm, although as he studied the sky he thought one unlikely. It was the tail-end of the dry winter season. If the land was lucky, there would be a few sooncoming days of hard and steady rain before the summer brought down more dry and killing heat. If any had water to keep their crops alive, they would have to race the brief autumn rains to get in their meagre harvest. Fall would find fewer families on the land. Like every other human endeavor, farming in this age amounted to a game of attrition, a losing proposition in the face of an increasingly severe and hostile Nature.

Levi unburdened his animals, gave them their food and water ration, almost enough, like his own, slung his duffle across his shoulder and headed toward his cot. As he passed his neighbors for the night, the two woolies were outside, stirring a pot of something over a feeble fire.

"Hey, Seed Man," the large red-haired one called, waving her wide hand at him. "How's your road, there?"

"How'd you figure?" Levi answered, faking a good humor he didn't feel. "Agent been gossiping?"

"Kathleen don't give out news for free," Big Red said. "You're an unattended male. That means you're either a Seed Man or an Enforcer. You look too gentle to be warding the Rule."

The other woolie, slender and dark, unwound from the

ground like a crepuscular vine, drawled across the settling dark. "How's your stock, gentle man? You carrying any spare short of pay or bribe for us?"

"You have sprouts?" Levi said, not really expecting an answer, but one came back.

"Two each, Seed Man," Big Red confessed, "and one of mine's a male, but he's withered like near all of 'em are." She spat into her fire, and added with a smirk, "Except for your kind, that is."

"I expect you pack a good punch under there," the Vine murmured, gesturing vaguely toward Levi's belt buckle. "We could show you some remarkable kindnesses would you share your surplus with us."

"With two sprouts apiece," Levi replied, "seems you've had your share already. I've a long road tomorrow, so if you'll excuse my company I'll go to my rest now."

As he turned away, Big Red called after him, "Seed Man, what do you ever do for fun?"

Levi stopped, turned around as if he'd heard an honest question. "I don't hear that word much at all on my round. I'm not sure I understand what it means."

Levi came awake after sunrise. It was full light outside and quiet. He felt rested and hungry. When he dressed and came out his door, the woolies had gone. The sheep's pen stood empty, gate open and dragging in the dust. Artemis heard Levi's approach or perhaps caught his scent and lifted her head from her water trough and neighed softly. Molly just gazed indifferently and wiggled her right ear.

A crow called from somewhere out of sight. Another answered from the dead oak just beyond the animal pens then flew away toward some avoidance or summons. The air was hazy, as usual, though no ominous clouds clustered above the horizon west. It might be a good day to travel.

Levi saddled Artemis, burdened Molly with her load, and led them to the Agent's shack to turn back his key.

"You're starting later than most, Seed Man," she said when he stepped inside. "Either you're sick or lazy or have a short road today."

"Not bad," Levi said, ignoring the speculation as to his personal condition. "I'll make my first call up by Twelve-Mile. Farmers generally show some hospitality, so I mightn't sleep on the ground tonight."

He pushed the cot key across the counter, and the Agent entered his duration in her book. Although he'd paid his stay in coin when he arrived, the Agent would draw stipend from the Congregation based on her occupancy rate.

"If you can't be good tonight, Seed Man, have a good time," she said as Levi turned to go.

He summoned a thin smile. "I'll be good," he said, adjusting his hat brim. He had his hand on the door handle when Agent called after him. "When you sow your seed in that close and holy dark think of my face, will you?"

Levi turned in the open doorway. Agent couldn't see his face for the bright day behind him, but his voice came to her like a truth, "I'll see your face often on the road, Kathleen, but when I sow my seed, I try not to think of anything at all."

BREAKDOWN

Keith Woodrow stops by the Drovers Gap Signal on his way to the bank. Today is his day off but yesterday he left his rain jacket hanging by his desk and gathering clouds are confirming the forecast of afternoon showers. Keith has plans to get in a little fishing at Lake Sharon before he meets Hazel in Hendo for supper at Kotobuki. He is not much for sushi himself, but Hazel professes a fondness for it. He teases her about an addiction to eating things raw and not quite dead, although Hazel never eats a large portion of anything, being extremely conscious of her weight and shape, which, apart from her sharp wit and insightful conversation, first caught Keith's notice. He would have invited Hazel to join this little expedition, but she has English classes to teach today at Marshall County Community College.

Keith is looking forward to this, his thirtieth birthday. His head is full of special plans beyond fishing, although catching some fish is no small part of it. His little boat has been parked on its trailer in his garage since he signed on with the bi-weekly Signal three months ago. He had no notion when he took the job that there would be so many newsworthy happenings in an erstwhile railroad town on a line that carried its last train thirty years before, but the surrounding mountains home trails to hike and streams to fish and clean air and long views. Folk who in a former era might have passed through on the train now park their cars and pickups and trailers and stay awhile at the campgrounds and quaint and cozy faux vintage inns that proliferate year by year. Drovers Gap is one of those not-quite-on-the-way-to-anywhere mountain towns that has to re-invent itself every generation or so in order to survive and so manages in one decade or another even to prosper.

The tourists and day trippers are not much in evidence on this early-season morning as Keith pulls his dusty Dodge into a parking space beside the Signal building on Commerce Street, home to all Drovers Gap's major businesses and sole traffic light. Keith figures there is probably more traffic on the hiking trail that emerges from the mountains at the west end of Commerce Street and, at the far limit of the village, plunges between two ridges following Sorrow Creek down into Dismal Gorge where it meets the Dark Fork.

He takes a deep breath, peers through the Signal's glass door, and seeing no sign of his employer, opens. "Morning, Maribeth."

Maribeth Pearson looks up from her computer screen and glares at him as if he just committed a grievous sin. "You ought not be here," she pipes in her child's voice, although Maribeth was never a child in Keith's lifetime. She is sixty if a day, although she contrives, with minimal success, to appear thirty years younger.

"Yep, I know that, Maribeth," Keith assures his colleague, "but I left my rain jacket here. Looks like I might need it."

"Well, don't let Webb catch sight of you," she shrills. "He's been looking for you." Maribeth is the Social News reporter, the only reporter beside Keith the Signal can support, and only supports her three days a week covering weddings, church suppers, high school graduations, Senior Center galas, baptisms and funerals. As editor and publisher, Ed Webb, explained her job description when he hired her, "I want you to cover all the hatchings, matchings and dispatchings in our fair village."

Keith occupies the Hard News desk. Hard News in Drovers Gap translates as DUI's, house fires, vehicle accidents, incursions by bears and other potentially hostile wildlife, as well as injuries and deaths to humans by assorted misadventures out on the mountains or in kayaks down on Dark Fork. So far, Keith has not been called on to chronicle any serious or fatal mishaps, but he lives in hope that eventually he will find opportunity to write up some disaster sufficiently significant to get his by-line in news media outside Marshall County.

He can hear Ed in his office down the hall shouting at somebody on his phone. Keith makes a silent dash for his own cubicle intending to grab his jacket and be gone before his editor emerges from his lair to vent his pique upon the larger world.

Keith grabs his jacket and turns to flee just as Ed Webb's considerable bulk occludes his escape route. "Good, you're here, Woodrow," the editor growls. "Pap Sumner, up on Slick Rock Creek, is a hundred years old today. I want you to go up there and do a birthday interview."

"It's my birthday, too, Chief," Keith says, clutching his jacket to his chest as if it might shield him from editorial interventions. "That's why you gave me the day off. I'll run up there first thing in the morning."

Webb stands unmoved. "It's a birthday interview, Woodrow," he says. "Today's Pap's hundredth. On your hundredth birthday, I'll give you a week off. Turn in your story today and you can have tomorrow off."

"Yes, sir." Keith exits before Editor has a chance to think of something he needs to cover tomorrow.

Slick Rock Creek tumbles at the far end of seven miles of discouraging mountain road and, beyond the creek, almost another mile of mud and sparse gravel to Pap Sumner's little farm. Most of Pap's acreage is too steep and stony to plant. Besides scrub pines and chinkapin, Pap holds title to not quite enough tilted pasture to sustain two cows and a half-dozen sheep.

Pap has entertained a Signal reporter on his every birthday since his ninety-first just in case one might be the last. This is Keith's first foray up past Slick Rock. Barry Bennett, his predecessor, never returned from last year's interview. No one admits knowing what became of him. Pap told Ed Webb that Bennett never arrived, that he was disappointed his milestone had not properly been communicated to the Signal readers. "Ganny I'll have to hang on here another year," he told Ed the day after, "so youns can do it right next time."

Pap has indeed hung on and become Marshall County's newest centenarian assuring that Keith's little fishing craft will remain parked in his garage for yet another day, and that he will likely be late for his supper date with Hazel. He texts her to that effect, checks his gear bag for camera and recorder, and starts his reluctant Dodge.

The fog hanging over Drovers Gap since dawn begins to lift and condenses into a steady drizzle crazing the windshield with writhing rivulets. Keith sets the wipers to *INTERMITTENT*, whereupon the drizzle accelerates into a steady shower. He turns up the wipers a notch, and as he drives past the Library, the last building on Commerce Street, he switches on the radio. The local NPR station, based on the campus of the State University in Asheton, rewards him with a barrage of folk music. It doesn't quite fit Keith's definition of folk, although the announcer periodically insists it is, but it isn't country and it isn't rock or rap, so Keith leaves it on hoping the play-list might eventually deliver a song that is cheerful and encouraging. After three miles of murderous siblings, runaway trains and false-hearted lovers, Keith feels an ominous vibration through the steering wheel. As soon as the Dodge lurches to a stop barely off the pavement, Keith climbs out of the

171

vehicle to have his worst fears confirmed. His left rear tire is flat. He stands there cursing his fate as the shower morphs into a deluge.

Twenty-seven terrifying minutes later, that seem like hours to a thoroughly soaked Keith Woodrow wrestling with jacks and tires while vehicles slosh past within inches of his backside, he pounds the hubcap in place over his spare – just in time for a big truck laden with gravel from the quarry down in Macedonia to douse him with a plume of mud and wet. Keith crawls back into his Dodge where Dougie MacLean is singing about going to America. Keith switches off the ignition, prays there is enough reserve left in the battery to start his car. He thinks about crying, debates with himself whether he should go back to town to have his flat tire patched. If he does, he will likely miss supper with Hazel tonight. He decides to trust his spare for a day. It never occurs to Keith that his world will not end if he disappoints his editor just this once.

When Keith turns the key, his faithful Dodge hardly hesitates. He carefully pulls out onto the road and drives another two miles before the rain stops and a scrap of blue sky reminds him that he left his deflated tire lying beside the road. It is out of character for Keith to take any chance he can avoid, but supper with Hazel is crowding his mind, and he drives on.

While Keith Woodrow plunges deeper into his disastrous day, Oren Taylor, Drovers Gap's official town character, who spends a good share of his waking hours walking the back roads of Marshall County, comes across the strayaway tire among the wayside thistles and doghobble and thoughtfully hangs it on a sign imploring motorists to *Watch For Falling Rocks*, where it will be visible and accessible to its forgetful owner should he survive to return and collect it.

If Keith had been paying more attention to his GPS, he might not have missed the turn-off past Slick Rock Creek that wound up the mountainside to Pap Sumner's place. As it is, he must drive nearly another mile along a narrow and treacherous convolution that reminds a driver somewhat of an actual road, before he can find an opportunity to turn around. Keith still hopes he might get his interview and be back in town by early afternoon. He won't get any fishing done today, but at least he will have a couple of hours to ready himself for supper with Hazel tonight. And since it is his birthday, and since he intends to give her a special present during dessert, he hopes that after supper she might have a wee gift for him that he would never tell anyone about.

It is past eleven when finally Keith's Dodge growls and groans to a halt before Pap Sumner's gate, an improbable improvisation of welded iron pipe, bent and rusted, that over its tenure has been painted several colors barely discernable now. The barrier sags and drags in the muddy track, half open, enough for a person to walk through but not enough to allow passage for a vehicle. Keith sits for a minute nurturing more uncharitable thoughts about his editor while trying to decide whether to get out and try to open the gate, or to leave his car and walk up the muddy hill to Pap's house which he can see partly obscured among a nest of poplars fifty yards farther up the slope. Either way, Keith is about to baptize his new boots in Appalachian clay rendered on this showery day too thin to plow and too thick to drink.

He slogs half-way up the hill to Pap's house, when the biggest German Shepherd Keith had ever seen rises like the shadow of Death and bounds off the porch in his direction. No bark, no growl, just movement, swift and intentional. If the dog were a dragon, Keith's heart could beat no faster. He glances over his shoulder. The gate is too far. He turns back to face his fear, and the animal is upon him. It opens its mouth wide, wide enough to swallow a bus, and closes its jaws on Keith's wrist. Terrified, Keith loses his balance and collapses into the slippery mud. The dog holds on, not crushing his bones as Keith expects, but gripping firmly as if the reporter were a stray puppy. The beast indicates no intention of loosing its grip, and Keith has barely presence of mind not to resist.

"Hello, there," he says in what Keith hopes is close to his conversational voice. What else do you say to a carnivore that may decide to eat you alive? He tries to look pleasant and unafraid. "What's your name, boy?" The big shepherd gazes at him with eyes that convey neither pity nor curiosity, reflect no hint of Keith's immediate fate. Somehow, he has managed not to fall on his expensive gear in his waterproof bag.

After a minor forever, a door opens up at the house and a diminutive woman of indeterminate age steps out onto the porch and calls, "Simondog, Be friendly."

Simon releases him promptly and watches waggy-tailed as Keith clumsily regains his footing, trying to prevent his gear bag from accumulating more mountain mud than it has already. The state of his new boots, at this point, the least of his concerns. Simon leads the way, looking back now and then to assess Keith's obedience. When they reach the porch steps, the old woman – Keith can see now that she is indeed old – inspects him silently, her mouth thin and serious but her pale blue eyes full of sky and laughter.

"Miz Sumner?" he ventures. In her small quiet way, she is as formidable as her dog. "I'm Keith Woodrow from the Drovers Gap Signal. I've come…"

Her voice sounds as young as her face looks old. "Oh, yes, I know. The birthday boy Ed sent to us. Well, Pap ain't to house. He's up the mountain ahind the barn mending fence atter last night's stormation."

174

"Will he be coming down for the interview?" Keith asks.

The old woman launches a laugh bigger than her. "If youns want to take his birthday picture, you'll have to go up there. Once he's made a start on something, Pap won't quit until dark or done."

Keith suppresses a sigh. At this rate, he is going to be worse than late for his supper with Hazel tonight. He tries to keep his frustration out of his voice. "How do I get up there?"

"On your feet, if you're lucky," the old woman says. "There's a logging road up past the barn. If you don't see Pap, just give a holler and he'll come deliver you from your lostlyness." She looks at the big shepherd and points across the yard. "Simon. Take this here boy up to Pap yonder."

Simon looks at Keith, emits a soft growl that might or might not be friendly, and trots off the porch. Tail wagging, he stands by the steps and gazes back at the reporter until Keith follows.

"Thanks, Miz Sumner," Keith says as he hoists his gear bag to continue his quest.

"Watch for the bear," she says, a towel in one hand and a cup in the other. Her eyes inform that she is laughing inside herself.

Down the steps and across the yard, through a wooden gate leaning toward collapse and around a dilapidated barn that has never tasted paint and tilts as slanty and crooked as the mountainside where it perches. The barn, the house, a shed, the rambling straggling fences, every human-made structure on the place looks make-do, temporary, transient and fragile, yet they have stood their ground for years, likely since before Keith was in the world. Patched and shored, propped and mended, they endure, like the people that wrought and placed them, under the mercy and sufferance of the changeless mountain.

Of course, the mountain has been ever changing too, but slowly, slowly, according to a timeliness far too long and deep for a human span to begin to grasp or measure. Three generations in the past and the pastures are forest, three into the future and the house is a grove and the barn not even a notion in a wandering mind. The rutted track where Simon herds Keith now had not even been a footpath before Pap Sumner thought of it. If no one comes to walk it after him, the mountain will claim it back and trees will grow too close for tractor or wagon to pass.

As he trails Simon past the ramshackle barn and up the uncertain and dubious track toward a fringe of forest higher up the ridge, Keith feels exposed, vulnerable. He wishes Annie Sumner had kept her bear to herself and is grateful that he neither hears nor sights any evidence of ursine presence. Had the Sumner's been visited by a bear, or was Annie's warning just a joke on the city boy? Simon pauses and looks back every forty or fifty feet to ascertain Keith's status, and Keith valiantly attempts to quicken his ascent for fear the big canine will come grasp him by the arm to haul him up the hill to Pap. In truth, Keith Woodrow's condition is as hard for him to discern as the rambling and diminishing path under his feet. Sweating, winded, sore as if he had been brawling through the previous night at Drovers Tavern, Keith only knows for a certainty that he doesn't feel well.

When he looks back down the slope behind, he sees no sign of barn or house, only trees and more of them. The view ahead he finds also populated by trees, close and multitudinous. He climbs Pap's mountain for minutes that pass like hours, when around another turn the woods begin to thin, and he glimpses what Annie Sumner had called the upper pasture. It doesn't look much like a pasture to Keith, just a narrow clearing of waist-high grass and bramble half-concealing a straggle of cedar and locust fence posts, angled and unwired.

On the upper verge of this purported pasture, Pap Sumner himself emerges from a swath of mixed hardwoods and conifers and descends the slope in long deliberate strides with a split locust fence post balanced on each shoulder. The old man calls out with more voice than Keith can muster in himself at the moment. "Hello, there. Reckon you're Webb's new writer-upper at the Signal."

Keith swallows air and manages to push a faltering warble past this mouth. "Yessir, Mister Sumner. They tell me you're a hundred years old today."

Pap roars a laugh that would do fair credit to a lion or a dragon. "Yup, that's so, and I'm done broke down already." He lets the posts roll off his shoulders, and they slide precipitously down the slope in Keith's direction. Tired as he is, he hops nimbly to avoid having his left foot bashed and mashed by one of them. Pap appears to find this frantic maneuver hilarious.

"Hand me down one of them locusts, son," Pap says, picking up his shovel. "Plop the end in this here hole," pointing to the neat dark opening in the grass at his feet. Keith holds the post upright, as Pap shovels earth around the post, taps it down with the handle of his shovel, repeating the ritual until the hole is filled and the post emerges from the mountain amid a tight compact mound of red highland clay that given three sunny days will become hard as brick.

Pap gestures at the other post, and while they perform their rite one more time, he says, "You going to ask me the question?"

"The question?" Keith echoes.

"The question I get asked every birthday for the past ten," Pap says. "You're the last in line. You gonna ask it?"

177

"Will you tell our readers how you've maintained such a long and vigorous life?" Keith recites dutifully. "What's the secret of your longevity?"

"I owe it all to this here mountain," Pap says, waving his lean and muscled arm at the trees and blue sky behind and above. "Me and the Fairy Knob have an agreement."

"Fairy Knob?" says Keith.

"You sound like an echo, boy," Pap remarks because Keith does. "The sign down at the forks says Mary Mountain Road, but them what been up here long enough to see what rides the fog down from the trees on moonful nights call her the Fairy Knob."

"That sounds like a good story," Keith says hopefully.

"Too long for this day," Pap says, "but like I said, me and the mountain have an agreement. "I keep her ways, and she keeps me sound."

"You keep her ways?" Keith says, not precisely a question but another repetition to disguise his lack of appropriate query.

"My hearing's still good, too," Pap murmurs, a veiled commentary not entirely lost on the young reporter. "Of course, Annie and me take right living to heart. The mountain tells us that whatever we take from her will nourish and preserve, so, as far as we're able, we avoid what comes from down below. We grow our own vegetables and such in the mountain's good soil and give back to her all we don't keep. We eat only meat what's been killed and bled right here on this holy mount, so's we get nourished by the flesh and the mountain takes the blood to heart. We grow our grain and grind it here and the bread we bake and break, has the mountain in it. The mountain gives us all we are. and we take nothing away from this place. That is our continuance." Pap stares intently at Keith, as if to discern the young man's understanding, then continues, "and, oh yes, I drink a glass of spirits after supper of an evening."

"Do the spirits come from the mountain, too?" Keith asks. "Do you make that yourself?"

Pap tugs at the post to confirm it is solid and steady in the mountain and allows a satisfied chuckle. "Now that would be against the law, don't you know?" Another question that wasn't.

Keith figures the interview has concluded, but every time he makes to go back down the mountain, Pap assigns another task: "Hand me that digger," or "Fetch me that roll of wire," or "There's a hammer and a bucket of staples yonder, Son. Bring 'em here, if you will."

Afternoon creeps toward evening, shadows slowly slowly start rolling downhill, and Keith is beginning to fret he won't see Drover's Gap in time for supper with Hazel after all, when Pap proclaims, "I've had enough today for an old man. Let's get to the house and have a big glass of Annie's herbal before you go back to town."

Keith's gear bag weighs a lot heavier going down the steep path, still slippery damp from the morning's rain. Twice his feet slip from under him, and he goes down, injuring his pride and further muddying his new jeans. He has forgotten about the hypothetical bear until passing the barn the path begins to level, and Keith hears stones rattling down the slope behind him. He turns to see if Pap has lost his footing, and there it looms, huge and bristle-shouldered, the bear, standing on its hind legs, front paws stretched toward Keith, wicked claws poised to rip and grasp, mouth gaping, all teeth and slobber below tiny red eyes full of meanness and hunger.

Maybe Keith screams, he isn't sure, but he jettisons his gear, runs for the house, falling, running again, slipping and going down again on his knees, staring at Annie laughing on the porch. He clambers to his feet and looks back to see

179

not Bear, but Pap Sumner, holding the abandoned gear bag, apparently sharing fully in his wife's bout of hilarity. Pap wraps a heavy arm around Keith's shoulders and guides him to the porch, where he collapses on the steps, spent and empty.

"Youns run like you'd seen a ghost, young feller," Annie says, her mirth subsided now to a hint of smile.

"That bear," Keith gasps. "Didn't you see it, too?"

Annie shakes her head. "I just saw old Pap," she says, "and he didn't look like he was achasing you 'tall. I'll fetch you a glass of herbal. That'll settle you."

"Sometimes this mountain light tricks on a man, don't you know," Pap said, dropping Keith's bag on the porch. Keith, with his head in his hands, doesn't see Annie standing in the doorway, a small bottle in each hand, gazing expectantly at her husband as she lifts the green bottle. Pap shakes his head. Annie looks puzzled then holds out the brown one. Pap nods, and she vanishes into the kitchen.

Pap sits on the steps beside Keith and launches into a rambling narration about the history of Marshall County in general and her most notorious citizens in particular, when Annie reappears and hands them each a tall icy glass of something the color of autumn leaves that makes Keith's teeth hurt with its sweetness and with each swallow washes the soreness from his limbs and calms and clarifies the chaos in his head. By the time his glass holds only ice, Keith feels fit to finish his long day. He thanks Annie for the tea and Pap for his time, picks up his bag and turns at last to go find supper with Hazel.

"You going to take my picture?" Pap says.

"Picture?"

"It's a newspaper article. You oughta take my picture." Pap repeats.

Keith rummages in his bag. Somehow, in the day's

hustle and tussle, his camera has dislodged from its cradle, and the lens now projects from the camera body at a decidedly dysfunctional angle.

"It's broken." Keith whispers.

"Use your phone." Pap says.

So Keith uses his phone to take a photo of Annie and Pap Sumner standing arm in arm on their porch with Simon sitting beside them, ears up and tail lazily waving at the photographer. Keith murmurs again his thanks. Pap says, "Happy birthday, Pilgrim," as Keith begins trudging down the long drive toward his Dodge. *How did he know?* Keith wonders, almost stops to ask aloud, but keeps walking, figures he's asked enough questions for one day.

Annie and Pap watch him in silence as he goes. Simon barks once, as Keith starts his car and drives away down the road. Annie turns to her husband and says, "That one looked tender. I'm surprised you let him go."

"Our grandbaby's got eyes for him, don't you know," Pap says. "We still got a ham that Bible salesman left us with, and there'll be some Witnesses and Mormons come along now that tourist season is 'bout over. No need being greedy now."

"I suppose not," Annie says, "but what if he winds up being family?"

"That being, we'll have to teach him how to eat proper," Pap says, "but that much is up to Hazel, ain't it?"

Keith's drive back into Drovers Gap proves no more eventful than typical. Two deer, does, dart across the road in front of him but not so close he needs to brake. He slows when he thinks he is near the place where his tire went flat. He sees it hanging on the roadside sign where Oren Taylor left it. He retrieves the tire and stows it in the trunk of the Dodge, thanking whatever local deities might be watching over this stretch of mountain highway. He is in his car, pulling back onto the tarmac before he sees the bear standing amid the trees, watching him. Keith waves at Bear as he passes. Looking in his rearview mirror, he thinks he sees Bear waving back. "Couldn't be," he says to the trees and drives on to town.

Ed Webb makes enormous sport of Keith trashing his camera in his panic, since it is Keith's personal property and not the Signal's camera. The publisher also makes fun of him using his phone for visuals, but when he sees the shot in the photo app, he says, "We ought to submit this to a magazine." The mountain light has tricked the photographer into a minor masterpiece of nostalgic Appalachia. Keith will eventually win awards for his portrait of Pap and Annie Sumner, and it will be seen with appreciation by strangers far from Marshall County.

Keith barely has time to go by his apartment, shower, change into older but clean clothes and meet Hazel for their supper date. She has been waiting for ten minutes, when he finally sits breathless at their table.

"You're late for your birthday celebration," she says, teasing. "You're thirty years old now, old man."

"Yup," he says, imitating Pap Sumner's twang, "and done broke down already." He tells her about his mission to Pap Sumner's farm.

"Pap and Annie are my grandparents, don't you know." She says it like a statement.

"Really?" Keith says it like a question. "I had no idea."

They have a good meal. The food is fresh and tasty, the wine decent but not terribly expensive. While waiting for dessert to be served, Keith pulls from his jacket pocket the little box that made him late. He forgot it until he was half-way to the restaurant and had to rush back home to get it.

Hazel looks surprised, though she has been expecting

this. Her best friend Marcie runs Stone and Thistle Jewelry, so Hazel already knows what is in the box. She opens it and makes Keith feel like he is watching a sunrise. "You sweet, delicious man, Keith Woodrow," she murmurs. "Of course. Certainly. Absolutely. Yes."

STAY

The smiling woman hands her copy of *Aimless* to Riley, and he dutifully opens the front cover to sign it. She is the last in a long line of literate humans winding back through a three-week book tour. The reading has gone on later than Riley intended, and afterward, there will be hours of driving between this town and home. He's tired of it all but still committed to making the effort.

He poises his pen above the title page, gazes up into a plump and appealing female face and says, "How should I inscribe this? To you?"

The woman gives him a little laugh, as mellow and round as her face, and says, "Not me. To my daughter. Her name is Maria, and she reads all your books." Riley is about to ask something about Maria to guide his inscription, when her mother adds, "I don't read fiction, you see. Well, just a little. Maria wants to be a novelist. She writes every day. Pages and pages."

Riley writes, *To Maria – I want to write like you when I grow up. -Riley Nash.* He holds out the open book to Maria's mother. She looks at it, a satisfied smirk on her face, then closes the book and peers across the little table at him. In her thoughtful gaze, Riley sees the question coming. He's heard one variation of it or another ever since his first stop on this book tour, except this time it isn't a question. "I'll see you in Drovers Gap," she says.

Riley doesn't try to curb his laugh. "I doubt it," he says to her big blue eyes. "You won't find Drovers Gap on any map, unless maybe you go to Australia. It's a made-up town. A fiction, inhabited only by stories."

Plump Mother laughs back at him. "You don't fool me, Mister Nash. You describe it in such detail. I know you've been there."

Riley tries to look serious. "Only in my mind. I throw in enough generic detail to remind a reader of some place they know and left and might want to go back to. Drover's Gap is a literary device to draw readers in, get them hooked on a story."

The mother puts on a convincing show of annoyance. Riley figures she is putting him on. "It's a real place, sir," she says. "I live there."

"In that case... Pardon me. I don't know your name." Riley needs a name to assure himself he is conversing with a real person.

"Tsula," she says, laughter still flickering like firelight in her eyes, "Tsula Stone."

"Well, in that case, Tsula, You're just a figment of a writer's imagination. I thought you up."

Riley senses the touch of anger in her reply, sees the changing light in her eyes, though her voice flows soft and sociable when she says, "God thought us up. You haven't imagined anything that wasn't breathing in the air before you. Drover's Gap is real. You'll see when you get there."

I'm sorry. I wasn't trying to upset you, just being the clever, cantankerous writer my public has come to expect, Riley is about to say, but by then, Tsula has turned and walked away, merging toward anonymity in the vague crowd.

Riley turns to look for a drink and comes face to face with his wife. A tinkling little laugh escapes her as she hands him a glass filled with a red liquid. He takes the glass and sips. The taste reminds him of real wine. The thought flashes behind Riley's eyes and is gone. Does any woman ever take him seriously? Or do they regard all males as optional accessories for convenience and entertainment? Riley knows better than that, though. Valerie always takes him seriously. She has saved his life. Whenever she laughs at him, and such occasions occur fairly frequently, it is so that he can laugh with her.

"That woman looked like she knew you, Riley," Valerie murmurs over her own glass, the contents not quite as clear as water. "A former student perhaps? She seemed to make an impression." Riley had indeed been impressed, not by Tsula's appearance, which was agreeable enough, but by her claim to be from the place he'd thought existed only in his book. Tsula, he is now convinced, was sincere. Drover's Gap is real, at least in her world. She lives there. Maybe sometime he's been there too and forgotten. Maybe that's why he's been able to describe it so convincingly on the page. But when or where, he can't remember.

"She claimed to be a character in my book," Riley says, taking another sip from his glass. He decides it might be wine after all. "She said her name is Tsula and she lives in Drover's Gap."

"There's no character named Tsula in *Aimless*," Valerie says, holding out her cookie, inviting Riley to take a bite.

He does. The cookie has more to recommend it than his wine does. "She seemed awfully real just now," he says. "I must have forgotten to write her."

Dusk settles prematurely as they carry their bags to the rental car. The sun is still hanging just above the horizon but obscured by gathering thunder clouds westward. Lightning flashes among these clouds, too far yet to sound threatening, just loud enough to plant a seed of caution. Riley guides their rented Prius out onto the road and heads toward the interstate access ramp visible a block ahead. Valerie offers to drive. She knows her husband doesn't like to drive at night, tries to persuade him to wait until morning to start home, but Riley says he is homesick and reminds her that it will all be interstate driving except for the last thirty miles on familiar local roads.

"I'll be fine," Riley insists. He doesn't tell his wife that as long as he concentrates on his driving, he won't dwell on the possibility, real in his mind, that his current novel-in-progress may not progress to a conclusion, publisher's advance notwithstanding.

Two hours later, they pull into a rest area where Riley empties his bladder and buys a cup of hot liquid that doesn't quite convince him that he is drinking coffee. They stop again at the next exit to fill the tank on their rental. Valerie offers again to drive, fairly insists on it, but Riley is adamant. Adrift in an undefined darkness, he needs to maintain the illusion that he might control his trajectory. Valerie sees how tired he is, fears her husband might fall asleep at the wheel, so puts on some music, lively and dissonant enough to discourage relaxation. When she begins to think the playlist might be losing its efficacy, she starts talking to Riley.

"If you're going to talk to me, Val, turn off that racket please," he snaps irritably. Valerie prefers irritable to sleepy, turns off the radio and continues talking, too loudly for comfort without the background noise.

Before Riley can complain again, she lowers her volume and continues, "We have a lot to do when we get home."

"Yeah," says Riley, wincing as a truck, headlights beamed high, meets them and passes behind, "I have to finish my book."

"This trip has been rather grueling," Valerie counters. "I think you ought to take a few days and rest."

"You just said we have a lot to do when we get home," Riley grouses.

"Yes, but it doesn't all have to be done tomorrow." Valerie says, changing tack mid-stream. "Seriously, Riley. We ought to take a couple of days just for ourselves without having to answer emails or talk to people. Just us. Just…"

"Just what?" Riley says, thinking maybe he ought to turn the radio back on. Conversation requires thinking and tonight he feels about thought out.

"I don't know," Valerie murmurs, recalling times when just being in the same room was enough to render them both content and happy.

More miles pass in silence, except for the metronomic swipe of the windshield wipers and the slurry sigh of tires on wet asphalt, punctuated by the occasional flash and flurry of a big truck two lanes over racing into their past. Riley and Valerie are both wrestling thoughts it wouldn't do to say aloud. They love one another, but they are both feeling unspecified hurts that were for the most part undeserved, and nursing vague guilt over unintended wounds they may or may not have inflicted. They are not sure. This night they are not sure of much; except they are hurtling through the dark together and together is far preferable to any imaginable alternative.

Raining heavier, now. Riley turns up the wipers a notch. Valerie turns and leans across the back of her seat, rummages in a bag. She knows what she is looking for, finds it by feel, turns back and plugs in their favorite play-list, the one that holds their road music. Mary Black begins singing about *a fine man, a dainty man, and a spicy one, too.*

The song gets Riley's attention, as his wife knew it would. He glances over. The lights from the instrument panel are barely bright enough for Valerie to catch a glimpse of his smile.

"You still think so, after all these miles?" he says.

"After miles and years I quit counting long past," Valerie murmurs, reaching out to touch Riley's arm, "I know it."

188

"I'm not as spicy as I used to be," Riley says, his tone a touch wistful.

"But you're still fine and dainty," Valerie says, is poised to lean across and kiss his ear, when Riley shouts in hers, "Damn."

"What's wrong?" she says, startled, searching for some sign of impending crisis.

"I just missed the exit to Pearis Falls," Riley said. "I shouldn't be spicy when I'm driving in the rainy dark."

"Will we have to go back now?" Valerie asks, realizing she really is tired.

"I don't think so," Riley says, studying the little Navigator screen on the dashboard. "The next exit is just a couple of miles. This says the road there connects to our route. Looks crooked, but according to the app, it's only nine miles. We should be home before midnight if I don't miss another turn."

Mary Black hardly finishes her song, before they reach the exit and a marker declaring, *Pearis Falls – 32 mi.* Riley steers the rental down the ramp. Stops, turns right past a petrol station dark as the night and locked up tight. The rain falls harder now. Riley sets the wipers to *Max.*

Riley drives slowly, as the wipers are not quite keeping up with the deluge, but after a mile the rain stops suddenly and their rental is engulfed by a wall of dense fog. Riley clicks the headlights to low beam. The road reveals itself in grudging increments. Off in the foggy unknown occasional lights emerge, warm and encouraging, like friendly stars. Although this is the first time Riley has driven this road and the fog-filtered lights provide no clue as to landmarks or any local detail, the scene seems familiar to him.

"There's a little town, out there," Valerie says. "A village, at least."

"Some sort of settlement, anyway," Riley says. "The Navigator isn't giving it a name."

"The lights seem so welcoming, inviting," Valerie murmurs, gazing into the fog. "I wish we could just stay here tonight."

A sign presents ahead with an arrow pointing to the left. *Pearis Falls*. It doesn't say how far. Riley believes the sign. The rental turns left, lurches across a double railway track, begins ascending a long hill whose crest is concealed by the fog, as the rain commences again, flooding the street in sheets. The gutters roar like creeks, as if it has been raining like this for years. Riley is about to assure Valerie that there is no way they are going to stop in this maelstrom, when ahead on the right, a lighted sign appears suddenly, as if somebody just powered it on.

HIGH BALSAM INN
We left the light on for you.

Behind the sign a rambling Victorian hallucination rises above a lighted porch. The only thing that sets this B & B apart from a hundred others they might have happened upon in this fold of the mountains is the name. One of those coincidences that seem to defy possibility and thereby gain the status of a portent in the mind of a road-weary driver. Riley has never set eyes on this place until now, but High Balsam is the name he gave to the bed-and-breakfast he wrote in *Aimless*.

"I'm tired," he says. Valerie is not surprised.

"We are tired," she whispers. The rain stops again long enough for them to gain the shelter of the porch.

Riley peers through the door of frosted glass, etched with a design of leaves and twining vines and fruits and flowers, an incongruous blend of grapes and roses. He thinks he glimpses through the maze and haze a young woman inside, sitting by the fire and reading a newspaper, but when he opens the door, there is no reader and no newspaper lying on the empty chair beside the fireplace where a real fire, not gas, pops and sizzles in a bed of coals recently augmented by several sticks of wood, apparently just brought in out of the rain.

"Where did the girl go?" Riley says as they shake the rain off their coats and come through the door.

"What girl?" Valerie queries.

"Well, a woman, really, quite young. I thought I saw her through the window. She was sitting in that chair reading a newspaper."

"I didn't see her," Valerie says, looking skeptical. "Nobody reads newspapers anymore."

Passing through to a room beyond, they find a table already set awaiting tomorrow's breakfast, and at one end of the room, a woman sits behind a short counter shining a grand smile on them as they enter.

"Ah, here you are," she says. "We've been expecting you. Your room is ready."

The woman looks familiar to Riley. He's sure he's heard that voice before. But he's dead tired, has encountered more strange faces and voices over the past three weeks than he can sort. He's still trying to remember where they have met as he says, "We're not who you think we are. We didn't make reservations. We just saw your vacancy sign and hoped you could save us from driving all night through this storm."

"That's why we're here," the woman assures him in her hypercheerful voice. "Like I said, your room is ready."

Valerie reaches into her purse for their credit card. Cheerfulwoman waves her hand. "Wi-Fi's out. Happens every time it rains like this. We'll do that stuff when you leave."

Riley goes back to their car to fetch their overnight gear. The rain has commenced again, and he is sopping by the time he regains the porch. He stomps and shakes and looks through the door glass and finds no hint of the elusive reader. The fire is still burning brightly on the hearth. When he walks through to the breakfast/reception room, Valerie and Cheerfulwoman are chatting like long-lost sisters.

"Who was the young woman reading in there by the fire when we first arrived?" Riley says, dropping their bags on the floor and gesturing back toward the entrance.

He thinks Cheerfulwoman's smile falters for a split second before she replies bright as ever. "You're our only guests here tonight. You must have glimpsed one of our resident ghosts."

"Ghosts, of course," Valerie says before Riley can deliver a snarky retort. "Every respectable mountain inn must have ghosts." She and Cheerfulwoman laugh.

Riley is less amused. "Now you're about to tell me our room is haunted by some suicidal lover, I suppose," he says. "Like in one of my novels."

Cheerfulwoman finally finds her serious face. "All our ghosts are friendly," she assures him. "Nobody who stays here for a night ever wants to leave. Those who do, always come back eventually."

She leads them down a hall and up a narrow, angling stairway. Riley is tired. The bags he is carrying keep clunking on the stairs as he follows the two women. By the time they reach the upper floor and she opens the door to their room, Riley is lapsing into his default anti-social disposition. He says to Cheerfulwoman. "You don't have much accommodation for handicapped guests, do you?"

She turns on him a motherly gaze. "Any who are able to get to High Balsam can manage our stairs," she says.

The door is hardly closed behind them and Valerie is still opening her bag, when they hear a soft knock on their door. Riley groans, heaves himself up from the bed where he has just collapsed and opens the door to see Cheerfulwoman standing in the hall, holding a tray.

"I brought you some hot chocolate and these wee buns. I thought you might use some warming after being out in our weather."

Riley doesn't know how she found time to fetch her tray of goodies, but he thanks her and takes the tray. He is sincerely grateful. Cheerfulwoman backs away and closes the door.

"How sweet," Valerie says, reaching out to snare one of the buns. "This is really kind."

"I'm sure we'll have to pay for it in the morning," Riley growls, looking for a place to set down the tray.

Riley can hear Valerie singing to herself in the shower as he waits his turn. He downs the last swallow of Cheerfulwoman's hot chocolate and peruses a little bookshelf in a corner next to the ornate floor lamp with a Tiffany-style shade and multitudinous creatures resembling miniscule gargoyles clinging and climbing over one another up the iron base toward the light.

Valerie launches another verse of her Gaelic ballad which probably has at least fifty verses. Riley hopes she might leave him some hot water. The books in the bookcase are a motley assortment that look like they have been read hard and put away wet. Riley wonders if they have been left behind by previous travelers or bought by the pound at a junk store or estate sale. One volume, midway on the middle shelf, looks new, shining bright among its dingy, dinged and dog-eared neighbors. Even with only the spine visible, Riley recognizes it immediately. Unbelieving, he pulls it out and opens it to find his signature on the title page: *To Maria – I want to write like you when I grow up. – Riley Nash.*

Now he realizes why Cheerfulwoman seems so familiar. She's Maria's mother and she was the last reader whose book he signed back in Knox before starting the two hundred-forty miserable miles home. Why isn't this copy on its way to Maria, he wonders, and how did it get here ahead of him?

When Valerie at last emerges from the bathroom, Riley holds up the book and says, "Val, that woman at the desk…"

"I know," says Valerie, handing him her towel. "She was at the book signing. Dry my hair, please."

Being the obedient bear he is, Riley takes the towel and sets to his task. He's had years of practice. He knows how to please.

"How'd she get here before us?" he asks as he works. "She was still talking, when we left there."

Valerie's voice comes muffled from beneath the towel. "She might be an angel. Maybe she has wings. Keep doing that."

Riley keeps doing that as he murmurs, "She might have ridden her broom."

Chocolated and showered, Riley falls into bed and has hardly kissed Valerie goodnight before he sleeps as soundly as a dead man. Sometime during his deep slumber, he dreams they are still driving through the foggy dark. He wonders why everything they see outside their car looks upside down but before he can figure it out he is awake and the dream is forgotten.

Valerie is not in bed. Riley gets up, crosses to the bathroom door and knocks. He calls, "Val, you in there?" She isn't, which is fine with Riley. He feels an urgent need to pee. By the time he gets himself dressed, Valerie still has not returned to their room. He's been hoping she might bring him some coffee. Riley doesn't have a watch. He relies on his smart phone for the time, but the phone is dark and unresponsive. He forgot to charge it last night. He ventures out into the hall and down the crooked stairway in search of his wife and a caffeine fix.

Tsula Stone, cheerful as ever, greets him in the dining room. Riley sees the table is set for breakfast but only one place, a glass filled with juice, a plate stacked with blueberry waffles, a cup of coffee, filled, steaming.

"Where's my wife?" he demands.

Tsula shrugs, her smile unfailing. "She had to go out. Drink your coffee while it's hot."

Riley doesn't drink his coffee, he turns, goes out to the porch, Tsula catches the door so it doesn't slam behind him. There's no sign of Valerie. No sign of their rented Prius, either.

"What happened to our car?" he asks anybody who will answer.

Tsula does. "They took it away last night, since you'll be staying with us. Come eat your breakfast before it gets cold."

"The hell I'll be staying. What's going on here?" Riley shouts. Tsula doesn't say anything, bends and picks up the morning copy of *The Drovers Gap Signal* from the porch floor. Riley notes the headline and snatches it from her. It's hard to read without his glasses but he sees more than he wants to:

Local Author in Fatal Wreck

Author Riley Nash and his wife, photographer Valerie Maples sustained multiple injuries in a single car collision, when their car left the road during last night's storm and hit a tree on Pearis Falls Road. Nash was pronounced dead on arrival at Hardy Memorial Hospital in Hendo. His wife Valerie remains in serious condition but is expected to recover...

AMONG THORNS

Low clouds and mists obscured the heights of sloping woodland hemming the river and the road. It might have been an ocean out there behind the fog, or mountains. Lawless Thorn knew they were mountains as he steered his Jeep pickup along the winding road hugging the river. Tires slurred over the wet asphalt and wipers thumped like heartbeats across the windshield as Thorn drove. Not too fast, there was no need to hurry. Rebecca would still be putting their supper together right about now. It would be hot and ready for them when they arrived.

"Uncle Thorn?" piped Violet, the ten-year old who sat next to him, her nose almost touching the glass, making little clouds in front of her face that further obscured the fog-shrouded landscape she wanted to see, searching eagerly for some remembered landmark that would restore her to this occasional world. "Does it rain here all the time?"

"Only when we need it," Thorn said, laughing only behind his face. That was not precisely true. It had been a wet summer in the Valley. Sometimes much more rain than was needed. "Did it rain the last time you were here?" he said.

"Yes, said Violet, "and the time before that."

"It rains to make young souls grow," Thorn said, glancing at the earnest young face upturned toward him now like a flower to the sun.

"Rain makes me grow?" Violet sounded as if it were a dubious proposition.

Thorn's answer came out before he even thought of it. "It makes corn grow, and tomatoes, trees even. I can't imagine why it wouldn't work for children."

Rounding a blind curve, Thorn had to brake sharply as they came up behind a log-laden truck, moving slow on the narrow road. The cab was hidden from sight by the huge tree-trunks piled high on the trailer behind.

Violet's face became a mask of apprehension. "What happens if all those logs come loose and fall on us?" she murmured.

"They won't. Don't worry." Thorn reached over and patted her leg. His gesture of reassurance appeared of limited efficacy.

"I wish they'd go somewhere else," Violet said.

The truck ahead rounded another curve and disappeared behind a rocky cliff edging the road. When Thorn's pickup made the turn, the road ran straight and empty ahead of them for perhaps a quarter-mile.

Thorn glanced at his niece. "Where'd it go?" he said.

"I don't know," Violet replied, "but I'm glad it's gone."

Three miles further up the road, they had still not sighted the log-hauling truck when they reached the turn-off to Thorn's place. The gravel track wound off among the higher ridges back from the river road. Two houses lent their chimney smoke to the bank of fog hanging low over this narrow valley. Thorn's house sat out of sight beyond the nearest hill, at the end of the road.

Violet, solemn and silent, listened to the mutter of the engine and the crunch of tires on loose stone, until her uncle's house came into view, then she broke into a broad smile. "Nothing's changed," she piped in apparent delight.

Thorn laughed, laid aside his serious preoccupation regarding the day's previous events, and said, "Well, Violet, a few things have. Daphne has a new calf, and we have a new puppy, too. He's named Orville."

"What happened to Wilbur?" Violet said, her smile disappeared.

"Wilbur's buried down by the creek," Thorn said. He got snake-bit. Wilbur was old and didn't make it."

"Orville won't replace Wilbur," Violet said, not a complaint but a recognition.

"No soul can replace another," Thorn confirmed. "Orville will have to make his own place in our hearts, if we give him a chance."

"I'll give him three chances," Violet said. She had loved Thorn's old hound, and the feeling had been reciprocal. "And then three more, if he needs them," she added.

The sun, if they could have seen it for all the clouds, would have already dropped behind Warwoman Mountain by the time Thorn stopped his Jeep beside his back porch. Light from a kitchen window spilled down into the yard, setting the fog aglow. Dusk was well on its way to nightfall, although night doesn't fall between the mountains. It rises, as shadows swell upward from the creeks and bottomlands, climbing the ridges like a filling reservoir, until the last light left is the sky itself which is never quite dark, but silvered by moon or sparkling with stars. Even on overcast nights, the dark of the clouds above betrays the outlines of the darker mountains below.

Thorn climbed out of his Jeep and Violet slid out after him, pulling on her backpack as her feet planted firmly in the yard. Thorn retrieved her single suitcase from behind the seat and closed the door. Immediately the kitchen door swung open, and Rebecca Thorn stood silhouetted by the light behind her.

"About time you two showed up. I was ready to feed your supper to Orville," she called, her voice full of smile.

"You wouldn't have let us starve now, would you?" Thorn said, laughing. He might have said more but a small German Shepherd, five or six months old, emerged from between Rebecca's feet and bounded to the top of the porch steps where he stopped, puzzled by the new human presence

198

in his territory, tilted his head to one side and uttered a shrill piping bark, neither alarm nor warning, not quite a greeting, more of a question.

Violet shrugged off her pack, knelt on the ground, held out her arms and called, "Orville."

At the sound of his name, Orville tumbled down the steps and in three leaps and a hop, deposited himself in the girl's arms, nearly toppling them both in the process and commenced licking Violet's face prodigiously while flailing her legs with his tail.

"Friends for life," Thorn murmured, picking up the backpack in his free hand as he walked away toward the house and Rebecca and his supper.

Supper was simple – cornbread, kale, some roasted potatoes, and tomato slices. It was past season for tomatoes, but Rebecca had pulled the vines with the late green fruits still attached and hung them in the barn where the tomatoes continued to ripen. They were eating the last of them now with Violet.

There was no dessert. Sweets were rare in this household, although Thorn kept bees and Rebecca would stir some honey into the dough when she made bread. "To feed the yeast," she said. Whenever Rebecca would voice intention to bake a cake or a pie, Thorn would tell her, "You're all the sweet I need."

Violet ate all her serving and asked for more until her plate had been twice emptied. The child was possessed of a capricious appetite. She might go for days eating so little her mother worried she was unwell, then something within would click. As if suddenly recalling her body needed to be fed, Violet would eat anything and everything made available to her. Somehow, though, among the mountains with Rebecca and Thorn, her appetite always appeared unleashed.

After supper, Violet helped gather up the dishes and

carry them off to the kitchen sink. When Rebecca began to wash them, Violet picked up a towel to help dry, but Rebecca said, "Your uncle Thorn can do that. I don't want him to forget how it's done."

"I don't mind," Violet said. "We do the dishwasher at home. There's nothing for me to dry there."

"After breakfast, then," her aunt said. "You've had a long day already. Why don't you go upstairs and take your bath? I'll come up in a bit and tuck you in bed." The child's nightly ritual at home with her parents no longer included getting *tucked in* at night. She relished that ceremony here where Rebecca, or sometime, Thorn, would come up to her room after she was abed. They would straighten her covers and pull the quilt snug about her shoulders and chin, then sit for a while and listen to her tell about her day's adventures, and perhaps, if she still lay wakeful, they would tell her a story about life among the mountains. In these tales, creatures and trees were invariably the main characters, and mountains could talk and creeks and rivers could sing and bears and owls were wiser than humans.

To Violet, these stories were more true and real than the factual existence she led in the far-off town. True or not, these nocturnal tales were invariably funny. Laughter primed her for sleep, and when the light went off and the door closed behind a warm and gentle "Good night", she was immediately asail on the ocean of her dreams.

Orville roused from his station beneath the table and watched Violet climbing the stairs. He tilted his head and gazed at Rebecca and Thorn, either in supplication or apology, and when Thorn murmured, "Go on, then," bounded away up the stairs after the new member of his pack.

On this night, though, sleep proved fugitive. Violet lay awake and aware long after Rebecca had said her goodnight, and this time, left the door slightly ajar for Orville to follow when he was ready, for the dog had declared in no uncertain terms his intention to maintain his vigil with Violet.

Not long after Rebecca's footsteps whispered away along the hall and down the stairs into silence, the dog stood with his chin pressing into the quilt, his moist nose inches from Violet's face, until she patted the bed covers and Orville gathered himself into a leap up beside her, where he lay warm and close with her arm across his round belly.

Violet lay more still than if she slept, relishing the unaccustomed proximity of another breathing soul in this normally private and solitary space. She could feel Orville's heart pulsing beneath her hand. His breathing sounded like any human child's. He was, she believed in that moment, a presence as worthy and exalted as any of earth's creatures, whether they walked on four legs or two.

For a long time that seemed no time at all to Violet, she lay gazing at the night outside her window, a darkness just shy of sight. Waves of rain beat against the house from time to time. At other times, it was only wind. She felt the rise and fall of Orville's flank beneath her arm. She could hear, faintly, faintly, as dim as the light, the beating of his heart, not the measured cadence of a human heart, but a pattern if one listened for it. Like a code tapping out his life. Twice, he whimpered in his sleep, dreaming, just like old Wilber. Violet had asked Thorn once if dogs had souls same as people. Thorn said, "Anything that dreams is a soul."

Tired as she was, Violet wished fervently for some light, wished for a sky free of rain and obscuring clouds, and there it was, the light, beginning as a soft veiled glow through the thinning clouds, and then the moon emerged, the clouds shredding and turning around and around, drawn into that whirlpool of light until they were gone and there was only the moon, bright and huge and sharp among a scatter of stars. Violet thought she might count the stars in her window, but they were so many and she was asleep before she finished.

Downstairs, Thorn and Rebecca were turning out the lights and preparing to go up to bed themselves.

"Do you think the child has any idea she's responsible?" Rebecca asked.

"I'm sure she doesn't," Thorn said, shaking his head. "How could she?"

Rebecca shook her head, in a gesture that might have indicated sorrow or disgust or both. "John was crazy to marry." We all agreed this would end with us."

"He didn't get the gift," Thorn said. "He must've figured he was free of it."

"Why do we call it a gift?" Rebecca murmured. "It is a curse, and sometimes it skips a generation, but it always comes back." They climbed the steps together, then stopped at the door to her bedroom. Rebecca leaned out and kissed Thorn's cheek. "Goodnight, Brother," she said softly.

"Goodnight, Sister," he replied, reached up to touch her hair lightly, then turned and walked toward his room at the other end of the hall. Violet dreamed his footsteps as he passed her door.

Orville was gone next morning when Violet woke to the sun in her face, shielding her eyes with a hand that still tingled from being slept on. She looked around the room, beside her bed, even under it, but no Orville. By the time she was dressed and down the stairs, the table bore the remains of Rebecca's and Thorn's breakfast. They had eaten without waking her, but Rebecca had heard the child stirring and was turning out a scramble of eggs and sausage as Violet descended into her day. Two biscuits waited hot in the oven.

"Morning, Sunshine," Rebecca said with unfeigned cheer. "Pour yourself some milk and juice and sit down there so I can feed you."

"Thanks. I'm hungry," Violet said, setting her two full glasses at her place and merging with her chair. "Where's Orville?"

Rebecca set the child's food before her, poured herself another cup of coffee, then sat opposite at table. "Your dog has gone up to the high meadow with Thorn."

Violet took a swallow of her grapefruit juice, picked up a strip of bacon with her fingers, and bit off the end. This lapse in table manners would have brought a mild reprimand from her parents, but her aunt just smiled and sipped her coffee.

"What's Uncle Thorn doing up there?" Violet asked, soon as she'd downed her bacon bite.

"Bear's been at our bees again," Rebecca said. "Thorn's putting up an electric fence around the hives. It's got a battery and solar charger and all that good stuff. He brought it up here from town with you."

"I wondered what was in that big box in the back, but I thought I'd be impolite to ask," Violet said between bites of her egg.

"You ought to ask your uncle anything you're curious about, and he'll tell you," Rebecca said. "If it's a secret, he'll tell you that, too."

"Can I go up there and help?" before a sip of milk.

"Well, you can help me feed the chickens and gather eggs," Rebecca said, "then we'll turn them out into their pen. The bees will be upset after the bear maraud. I wager Thorn and Lance might garner a few stings before they're done with it."

"Who's Lance?" Violet asked, wide-eyed and curious.

Rebecca laughed. "Lance is an old man who lives all by himself over across the river. He's a right strange one, but harmless, I reckon. He's a hard worker if somebody's around to instruct his every move. He's good with bees and he's helping Thorn put up the fence."

"The man who broke into our class at school was named Lance, but he was young," Violet said.

"The man with the gun?" Rebecca queried.

"Yes, but he went away before he could hurt anybody, Violet said. "Just like the woman who came to our house to take me away to the district boarding school at Laurel Creek Containment."

"What happened then?" Rebecca asked, as if this were news to her.

"I don't know," Violet said. "She said I had to go with her, and I ran up to my room and hid in my closet. I just wanted her to go away. After a while, Dad came up and found me, and said the woman had gone. I don't know where. They phoned Uncle Thorn, and the next day he came and brought me here. I'm glad. Mom and Dad told me that when I come back home, we'll be living somewhere else. They didn't know where, exactly. I like it here with you and Uncle Thorn, though."

Rebecca got up and stood behind Violet's chair, put her arms around the girl and kissed her tousled head. "And we like having you with us, Violet," she said. "We like it very much."

Lance Weathers was tired walking down the hill behind Thorn. That man had worked him harder than he figured the dollars Lawless would pay him entitled. Truth be told, though, Thorn worked harder than Lance, never asked more or other that he wouldn't put a hand to himself. In fact, Lance felt some gratitude toward Thorn, who had found him camped out down by the river, homeless, half frozen and half starved, fed him, found him a place warm and dry to stay a mile down the road, and even paid the old couple who owned the shack to let him live there until he could pay for himself, and then gave or found him odd jobs so that he could. Yes, Lance was grateful enough, but right now he was tired and sore, and out of sorts.

As well as Lance could calculate, he was getting close to the time when his life got broken into two pieces. It wasn't fair. He'd been just a kid when it happened. He should have known better. He would have known better if his own kin had not brought him up like a yard dog on a chain. Looking back on it now, he wondered if he could have really killed those kids. They were rich and privileged and soft and deserved to suffer as much as he had, but he didn't think now he could have actually pulled the trigger. He scared them right enough, but he didn't know if he could have gone beyond his yelling and threatening.

As it turned out, he never got a chance to find out. That little girl in the middle of the third row looked him in the eye and she wasn't afraid of him at all. Just as if she spoke to him, he heard her voice in his head, *You shouldn't be here now*, and he wasn't. He was in a place he never knew at a time before ever he was born. He grew up and grew old orphaned and strange. Seventy now, if a day, although it was hard to figure his divided life, like an old photograph ripped in two, and tossed about until the edges were worn and didn't fit any more.

And now he was coming back around to the time where everything flew apart, back to the day and year that awful schism happened, except he wasn't and never could be. The fourteen-year-old he was over fifty years ago had been lost forever on the other side of that little girl's blue eyes. The old man that was him now was as crazy as the boy had been, maybe crazier, Lance figured. Lord, how could he not be, after all that had been done to him?

Thorn led the way down the hill toward the house and barn below, the red clay of the farm road still slippery from the recent rain. He lifted a hand and waved at Rebecca as she emerged from behind the barn, carrying a basket of laundry. She looked up, smiled and waved to the men as Orville bounded down the slope toward her. "About time," Rebecca called. "You boys ready for your supper?"

Lance, loosed as always by her easy welcome, lifted his arm to wave back. He was more hungry than he was tired. He would welcome a hot meal prepared by somebody who knew how... He would have said, "Yes, Ma'am," but he saw the girl following behind, trotting to catch up with Rebecca. The child gave Orville her first attention, and when he was in her arms, she turned to look at her uncle and the strange man with him, and Lance stared into the same pair of deep blue eyes that were the last thing he saw before his life was split in two.

"It's her what done it to me," he gasped, strangling on his words.

"What?" Thorn said, as if he hadn't quite heard. "That's my niece, Violet."

Lance wanted to shut his eyes, but he couldn't. The blue eyes peered into his soul, and he cringed, knowing he was about to be sent back there again, but the terrible little girl only smiled at him, innocent as a baby bird, like she didn't know who he was. Lance threw down the shovel he was carrying and started running.

Thorn called after him, "Wait, Lance. I haven't paid you yet." But Lance didn't hear him. The three Thorns gazed after him until he had run out of sight down the county road. A mile farther on, he staggered past his little shack, still trying to run, his ragged breath shredding his chest, his heart pounding in his head, about to burst his skull, and the only thought in his mind, *I shouldn't be here now.*

DOWN TO THE RIVER

Every morning before breakfast, Jeremy walked down by the River to pray. He didn't pray to the River. Jeremy believed in God. But in his mind, to look upon the dark face of the River was to gaze into the face of the Unknowable, and the boisterous water tumbling and surging, roaring and singing between boulders there was the Voice that had birthed the world. He could feel the Power of Creation in his feet as he stood upon the frozen ground, and when he lay his ungloved hands against the ice-glazed stones, he could feel the Presence that wrought all undoing and becoming pulsing like a cold fire in his fingers.

Jeremy would stand there beside the rushing waters in the shadow of the mountain until his breath became frost in his beard and his poor fingers, numbed by divine proximity, screamed beneath his armpits and the terrible music of the River began to form words to warn or comfort his troubled mind. Summer prayers were easier on his body, but the summer music was vague and uninformative in good weather, and in storm and flood, just a frightening rage that told him nothing about his life except he was a frail and temporary creature of not much consequence in the scheme of the world. In summer, there were bugs and other numerous slithery crawly creatures to distract and unsettle him with sting and buzz and bite.

In winter, in the cold where the birds didn't sing, there was just Jeremy and the River. Then, God spoke clearly to his need in the dark voices of the troubled and hurried waters. Then, Jeremy sensed what the preacher up at the church kept trying to say about Trinity, how God was One but more than one. A single voice could not begin to tell all that was in the Maker's mind, more than a human ear could hold in an hour. To know the smallest part of God's will and purpose in a life, one had to listen every day, through all the sounds and silences of a lifetime.

The one River was at once a sound and a silence that swallowed all other sounds. Not just a voice, but a choir of voices, singing forth the soul of all the days and nights to anyone who had patience and courage to keep listening. Jeremy was patient, persistent, and long ago he had forgotten how to be afraid.

Until the cold got inside of his clothes and he began to shiver almost to pain, Jeremy stood on a boulder looming out over the river, waiting for some word of instruction to guide his day. This morning, the River was not forthcoming. The waters sighed and shushed and warbled and whistled, but no words came. Some days were like this, when Spirit offered up no words at all out of the River's music. Like Mama had always told Jeremy, and he believed her, a body could not choose their moments of revelation. One had to pay attention and watch and listen all the time until the Moment chose them.

Jeremy pulled on his gloves. His hands were so cold that he dropped one, the right-hand, and as he bent to retrieve it, breathed a thanks to the Power upholding the world that the glove landed on the stone at his feet and not in the River, which would have carried it swiftly away beyond all use and sight without any thanks at all. In fact, that was what the River usually said about any problem or object he presented for guidance or intervention. *Give it me*, the waters would tell him, and invariably, when he heard the directive clearly, Jeremy would obey, and whatever he yielded to the River, it never gave back to Jeremy.

His mind as blank as the flat gray sky, Jeremy turned and began trudging up the winding path toward Mama's house. The sky was waiting for snow. Jeremy was waiting for what he knew not. In summer, the path would have been choked with burr-bearing weeds, and Jeremy would check his legs for ticks when he reached the house and pull the burrs from his pants. The weeds now lay brown against the ground, pressed flat by ice storm the week before, the only winter hazard now, slippery mud. Jeremy would take his boots off before he went into the kitchen. Mama got mad at people who dirtied her floors. Mama used to mop her kitchen floor every day. Since her back got so stiff that she couldn't do it, Jeremy did the mopping. Not every day, but often enough to keep Mama quiet. Mama never had a lot to say when things were going to please her. Sometimes Jeremy would do something to aggravate her just to get her to talk to him. Then Mama got sick. These days, Jeremy strove to satisfy her in all things in their life together. He did not want to add in the smallest way to the pain and upset he had already caused her with his wild and strange ways.

When he reached the yard, Jeremy stopped at the hen house he had built for Mama when their old one began falling apart faster than he could mend it. Their five hens perched in their nest boxes inside, Alice, Betty, Cynthia, Doris, Evelyn. Frances had died the month before when she got loose, and a coyote ate her. This time of year, the hens didn't give up much, but Jeremy had rigged a light in the hen house to encourage them, and he apologized to each by name as he slipped his cold hand beneath their warm feathers. They shuffled and chuckled, and Cynthia pecked him peevishly, but he found an egg beneath Betty and one from Doris. That would be enough for breakfast. Mama probably wouldn't eat hers and Jeremy would end up eating them both.

Jeremy crossed the yard, stepped up onto the porch, and carefully cradling the eggs in one hand, reached down with the other and tugged off his muddy boots before he opened the door.

"Morning, Mama," he said, backing against the door to close it. Mama just sat there in her chair by the table, a blanket draped over her shoulders, as if she hadn't heard him come in. Mama was that way. Especially since she took sick, it seemed to Jeremy she had talked less and less until he was left doing all the talking for both of them. He put the eggs in a bowl and went to the old wood range, opened the fire box and added two sticks of wood. Mama had a new electric range, but they'd kept the old iron one for heat, and when there was a fire in it, Jeremy would cook on it to save on the electric. Wood only cost time and sweat. Mama liked to say, at least she did when she bothered to speak to him at all. "A body who splits their own wood, warms theyself twice."

Jeremy took the skillet from out the sink, wiped it inside with a rag. He hoped Mama hadn't noticed that he forgot to wash it after supper last night. She wouldn't eat a bite if she knew her egg had been fried in a dirty pan.

Pete Tankersly, the mail carrier left Mama's government check in the mailbox, and before he drove away, waved at Jeremy, who had been sitting on Mama's porch for an hour waiting for him. Jeremy took the check inside and showed it to Mama. She couldn't use her hands anymore, and he signed it for her on the back, so he could take it into town and get it cashed at Dolf's Market and buy their month's groceries and sundries. He pulled on his coat and *Morton's Lumber* cap.

"I'm going into Drovers Gap, Mama. Cash your check and get our goods. I'll come right back soon's I can," he told her as he took Mama's car keys down from the ring by the door. Mama didn't say anything, just stared at the door, as he went out. Jeremy made sure he pulled it to behind him. Mama couldn't abide drafts.

Mama's old Plymouth started with considerable reluctance. Jeremy thought the battery was about to give out, when the engine finally coughed and sputtered and growled to life. Mama had told him time and again that he ought to go out once a week and let it run for a minute to keep the battery up, but if Mama didn't remind Jeremy of things, he would forget, and lately Mama hadn't been reminding him of much. He figured, with her being old and sick as she was, Mama's memory was worse than his.

Jeremy did remember to fetch the gas can from the shed and throw it in the trunk, because he'd forgotten to buy gas last time he was in town and the gauge when he looked at it was nearly on empty. He was afraid the Plymouth might leave him a mile or two to walk this morning. Jeremy's instincts were sounder than his memory. The gas gauge in the Plymouth had been stuck on nearly empty for years. He wasn't two miles down the graveled county road when, as he downshifted for a sharp bend, the vehicle wheezed and heaved and sighed to a stop. He had to get out and push the car far enough to the verge that another car might pass. In the process he slipped and ripped the knee on his jeans, his good pair for church and town. *Don't go down there looking shabby like you are*, Mama would say when she would still talk to him at all. There was still nearly a mile between Jeremy and the highway where, if he was lucky, which Jeremy usually was not, he might catch a ride into Drovers Gap, four miles beyond.

He hauled out the empty gas can and had just begun his trek to civilization, when a big Dodge came careening around a curve in front of him, forcing Jeremy to leap for the ditch, the gas can clattering across the gravel after him. He barely caught a glimpse of the man driving and his passenger, a woman Jeremy thought might look like Marilyn Monroe, although he couldn't see her long enough to be sure.

211

He watched them out of sight, retrieved his can, and as he resumed his walk, heard a noise like a tree falling some way back behind. Jeremy hoped it was that Big Dodge and he hoped they had hit a tree and not Mama's Plymouth.

The rest of Jeremy's morning went well. Jeremy, unused to things going well for him, couldn't shake the feeling that he must have done something wrong. But hardly had he reached the paved highway than Wilson Redding, the preacher at Slick Rock Creek Baptist Church, came along in his muddy Subaru, recognized Jeremy, and pulled over to the shoulder about twenty yards ahead. When Jeremy came up alongside, Wilson rolled down his window and said, "You need a lift, Jeremy? I'm heading into town."

"Yessir, Preacher Redding. Mama's Plymouth ran out of gas back yonder. I was on my way to cash her check and get some groceries."

Wilson reached across and unlocked the passenger door. "Well, hop right in. I'll drop you off at Dolf's. I'll only be in town for about an hour. I can bring you back on my way home, if you like."

Jeremy climbed into the Subaru, had to slam the door twice before the latch caught. "Much obliged, Preacher," Jeremy said as Wilson pulled back onto the road. "I weren't looking forward to walking all day."

"Walking's more fun when you don't have to," Wilson said. The preacher had a habit of saying strange things like that. Jeremy found his remarks unsettling, and wished he would just stick to plain conversation.

Jeremy was content to ride in silence, as he had nothing on his mind that required saying, but the preacher seemed to have a prejudice against silence, or maybe, Jeremy thought, the man just liked to hear himself talk.

"I hope we'll be seeing you up at Slick Rock come

Sunday," Wilson said in a tone that conveyed as much command as hope.

"I'll be there, Preacher," Jeremy said. "Mama will want to pry me about your sermon when I get home. She always wants to know, since she don't get out for herself anymore."

"Well, we miss her, Jeremy," Wilson said, sounding for all the world like he actually meant it. "Your Mama was the prettiest voice in the choir. I need to get out to your place and pray with her. I apologize not to have been there already."

Now that won't do at all. Aloud, Jeremy said, "Since Mama's been so sick, and the Corvid's been going around, she don't feel like seeing folk come by the house. She fears catching something, weak and frail like she is."

"I understand, Jeremy," Wilson said. "You tell your Mama I asked about her, and that we're holding her up in our prayers." Jeremy thought the preacher sounded relieved, somehow, that he had an excuse now not to make the visit. He wasn't nearly as relieved as Jeremy.

"How's your Mama?" Dolf Thomas said as he began counting out the cash for Mama's government check.

"Ganny about the same," Jeremy said, watching the twenty-dollar bills stack up on the counter. "She don't get out of the house now. She's fearful of anybody coming by that might bring in the Corvid."

"I know you're taking good care of her up there," Dolf said, as he put the check in his cash drawer.

"Yessir," Jeremy said. "She's my Mama." He bought a bag of groceries, filled the gas can from the pump in front of the store and sat on the bench by the door while he waited for Preacher Wilson to pick him up. The sun had come out, and the bench was warm and felt good to Jeremy's stiff back. He finished his *RC Cola* and was eating the last bite of his *Little*

213

Debbie cake, when the muddy Subaru stopped beside the gas pump. Jeremy loaded his gas and groceries in the back while the preacher filled his tank and went inside to pay Dolf. He didn't have to make conversation on the way home, as Preacher Wilson turned on the radio and they listened to some other preacher talk whose name Jeremy didn't know. He forgot most of what the preacher said, although when he went to church the next Sunday, he would think Preacher Wilson's sermon sounded a lot like the one they had heard on the radio.

The radio sermon got interrupted, when they came upon two sheriff's deputies doing a road check. One of the deputies knew Preacher Wilson. Jeremy recognized him from church but only knew the man to see him.

The deputies were looking out for a man and a woman who had robbed the credit union in Hendo right after it opened that morning. They thought the thieves were probably still in the area and were urging the public to be on the lookout for a red Dodge. Jeremy wanted to tell them about the car that nearly hit him after he ran out of gas, but he didn't say anything. Talking about anything at all to people he didn't really know seemed to Jeremy the best way to get into trouble. The deputy didn't remember Jeremy from church, and when preacher Wilson explained who he was, the deputy reached a big hand through the window and Jeremy had to shake his hand.

"I remember your Mama right well," he smiled on Jeremy. "She taught me in Sunday School when I was eight years old. I had no notion she was still alive. You tell her Jimbob Akin was asking about her, now." Jeremy nodded and held his breath, until Preacher Wilson started up the Subaru and pulled away. Jeremy looked in the side mirror and saw the two deputies talking to each other and laughing. He wondered if they were laughing at him.

When they reached the turn-off for the river road,

Preacher Wilson offered to take Jeremy to where he left Mama's Plymouth, but Jeremy said, "'Tain't far. I can manage." Preacher Wilson didn't argue. By the time he got to the car, Jeremy wished he had. He hadn't counted on the gas or the groceries getting heavier the closer he got to the Plymouth. He had some practice at running out of gas and knew what to do. With minimal tinkering, he got the machine running again and managed to turn around in the narrow road without backing into the ditch, something he also had some experience of.

He hadn't gone far at all toward home when he spied some broken down knotweed bordering a sharp bend in the road where it turned up a steep bluff above the river. He was in a hurry to get home to Mama and drove past before the thought caught him. Jeremy stopped, backed up to where the weeds and brush were flattened. It looked to him like tire tracks going off among the brambly growth. He got out of the Plymouth, walked to the edge of the gravel and peered off down toward the river. He could see where something big had torn a path through the tangle of laurel, and two old hemlocks stood freshly barked, their wounds white against the shadows. It took him another minute, though, before he could make out the big red Dodge turned up on its side, half in the water.

Jeremy stood there at the verge of the gravel and looked and listened for a long time, maybe five whole minutes. Nothing moved inside the Dodge. Nobody was talking except the River, clinging to the Dodge, chortling and chuckling, *Give it me, give it me...* like the water was hungry for something that didn't belong to it. Jeremy looked up the road and down the road and saw nobody to tell him what to do. From the road to the River was a tilted tangle of laurel and rhododendron. Jeremy did not like tangles and thickets, and normally did his utmost to avoid them but he remembered the

215

woman in the Dodge who might have looked like Merilyn Monroe. Being winter, the creepy slimy creatures he thought likely to encounter in such places were hid away in some place dark and warm where a body wasn't prone to step, so he began slipping and sliding, crawling and slithering through the laurel and ivy down toward the Dodge, getting snared and snagged in the process, ripping his jacket and raking his hide, until he stood panting and sweating, with his shoes full of water, next to the car.

The Dodge was tilted up sideways against a boulder. Jeremy had to climb up and stand on tiptoes before he could see through the window. The driver, a thin man with a mustache, sat in his seat, wearing an expression of vast surprise, his chest impaled by the unwheeled steering column. The woman passenger slumped forward against the dashboard, her head embedded in the spiderwebbed windshield. Judging by her hair, Jeremy thought she might have looked a bit like Marilyn Monroe after all if she'd still had a face. It seemed to Jeremy there was a lot of blood splattered around for just two people.

He shifted around on his slippery perch until he could see into the back seat. The steering wheel, resembling nothing so much as a pretzel, was wedged up behind the seatback against the rear window. Jeremy was wondering how it got there when he spied what looked like a doctor's medical bag lying in the seat. The bag was partially open, and Jeremy could see it was stuffed with money. A couple of bills had escaped and fluttered feebly in the light. Jeremy, stunned by all the horror, suddenly felt afraid and sick at his stomach and ejected his cake and cola against the door of the car. When he looked one more time into the back seat of the Dodge, the sight of money helped a lot to settle his stomach and focus his mind.

Jeremy was surprised and relieved when the rear door

of the Dodge opened pretty much as it was designed to do, and he found, after some tentative clamber and maneuver, that he could use a broken laurel branch to snare the bag without falling in on top of it. He didn't attempt to retrieve the loose bills. Jeremy wasn't greedy and the bag had more money in it than he figured he could count. Besides, he was eager to put some distance between himself and the car with its demolished humans, which had an odor about it now that reminded him of how Mama smelled at the worst of her sickness. Holding the bag close to himself, like a newborn babe, Jeremy began making his tedious way back up to the road. The River kept sighing and singing, *Give it me, give it me...* and Jeremy kept saying with every tortuous step upward into light, "Mine now. Mine now..."

When Jeremy showed Mama his bag of money, she didn't say a word, just glared at him vacantly out of her dark eyes, exuding disapproval. Jeremy knew what she was thinking, *That ain't yours, boy. It's stolen. Bloodcursed. Keep it and you'll bring down on us grief untold.*

Jeremy left the bag on the floor by the door where his torn jacket dripped on it and cooked their supper. As usual, Mama refused to eat any of it, so Jeremy had to eat it all himself. He'd anticipated that and had not cooked more than it took to fill him. After supper, he took the bag of money, put on his jacket and cap, and walked down to the river.

He stood by the water, holding the bag, listening to the indecipherable wisdom of the river flowing past. The water was dark, darker than the dark on land, although the moon here and there silvered the contour of a wave or ripple, so that the river looked full of stars, like the sky. Unlike the sky, the stars in the river shifted and danced, in and out, here and there, in time to the singing of the water. When,

217

after a longish spell, the River had told him nothing he could understand, Jeremy held out his bag and queried, "What on God's good earth am I to do with this?"

Give it me… give it me… the River gurbled and garbled. Jeremy upended the bag and watched the contents flutter like untreed leaves down into the current. When the last of them had dissolved away into the night, he threw the bag as far as he could out over the water. The river was singing loud enough that he couldn't hear the splash.

Jeremy waited until he was sure he had done the right thing, and his fingers were too cold to pain him, and slowly made his way back up the hill toward Mama's house. Behind him, he could hear the River still demanding offerings, but on this night, Jeremy had nothing left to give it.

He stopped at the woodpile on his way across the yard, picked up an armload of sticks to carry in to feed the stove. Mama never complained about the cold anymore, but Jeremy knew it hurt her. When he had built up the fire and was hanging up his jacket by the door, he said, "Mama, I didn't keep the money. I did like you wanted me to."

Mama didn't say anything to that, but Jeremy could feel that she was pleased with him.

THE WOMAN ON THE BRIDGE

Clive was just going for a little walk before breakfast. Around the block and maybe one turn through the park at the bottom of the hill. By the time he returned home, the morning newspaper would be on his steps, and he'd go in and drink the coffee Sandra had fixed for him and read the headlines while he waited for his breakfast. There was nothing to hint that this walk would be any different from a hundred morning walks before.

As he came down his front steps, the sun was about to rise, crimsoning the underbelly of incipient overcast. Looked to Clive like rain on the way. He would be long home by then though. Turning up the street, he saw the woman about a block ahead on the opposite sidewalk, standing motionless as a tree, watching him. At least, that was his impression. At the distance, he couldn't be certain he saw a woman. The form in the long black raincoat looked womanish to Clive. Her face under her umbrella, he more imagined than saw. She had dark hair, or it may have been just a black hood on her coat. Clive's eyes weren't what they used to be. He didn't want to stare, so studied his neighbor's flowerbeds until he was closer, then looked again, but she wasn't there.

Clive walked on. When he reached the spot, more or less where the woman had been standing, something plopped on the sidewalk right at his feet. He looked down and saw a bird. Clive thought it might be a robin. He wasn't certain. Birds weren't Clive's thing, especially. The maybe Robin looked a picture of birdly health. It was plump and sleek and very still. One shiny eye, moist and lustrous, like a fresh-plucked berry, gazed up at Clive with some kind of longing, it seemed to him. As he watched, standing there in the middle of the sidewalk, the bird's eye faded flat and

219

dull. He prodded the feathery corpse with the toe of his loafer. No reaction. No more life in it than yesterday's newspaper. "This bird is dead, Jim," Clive announced to the morning, trying to sound like that Forest whatever-his-name on the television show.

Nearly being bombed by a dead bird made Clive forget all about Umbrella Woman. The gathering breeze came on him not so much chill as merely damp. He walked faster than usual, even though walking fast made him wheeze past the knot in his chest. Still, Clive made his regular morning circuit without taking any short cuts. He was in sight of his house before rain drops began dotting the concrete ahead of him. Just a smatter of splatter. Clive held out his hand to make sure it was really rain, felt three drops before he put his hand back in his pocket. He opened the front door just as the shower commenced in earnest. He could hear it drumming the roof as he hung up his jacket, hardly wet, in the hall.

"Survival is contingent on timing," he said aloud, imitating the voice of another character with prosthetic ears from the same sci-fi series. Clive had always been prone to letting other people, even make-believe ones, put words in his mouth. His accumulation of quotes and paraphrases had become so vast over the years, that nowadays he seldom had to strive for something original to say to any situation that presented.

"What's that, dear?" Sandra called from the kitchen. "Is somebody with you?"

"Just me and Doctor Spock," Clive answered. *No*, he thought. *That's the guy who writes those children's books.* Clive stopped midway to the kitchen, trying to sort his familiars. *Seuss. That's the starship officer.* Somehow, the names still didn't rest quite right in his mind, but the smell of coffee supplanted with a new urgency. "Don't worry. I

220

was just talking to myself," he told Sandra as he came into the kitchen, where his wife was gazing at the door as if she expected she might need to set another plate. It didn't happen often, but more than once, Clive had returned from his morning walk with another hungry early wanderer in tow. If Sandra minded the occasional unannounced breakfast guests, she never protested to Clive. She was what Clive called "a real people person". Her only kitchen complaint ever to Clive, and that delivered only half-seriously, was that "It hardly seems worth the mess, cooking for just the two of us."

Once, he had responded sincerely, "Let me take you out for breakfast at Wardlow's," and Sandra had shown him that face she wore when he forgot to carry out the trash, and said, "Why waste money on something I can cook better." That settled the matter in Clive's mind. Sandra was happy. He never asked again, although he thought breakfast at Wardlow's now and then might be fun. Sandra was one of those people who was driven to do for others but couldn't abide being done for. He wished his wife thought better of herself. She was a compulsively kind person who deep down felt she didn't deserve the kindness she bestowed on the world.

Next morning, an unembodied male voice greeted him as he came in from his walk. *Viewer discretion advised. The graphic trauma captured in the following viewer-contributed footage may be distressing...* It had been a good walk, sunny, with a pleasantly cool breeze and no dead birds dropping on him and no strange women with black umbrellas crossing his path. He had stopped to chat with Old Anna Cybert, admired her peonies, and farther down the block exchanged some weather assessments and speculations with Derek Koons, retired, same as Clive, a

221

year or so younger. All the people Clive talked to on his morning walks were either small children or elderfolk, all the rest of the population being already on their way to school or jobs. Clive's friends and acquaintances, almost unanimously, enjoyed their shared state of still being in the world but no longer quite of it. A few of them claimed it was a dull life, but most agreed with Clive that being so unattached from what the majority of humans considered important and necessary endeavor was mainly and mostly liberating.

The voice commanding guarded attention emanated from Sandra's little television fastened beneath the wall cabinet over the kitchen counter. She stood transfixed, as if beholding a vision, in each hand a plated breakfast. Clive squinted over her shoulder at the tiny screen, recognized the Fifth street Bridge that carried the through-town freeway over the railway switch yards where Clive had worked for over twenty years. The view kept bobbing and weaving, so it was hard to see what was actually going on. It took Clive a moment to realize the man standing on the bridge was outside the rails. Maybe thirty feet to his left, a uniformed policeman was apparently talking to him, although the only sounds coming from the television now were the noises of nearby traffic. The contributing viewer must have been standing somewhere beside a street below.

Ensnared by the drama now as much as Sandra, Clive watched as the policeman inched closer to the man clinging to the railing. Behind the suicidal man, on the far side of the bridge, stood a woman in a black coat, holding what appeared to be an umbrella. The cop was apparently so intent on the potential jumper, he didn't see the woman. The woman opened her umbrella, and the man turned loose the bridge railing and leaned out into space. The camera, probably on a phone, zoomed in with jerks and starts, following the body as it fell, stiff as a child's doll, bounced off the top of a boxcar, and disappeared from view. The camera panned up again to the bridge, where the policeman stood at the railing, peering down toward the tracks. The woman was nowhere in sight.

Sandra gasped, her plates tilted, their breakfast would have landed on the floor had not Clive reached out and taken them in hand.

"They shouldn't show stuff like that on the TV where children might see it," Sandra whispered.

"I know that woman," Clive said, setting their plates on the table.

"What woman are you talking about?" Sandra said.

"That woman on the bridge, with the umbrella. I saw her here yesterday, on our street."

"On the TV just now?" Sandra snapped. "I didn't see any woman with an umbrella. Just that poor lost man. That hopeless soul."

Clive marveled at his wife's capacity for compassion toward total strangers. Indeed, he wondered that she held so much merciful kindness toward him. More, actually, than he considered himself worthy of. He knew he was not her first and only. There were others before and after his arrival who in their own time tired of the game and drifted away. He stayed. He played the game for keeps. Eventually, his was the only offer left on the table. Sandra decided that was the best offer she would get and asked him not to go. Convenience bred tolerance bred affection bred love. Love rewrote their history. All their friends now said theirs was the perfect marriage. It was a flawed marriage, he knew, but a marriage that had survived all their shared failings and infidelities. What remained between them was good and sustaining. More than they deserved and everything they needed. At least, it was everything Clive needed. What did he really know of Sandra's needs, he wondered. She never spoke of them at all.

Clive mulled these thoughts as he made his morning walk, thoughts he never spoke of to Sandra, and certainly not to anyone else. Thinking was not an exercise Clive was proud of. Whenever he indulged much in it, he came away tasting something close to shame, with no clear notion as to why he felt that way. As Clive rounded the corner onto Wilderness Way, he was trying hard to escape his ruminations, just to take in the day, the clearing sky, wet pavement, the rising light, scraps of blue overhead, springing green and flowers along the sidewalk. Clive was engaging with the flowers when he heard screaming brakes and a terminal sound midway between crunch and thud and looked up to see a minivan sitting crossways in the street a block ahead. Silence fell down solid as an anvil. Even the birds quit singing. Then somebody yelled, and there were several people running toward the minivan and one of the children inside the vehicle began to wail.

Clive wanted to turn around, put some distance between himself and this unprovoked unpleasantness, yet he found himself walking slowly, ever so reluctantly, toward accomplished disaster. By the time Clive closed the distance, two cops had arrived and ushered back a gathering fringe of spectators busily being glad it wasn't them or theirs under the van. Clive peered over the shoulder of a man in a suit, snared like him by the spectacle at the start of his morning route. Clive recognized the man as someone he had seen before, thought he knew which house he belonged to. He might have even waved on occasion as he passed the man's daily departure to an office in the next county, but Clive didn't know his name, had never even been curious.

Clive could glimpse through a reticulation of neighbors known and unknown the pretzled wheel of a bicycle and a shoe, almost hidden by the occluding van. Clive couldn't determine if the shoe was occupied by a foot, or if there was a leg attached. He watched a puddle of dark liquid slowly expanding from beneath the vehicle and wondered if it was oil, or perhaps blood. Most of the gory details and all informative action accumulated out of his sight on the far side of the van. Clive could hear a woman, presumably the van's driver, gasping out words between sobs to someone who must have been an investigating officer and spoke to the distraught woman in calm and calming tones that did not taste at all of crisis and destruction. The children in the van had been disappeared to someplace safe and removed, and Clive could no longer hear their shrill distress.

EMS arrived with blare and hustle, and after they unloaded a gurney, there were considerable indeterminate doings on the far side of the van, before Clive saw the crew re-load the gurney, discretely veiled to conceal consequences. At that point, the accident became old news, and the assembled audience began to trickle away toward their day's duties and preoccupations. Clive was about to move on with them as the EMS unit pulled away and he saw Bridge Woman, furling her umbrella as if she had just come out of the rain. Clive couldn't not stare. She caught his eye and smiled in seeming recognition, before he fled away to home and Sandra and breakfast.

"I saw that woman again," Clive shouted as he rushed into the kitchen, still wearing his jacket.

Sandra looked up from a glass she had just filled with grapefruit juice. "What woman?" she said, mystified at the outburst. This wasn't like Clive at all.

"That woman on the bridge," said Clive, his excitement ebbing now as he remembered to take off his jacket.

"What bridge?" Sandra said, still holding the juice carton. "Where did you go? I thought your walk was longer than usual this morning. I had to put your pancakes in the warmer. They'll be rubbery."

"There was no bridge," Clive clarified. "It was the woman we saw on the newscast, when the man jumped off the bridge. I only walked as far as Wilderness Way. I was watching the accident. That's what took so long."

"Accident? I heard sirens. What happened?" Sandra set the carton back in the fridge and pulled their breakfast from the warmer.

Clive sat at his place, unfolded his napkin. "Somebody on a bicycle got run over by a minivan. Nobody we knew."

"A woman or a man?" Sandra liked detailed narratives, whatever the occasion.

"I don't know. They were dead, I suppose. All covered up when the EMS people carried them off."

"So maybe we might know them." Sandra murmured as she picked up her juice glass.

Clive sipped his coffee distractedly, hardly noticing it was only lukewarm. It hadn't occurred to him he might know the accident victim. Somehow, he'd just assumed it was a man. Violent deaths never occurred among one's own acquaintances here. This was a safe neighborhood.

Clive slept poorly that night. He blamed it less on the deathly accident he'd observed two blocks from his front door than he did on the woman with the black umbrella. He dreamed her as he saw her on Sandra's TV, standing on the bridge, watching the suicide unfolding before her, the body falling away into oblivion. After an hour of wakefulness, Clive dreamed again, that Sandra's pet cat was sitting on his chest, watching his face with that piercing gaze cats have when they are close, as if they were plotting to steal your breath. Sandra only had a cat in Clive's dreams. In his waking world, his wife couldn't abide animals in her house, not even a caged bird.

When Clive woke again to daylight, he could still feel the weight of the feline dream, pressing subtly, just enough to stop him short of a full inhale. Sandra was already up, as she was before him every morning. He heard the vacuum shut off and then some preparatory clatter in the kitchen. He showered, dressed, and followed the scent of coffee.

"I don't think I'll take my walk this morning," Clive said when Sandra looked around, surprised to see him so early in her domain.

"You take a walk every morning, Clive," she accused.

"This morning," he admitted, "I just don't quite feel up to it."

Sandra set her spoon and bowl on the counter, turned her concerned face on him. "What's wrong? Are you sick?"

Clive shrugged. "No, I don't think so. I just feel off, somehow. Heavy."

"You didn't sleep well last night," Sandra diagnosed. "Tossed and turned, kept waking me, too. Go take your walk. It's sunny and warm out there. It will make you feel better, and you'll be out from underfoot while I make breakfast."

"I will," Clive said. He always made an effort to do whatever Sandra instructed, whether it made sense to him or not. He started down the hall to get his coat and hat. A knock at the front door inexplicably made him break into a cold sweat. *Why don't they use the bell?* Clive swallowed hard, opened the door and stepped out to see the woman with the black umbrella standing on his front steps. She gave him her almost familiar smile and said softly with his mother's voice, forgotten until he heard it now, *It's our time, Clive.*

The woman opened her umbrella and held it up over him. Everything was vague and shadowy under there, like a summer night. Clive suddenly felt very very tired. It took all his strength to lift his arms as he fell into the welcoming dark.

THE CAT AND THE PRIEST

It was the cat's favorite book. Every night, she would curl up atop the crimson cover embossed with a golden cross, and sleep. She couldn't read it, of course. Anyone knows that cats can't read, but proximity to the book gave her strange and spectacular dreams. She had become addicted to her visions. The priest she was living with had no awareness of Cat's inner life. Indeed, it never occurred to the priest that any creature so unlike himself might be possessed of an inner life.

The priest, of course, had dreams of his own. Some of them were quite dark and dangerous. The priest would never dare tell any person about those dreams, not even his Confessor. Sometimes, though, when he thought the weight of all that darkness would crush his heart, he would relate his nocturnal visions to his cat. He didn't believe the cat comprehended a word he said, but getting his darkness out into the air between them made him feel less burdened by his unconsummated iniquities. The cat, of course, understood it all and remembered everything.

The cat had not always lived with the priest, who had rescued the half-drowned kitten from a puddle during the worst storm of a stormy summer, when the priest was on his way home from the Wholly Spirits Pub where he'd spent the evening drinking with his only friend in Drovers Gap, who was an atheist. Cat had no memory of how she had come to be abandoned to Nature's indiscriminate mercies. The priest, for his part, had always generally preferred his own company, which was his primary motivation for becoming a priest. It provided an arrangement whereby he could live alone with means in place ensuring he might be looked after in case of a debilitating emergency. Since Cat's arrival in his life, however, the priest had developed a growing addiction to the pressure of that small furry body upon his lap. That concentration of feline warmth accompanied by the oscillating drone of a purr on a winter evening bestowed on the priest a sense of peace that eluded him even in the practice of his religious exercises. Amid his recurring debates and arguments with the Archdeacon, which of late had become more regular and frequent, the priest relied on Cat's presence to restore his calm and emotional balance.

Cat was ever aware of the priest's mood and disposition, often sensing the cleric's inner crises before the man was himself aware of his feelings. The priest expended a good portion of his daily energies attempting to maintain varying degrees of self-evasion and denial. Cat, on the other hand, never denied any condition, and naturally existed in a state of inquisitive alertness that sufficed to foresee and forestall most impending unpleasantries. An exception to this rule was the occasion when the priest, intent on the book he was reading, accidentally brought down the rocker of his chair across Cat's tail, whereupon Cat exploded in a paroxysm of unfocused destruction directed toward any and every living thing within reach, including the priest's ankle. The priest was surprised, then angry, and finally, when he forgot the pain of his injuries, remorseful. He was very careful regarding the placement of his rocker after the incident, but Cat, never forgetting anything, especially a thing hurtful, never came near the priest's chair again, except to leap into the man's obliging lap.

The priest took all his obligations regarding his fellow creatures with the highest seriousness. He never allowed the water in Cat's bowl to be depleted or go stale. Food appeared in Cat's dish at every appropriate time, and the priest took notice of Cat's preferences and aversions and adjusted her diet accordingly. Cat knew from observing the behaviors of humans who came and went from the house that her priest was by far more readily trained than most of his species. Their mutual accommodation might have continued until one of them died, had not the priest unwittingly committed a transgression beyond forgiveness or repair.

The priest's undoing began innocently enough, not with a sudden aberration and abandonment of respectable behaviors, but with the repetition of a guileless ritual the priest had been practicing for several years since his arrival in Drovers Gap, his weekly brainstorm with the town atheist down at the Wholly Spirits Pub. Every Tuesday, rain or shine, the two men would meet there at the end of the day and sit until their third beer was warm and flat, their fish had disappeared and the few remaining chips grown cold and hard, while they asked unanswerable questions and posed unprovable answers. At some point in their conversation, there would come a prolonged pause. The one of them whose turn it was to pay would pick up the check, summon the waiter, and they would arise and go.

On this occasion, while waiting for the waiter to bring the bad news, the atheist looked out the window at a view of the sun setting among blossoming storm clouds and purpled mountains and murmured, perhaps only to himself or to an unacknowledged God. "That is beautiful."

The priest, who had been lurking like Whitman's noiseless patient spider, jumped on it. "How can you say that?"

"Because it is," said the atheist.

"How can you know that?" said the priest.

"I can see it; therefore I know," a good answer, one would think, befitting an atheist.

"What do you see that makes it beautiful?" queried the priest, insistent.

The atheist gestured toward the window. "There are

colors, movement. It's a compelling combination," said the atheist, don't you feel it, too?

"Yes, certainly I do," said the priest, "but if somebody set off a bomb in here, there would be colors and movement. It would be compelling in a lot of ways. Would that be beautiful?"

"It would be painful for those who survived and nothing at all for those who didn't," the atheist said, "but beauty transcends circumstance."

"Oh, so you believe in beauty, then," said the priest.

"I recognize it when I experience it," said the atheist.

"If you've experienced it," said the priest, "can you define beauty for me?"

"Beauty eludes all definition, though many have tried," the atheist said. "You just have to be there to know it."

The priest lifted his glass, as if to drain his last swallow of beer, then thought better of it and put the glass back on the table. "So then, you just have to take beauty on faith," the priest said, smiling as if he'd won a point.

"Are you trying to drag me to belief in your God?" the atheist said, as he looked at the check, laid some currency on the table and pushed back his chair.

"Not tonight," the priest said, standing. "I just want to remind you that all our so-called knowledge begins with a faith-based proposition. You can't recognize beauty unless you believe it exists."

"So, Father, do you believe in everything you tell your congregation on a Sunday morning?" the atheist said.

The priest shook his head ruefully. "It is the duty of a priest ever to tell his flock more than he knows. It's how I keep my job."

"So do you even believe in God yourself, then?" the atheist said.

"My salvation is not dependent on my belief in God,

my friend, but on God's belief in me," the priest said, as the two men walked out into the cooling evening.

Neither had noticed the Senior Warden sitting quietly at the next table, pretending to listen to the conversation of his guests while straining to eavesdrop on his priest's conversation. He caught a snippet here and there, just enough to persuade him he had legitimate cause to report to the Vestry that their priest had admitted publicly that he did not believe in God.

By the time the rumor of the priest's apostasy filtered up through the ecclesiastical hierarchy it had assumed the guise of indisputable fact. When the Bishop heard of it, he instructed the Archdeacon to initiate appropriate damage control. The Archdeacon convinced the priest that his best course was to slip away quietly without ruffling further any congregational feathers, and suggested the priest be indisposed by a vaguely-defined illness while the Archdeacon arranged a temporary celebrant to cover his duties during the priest's incipient absentia.

Sitting in their darkened house on a Saturday night, the priest informed his cat that he would not be officiating at church next morning. "We'll have to leave here now, faithful friend," the priest said, "but whatever happens and wherever it does, I'll take care of you," he promised. As soon as the priest said that Cat jumped down from his lap and wandered off into another room.

Cat liked this town, had no intention of moving away. She canvassed the neighborhood looking pitiful and hungry, and a few days later the priest packed his old car and called for his cat, who didn't answer and was nowhere to be seen.

She watched from the window of her new home down the street, as the priest drove by on his way to some place Cat wanted no part of. *If the man expected loyalty*, she thought, *he should have got himself a dog.*

ACKNOWLEDGEMENTS

This author is exceeding grateful to Gill James at Bridge House, who has concluded these collected tales deserve to be read and gave them a book to live in. Deep thanks as well to my editor at Bridge House, Liz Cox, who repeatedly saved my book from my words and my words from me, and to Martin James who designed a just-right cover.

Special thanks to Scott Derks, David Longley, Frank Murphy, John Mitchell, Marianne Kinane, Julianna Welch. Stephen Drew, Thayer Fleming, Kristen Collins, Keith Davis, Chip Broadfoot, Jean Clarke, Charlie Nabers and the other Henry Mitchell who read these tales first and loved good writing enough to tell me where I didn't get it right. Stephen found enough right about it to merit a generous and insightful foreword.

Boundless gratitude to and for the Main Muse, a.k.a. Jane Ella Matthews, who heard them all more than once and still loves me.

ABOUT THE AUTHOR

Henry Mitchell reads and writes in the Blue Ridge Mountains of North Carolina. He has written six novels and three collections of short stories. Before he began writing fiction in 2012, he worked for fifty years as a painter and sculptor.

ALSO BY HENRY MITCHELL

The Summer Boy
Between Times
Dark on the Mountain – stories
Laurel Falls
Slick Rock Creek
Early Dark – stories
The Winged Child
Among the Fallen

See https://amzn.to/4ljbrA3

Like to Read More Work Like This?

Then sign up to our mailing list and download our free collection of short stories, *Magnetism*. Sign up now to receive this free e-book and also to find out about all of our new publications and offers.

Sign up here:
http://eepurl.com/gbpdVz

Please Leave a Review

Reviews are so important to writers. Please take the time to review this book. A couple of lines is fine.

Reviews help the book to become more visible to buyers. Retailers will promote books with multiple reviews.

This in turn helps us to sell more books... And then we can afford to publish more books like this one.

Leaving a review is very easy.

Go to https://amzn.to/3IZHebr, scroll down the left-hand side of the Amazon page and click on the 'Write a customer review' button.

Other Publications by Bridge House

White Moon
by Mehreen Ahmed

White Moon is a collection of avant-garde short stories, micro and flash fiction.

Together they bring a stronger message than they do individually. The incidents in this book depict imaginary characters and events underpinned by dreamlike, strong surrealistic, even esoteric connections. The narratives bring together a unique blend of absorbing, entertaining and otherworldly experience.

As ever Mehreen Ahmed brings a strong and convincing voice to all of the texts. Enjoy the surreal and dreamlike quality of these stories.

Order from Amazon:

Paperback: ISBN 978-1-914199-90-5
eBook: ISBN 978-1-914199-91-2

Between Worlds
by S.Nadja Zajdman

We all inhabit multiple worlds and the real person lives in the liminal space between them.

In this fascinating collection of vignettes and creative memoir, we are invited to explore several constructs of the times and places defined by the narrator, and also envisaged by those around her. These accounts have appeared in other publications, but gathered here the whole becomes greater than its parts and tells a larger story.

S. Nadja Zajdman brings her rich and unique voice to this story: *Between Worlds.*

"This collection will not disappoint...! Bravo!" *(Amazon)*

Order from Amazon:

Paperback: ISBN 978-1-914199-84-4
eBook: ISBN 978-1-914199-85-1

Once We Were Heroes
by Henry Lewi

Where do the gods of Olympus do their shopping?

Do the Old Gods live amongst us, and if so where? And which jobs do they do? Where do the Old Gods shop, or do they do it online? Which football clubs do they support? When Angels are sent down to Earth, how do they get home? How did Vampires cope with Lockdown during the pandemic? And finally, are Extra-Terrestrials dangerous, or do they just want to speak to us?

"Henry Lewi writes with confidence and with imagination. The story about the gods moving to North London provided an interesting opportunity to comment on modern times. The Pandemic features in many of the items in the collection."
(Amazon)

Order from Amazon:

Paperback: ISBN 978-1-914199-82-0
eBook: ISBN 978-1-914199-83-7